An American Family

Book 1 of
An American Family
by

JACKSON BAER

AN AMERICAN FAMILY
An American Family - Book 1

FIRST EDITION SOFTCOVER
ISBN: 1622530268
ISBN-13: 978-1-62253-026-7

Editor: Mike Robinson
Interior Designer: Lane Diamond

EVOLVED PUBLISHING™

www.EvolvedPub.com
Evolved Publishing LLC
Butler, Wisconsin, USA

Printed in Book Antiqua font.

BOOKS BY JACKSON BAER

AN AMERICAN FAMILY
Book 1: *An American Family*
Book 2: *Life after Death*

Clouds Fall Like Fire
The Earth Bleeds Red
The Lights Will Never Fade

Jackson Baer's Website
www.JacksonBaer.com

CHAPTER 1
A Situation like This

SHE NEVER RAN THIS LATE AT night.

The sun still waned on the horizon, yet Ramie must've been beyond its reach. Isaac peeked through the blinds on the living room window. Her mid-September, seven-thirty run came on a dimly lit evening in Woodstock, Georgia. During their nineteen years of marriage, Isaac Childs couldn't remember a time when Ramie wasn't back and showered by now, relaxing with a book, or making something to eat for him and the kids.

Ten more minutes, he thought, *ten more minutes, and then I'll call the police.*

"Mom's not home yet?" Carter joined his father on the couch; the clock now glared eight. He motioned for Rylee to join him, though she didn't really need the okay to do so. The one-eyed, fawn colored pug—a favorite of the family since they got her for free six years ago from a family who'd just had a baby. They'd kept the dog's name because having a dog with a human name made them laugh.

"No, son, she's not home yet." Isaac sensed that something was wrong, but what could he do? He'd watched too many crime shows. He imagined the police saying, "She's an adult. She can't be missing if she's only been gone for three hours. Maybe she went out with a friend." Isaac shook his head. She wasn't answering her phone, and that was not normal for Ramie. That was not his wife.

"Should we call the police?" Carter's nervous voice sounded more like a ten-year-old boy's rather than that of the eighteen-year-old man he'd become.

"Not yet. I don't think that enough time has passed yet for them to do anything." Isaac shifted uneasily on the couch. "You stay here with your sister, and I'll drive around and look for her."

I should have done this earlier, he thought. He called Ramie's cell one more time before leaving the house, but the call went straight to voicemail. Isaac hurried out to his black Nissan Titan pickup truck and backed out of the driveway, headlights on bright. He drove slowly down Bethel Drive, scanning both sides of the street, searching for anything out of place, any detail that might reveal to him Ramie's whereabouts.

His mind wandered down dark paths. Maybe a car hit her, and she was at the hospital. Isaac searched on his phone for Northside Hospital's phone number as he turned onto another street in the neighborhood, the route Ramie usually took during her six-mile runs.

Ramie was an avid runner. She had been for most of their marriage. They'd married young, right out of high school when they were merely kids themselves. Eighteen years old and married. Nineteen years old with a baby. Twenty-one years old with a second child. Life had progressed quickly for Isaac and Ramie Childs.

"Ramie, where are you?" Isaac whispered. He spotted a female runner up ahead, but it wasn't Ramie. At slightly over five feet, Ramie's petite frame couldn't be confused with this woman who looked to be closer to his height.

Isaac glanced down at the numbers on this phone and dialed the hospital.

"Northside ER," the front desk women answered.

"Yes, my name is Isaac Childs. My wife hasn't come home from her run, and I thought that maybe, well, that something might have happened to her. I don't know exactly, but I figured I'd call to see if anyone by the name of Ramie Childs has been admitted. Maybe someone who was hit by a car or something?"

"Let me check." The woman sounded unaffected, like she had heard and seen it all. *Sad,* Isaac thought, *this is my wife*. This stranger on the other end of the line should care more. "No, sir, there's no one by that name who is a patient here. I'm sorry."

She didn't sound sorry. Isaac prided himself in being a people person. He could read people, all the way back to his days at the University of Auburn. He and Ramie went there together after high school, a young, married couple in love. He studied Business while Ramie went for English and Education. She wanted to be a high school teacher, but the unplanned pregnancy of Carter put her education on hold, indefinitely. She finished her first year before dropping out, while Isaac worked full-time and graduated in four years. Two years after

Carter was born, they completed their perfect little family with baby Olivia. They said it would never last, but they had beaten the odds.

People change.

They said these things and other sentiments like them, but they were wrong. Isaac and Ramie proved them all wrong. They were happy. Who wouldn't be happy, to be married nineteen years and only be thirty-seven-years-old? Carter would be heading to Auburn in just a few days, and Olivia only had two more years of high school left before she went off and made her own life, hopefully at Auburn as well. Isaac and Ramie planned their future together without kids and dreamed of all the places they would go.

"It's like a Dr. Seuss book," Ramie teased Isaac one previous winter evening, both of them tucked underneath under a handmade quilt watching an episode of *Dateline NBC*. "Oh the places we will go, or see, or something like that." She always came close to remembering a title of a book or the name of a show, yet quite often, she would confuse one word with another. Isaac found this endearing.

He called Ramie's phone again, but it went straight to voicemail. The phone must be turned off, or worse. He tried not to think about what could have happened. He texted for at least the twentieth time, but there was no response. By ten, he'd driven all over their neighborhood, twice, and through the two other neighborhoods that connected to the back end of Victoria Landing, their neighborhood for the past ten years. They'd earned enough money to live in a newer neighborhood, but Isaac liked being away from the city and the traffic and Ramie agreed. They'd built their home a decade ago in the back of the neighborhood, tucked off to the side of a quiet cul-de-sac, and hidden behind a wall of towering trees.

Isaac's phone rang, and he looked down to find that it was Carter. "Is she there?" Isaac's voice trembled. He didn't give his son a chance to speak first.

"No, she's not here. I called to see if you found Mom or heard from her." Carter sounded calmer than when he first joined his father in the living room.

"Nothing yet, son. I'm still looking."

"Dad, I called the police," Carter said. He sounded like a child admitting he'd done something wrong, anticipating his parent's disapproval.

"I thought I said to wait," Isaac snapped a bit, not quite sure why. It wasn't like he didn't want to call the police. He just thought it was too soon, and he didn't think they'd do anything until more time had passed. That's what they said on the crime shows and the true crime mysteries as well. Forty-eight hours. That seemed to always be the acceptable amount of time before the police would step in and intervene. That's when it would become an investigation. Isaac did not want an investigation. An investigation meant that something was wrong. It meant she was missing, kidnapped, or worse. No, there could not be an investigation.

"I know, but I got scared. I'm sorry, Dad. The police are on their way. The person on the phone said they'd be here shortly."

"It's okay. I'm not mad. I'll be home in ten minutes. There's no one out here anymore." Isaac paused for a moment as he said those words. If no one was out there this late, that included Ramie. "Love you."

He hung up the phone and finished his search of one last side street, not expecting to find Ramie or any other person out walking or running. He drove around the curvy streets and switched between his brights and regular headlights, trying to spot anything on the side of the road. He turned back onto Bethel Drive and pulled into his driveway, greeted by the sight of two police cars parked in the otherwise empty and unlit driveway.

He parked in the grass and walked toward the front of his home, ill-prepared to have this conversation with real life officers.

"Hello." Isaac greeted the male and female officers who stood to their feet as he entered the house. "Thank you for coming."

"Hi, Mr. Childs. I'm sorry to meet you and your kids under these circumstances. My name is Officer Denton, and this is my partner, Officer Gonzalez." The male officer took the lead as his female partner observed from his side.

"It's okay, I don't even know what these circumstances are." Isaac tried his best to talk with the officers like he would during any other conversation.

"That's why we're here, Mr. Childs," Officer Gonzalez answered. He could see she was trying to make him feel at ease. "Now, when was the last time you saw your wife?"

"This morning, probably around seven-thirty, right before I went out for my morning run."

"Your son mentioned that your wife has been missing since around five this evening. Are you saying she hasn't been seen since seven-thirty this morning?" Officer Gonzalez continued while both she and Officer Denton took notes.

"No, Carter is right. I haven't seen her since this morning, but the kids saw her this afternoon. When I got back from my run, she had already left for the day." Isaac couldn't help but think of the hundreds of crime shows he'd watched, most with Ramie. The husband was always the prime suspect. He felt their suspicion aimed right at him. "She always runs in the evenings, but she's never out late, and she never goes without answering her phone. I can't tell you how many times I've called and texted."

"Do you know what she did today, where she went, who she was with?" Officer Denton asked the basic questions, and Isaac understood they wanted to track down people she might have met with and visit any places she could have gone. Carter stood in the doorway leading from the living room to the kitchen, while Olivia sat in the loveseat, on the other side of the living room. Isaac felt uneasy and tried not to rock in his recliner. He watched the officers observe him from the oversized couch.

"I know she went for coffee with her sister, Stacey, and then I think she said she was going to Hobgood Park to walk and read as well." Isaac tried to recall what his wife had told him. They were close, but they also lived their own lives. Neither he nor Ramie always knew where the other one was all the time.

"So, she went for a walk this morning and then for a run this evening?" Officer Gonzalez asked. "Did she normally exercise twice a day?"

"Sometimes," Olivia chimed in, "Mom is unpredictable. Well, she's not unpredictable like this. What I mean is she doesn't always have a set routine. She just kind of goes where she wants and yeah, sometimes she does exercise two or even three times a day. But she's never home late, ever. This is not like her. Something is wrong."

Olivia admitted what Isaac sensed as well. Something was wrong.

"I didn't mean it in a bad way," Officer Gonzalez answered. "I'm just trying to see if anything was out of the ordinary for your mother today. Mr. Childs, what time did you notice your wife might be missing or suspect that something could be wrong?"

"Right around seven thirty. I kept checking through the window to see if she was out there, but there was nothing. It's like she just disappeared."

"And the call came in a little after ten from Carter." Officer Denton took scrupulous notes as he spoke. He barely looked at Isaac or his kids. "Is there a reason you waited until then to call?"

"To be honest," Isaac answered, as if there were any other way he would answer, "I didn't want to admit that something might be wrong. I went looking for her around eight o'clock and kept calling and texting. I remembered all the crime shows we watched together. Ramie and I love crime shows, and I thought you had to wait forty-eight hours before the police would do something. I know that sounds stupid now." Isaac leaned forward and ran his hands through his slightly balding hair. His chestnut brown color clashed with his burnt umber recliner. Carter took after him, though he was not balding just yet.

"That doesn't sound stupid," Officer Gonzalez said dismissively, "you were looking for your wife. There's nothing to feel stupid about. Could my partner speak with you privately before we leave, Mr. Childs?"

Here we go. It's time for the good cop, bad cop routine, he thought. Isaac had watched this play out so many times on TV. He had nothing to hide, however, and he knew he would be fine.

"Sure, no problem." Isaac stood and glanced at his kids. He motioned for Officer Denton to follow him outside. The late-summer air still held a touch of humidity but nowhere near the amount that comes in the middle of a Georgia summer, usually before a pop-up thunderstorm.

"Mr. Childs," Officer Denton spoke like a friend. This surely didn't feel like a bad cop shift from the understanding officer. "There's just a few more things I need to know before we leave and begin the search for your wife. These are things I have to ask everyone in situations like this, so don't take them personally. Were either you or Ramie having an affair?"

An affair. This is something that couldn't possibly be true. Ramie loved him. They were looking forward to and actively planning their lives together as empty nesters. Yes, they had their problems, but they worked through them, and they were genuinely happy now. They would be the envy of all other couples, free of kids by the time they were forty, and the money and opportunity to do what they wanted in life.

Isaac had started an internet business back in 2003, using a monetary gift from his father for graduating from Auburn. He purchased domain names and had the idea to launch a company that sold them to the highest bidder, like an eBay for domain names. He made thousands of dollars selling domain names during college, and within his first year of the startup, he made nearly a million dollars. One year after the launch, he sold it to one of the big tech companies for a cool twenty million dollars.

"No, nothing like that. We're a happy couple. We've been married since we were eighteen. We were high school sweethearts. Hell, our kids went to the same high school we went to. Olivia is still in school, but Carter just graduated this year and is going to Auburn just like we did. There's no way she's having an affair. We've had our problems, like any other couple, but we are in a good place right now."

"And you, Mr. Childs? There's nothing we're going to find or stumble upon when we do a little digging? Because if she really is missing, we're going to have to search your computers and phones, and I just need to know now if there's anything that's going to turn up so there won't be any surprises."

"No, I'm not having an affair." Isaac just wanted this conversation to end. He needed them to leave and go find his wife. Someone had her, or she was hurt somewhere. He didn't have anything to do with it, and they were wasting their time on him.

Isaac watched the officers leave with their missing persons report and felt more hopeless than before they arrived. He walked back into the house, carrying his phone in case Ramie called or texted, and he hugged his kids. Carter stood two inches taller than him, north of six feet, and Olivia right in between his and his wife's height. She looked short compared to her father and brother, but she loomed over her petite mother. Olivia's dirty blonde hair matched her mother's, and Isaac saw every bit of Ramie in his sixteen-year-old baby. As much as Carter looked like him, Olivia resembled her mother.

"What do we do now, Dad?" Olivia broke the silence. Isaac knew what she was thinking. Their mother always texted her back within five minutes. She never went this long without responding and was always home by eleven. She was usually home by seven.

Isaac didn't know how to respond.

"You and I will go out and look for her, while Carter stays here and calls friends and family."

"But I want to help look, too," Carter said.

"We need someone here in case Mom comes back home. Plus, the dog knows something is up. We can't leave Rylee alone either, goofy dog. I need you here, and I need you to call everyone. Call all her friends, Aunt Stacey, and Uncle Josh. Call Ama and PaPa and NaNa and Pa. Let them know that we can't find your mother, that she hasn't been seen since she went for her run around five o'clock, and that we've already filed a missing persons report with the police. Tell them her phone is going straight to voicemail, and she's not responding to any text messages. See if anyone knows anything, has heard anything, or if they knew of any other plans she had that she didn't tell us about." Isaac tried to be as thorough as possible with his son. It's not that Carter was dumb. He was smart, in fact, but in the heat of such a situation, Isaac was prone to overcompensating.

Isaac and Olivia piled into the truck, while Carter started making phone calls from his room. They drove the same route that Isaac had previously searched only a couple hours ago.

As midnight arrived, they'd searched every neighborhood near Victoria Landing and decided to head into the heart of Woodstock, toward Towne Lake. It was too far of a run for her to make from their home, but Towne Lake contained no less than twenty upper class neighborhoods, and it was almost a city of its own within Woodstock. Isaac thought, feared really, that if someone had taken her, maybe they lived there. It was a stretch, he realized this, but he had nothing else to go on at this point.

Carter continued to make phone calls, but he texted his father that no one had spoken to or heard from his mother. Isaac and Olivia maneuvered their way through the neighborhoods within Towne Lake. They searched Eagle Watch, rolled through The Hills, looked all around Deer Run, and finished in Centennial Place, a mile past Etowah High School, close to Woodstock High School. They hit every neighborhood in between without seeing a single person on the streets. *Why would there be anyone out here?* he thought. It was nearing three in the morning, and Woodstock wasn't exactly Atlanta. Sure, it's not the country either, but restaurants closed by eleven, and most bars shut down at midnight. Ramie was nowhere to be found.

"Now what?" Olivia asked the question that had no answer. No good answer anyway. Anything Isaac said to his daughter would either be a lie or speculation. The speculation he had in mind was terrifying to him. He couldn't imagine what it would sound like to his baby girl.

"I don't know, precious. We go home and get some sleep. Then we start again in the morning."

Isaac and Olivia found their way home, looking on both sides of the street as they made the drive. They found nothing except for the occasional road kill and litter sprinkled along the way. Isaac checked his phone, but there was nothing from Ramie; only a few dozen texts and calls from worried friends and family members. He'd ignored them all while they were out searching, not wanting to miss anything, just in case they saw her. They walked into the empty home and embraced Carter, who met them at the pearl white front door. Isaac painted it every summer. It didn't need the fresh coat yearly, but he did it anyway. He liked the way it looked in the middle of the brown, wood-sided house, though you couldn't even see it from the street.

"I'm sorry, guys. I don't know what to say." Isaac led his kids into the home and tucked them into bed, something he hadn't done in many years.

Carter had slept in their room until he was ten, Olivia until she was eleven. "They won't be young forever," Ramie used to remind him whenever he said they were too old to sleep with them. Still, it felt like an eternity since they'd needed his protection and a goodnight kiss. Isaac stared at the ceiling, his phone in hand, and simply waited. He waited for Ramie to walk through the door or for the police to call and say they'd found her. *Why?* Why is all he could think as he finally drifted off to sleep just after four in the morning.

CHAPTER 2
Nine

"AUTHORITIES IN WOODSTOCK ARE SEARCHING for a missing person. Ramie Childs was last seen yesterday around five o'clock in the evening, before she went for her nightly run..."

From his bed, Isaac watched the Atlanta morning news. No, this wasn't a dream. Ramie really was missing. This was no longer an if. It had actually happened. She was on the news. How did they know already? Isaac woke Carter and Olivia and headed downstairs to call the police for an update.

"Officer Gonzalez?" he said. "Yes, I just wanted to see if you guys heard anything. I saw on the news that they announced her as missing." Isaac stumbled along, growing more anxious with every word, every word that just made this more real, and cut him with a sense of loneliness he'd never felt before.

"Hi, Isaac. No, we haven't heard anything from Ramie. I see that you contacted the news. That's a good way to spread the word so we can locate Ramie quicker."

"I didn't contact the news." Isaac assumed the police were the ones who'd contacted the Atlanta news. He figured it was the next step in this whole process.

"Okay, well I'm not sure who did." Officer Gonzalez sounded somewhat surprised. "Either way, it's good that it's out there now since she hasn't returned home. She hasn't returned home, has she?"

A strange question to ask, Isaac thought. "No, she's not here. My daughter and I looked until three in the morning, but we didn't find her, obviously."

"I understand," Officer Gonzalez said. "Two FBI agents will be coming over today to talk with you more and give you some details regarding the case."

The case. What did that mean? How was this already a case and one that required the assistance of the FBI? On TV, it took forty-eight hours before they'd even look into a missing adult case. They didn't start cases the day after someone supposedly disappeared. The FBI didn't show up right away.

This felt more like a bad dream rather than his actual life.

"The case?" Isaac asked, prying for any information that Officer Gonzalez might give up. "Are there reports of Ramie being sighted somewhere or something like that? Why is the FBI involved?"

"I can't tell you more, Mr. Childs. Two agents will be in touch with you later. This is being led by the FBI now. I only found out this morning, so my knowledge is extremely limited at this point. I do know they'd like to come by around noon, if that works for you."

"Yes, that works for me," Isaac answered, as if he had any choice in the matter. His wife was missing, and they already had a case with agents assigned to it. He knew that this was not good. This surely meant that something bad had occurred, and he might not ever see his wife again. He knew he was being cynical and pessimistic, but hell, life was not fair. Maybe this was bizarre karma for their morbid fascination with all those crime shows. Isaac felt guilty for making this about him. This was about Ramie. He had to find her. The whole ordeal had put in painful, stark relief just how much he loved her.

When noon rolled around, there were people all over the house and overflowing into the front yard. All their immediate family and a handful of friends showed up to form a search party. Isaac hugged his parents and hers as well. He shook the hands of a few of his male friends and hugged their wives. He embraced his brother, Josh, and Ramie's sister, Stacey. They broke off into groups of three and took several different routes, beginning at the Childs' driveway on Bethel Drive.

They went out, accompanied by at least ten officers and a dozen FBI agents, plus search dogs. Isaac remained behind at the house to answer questions from two FBI agents. He stared from the front porch as people made their way through his neighborhood, while others dispersed into the woods that surrounded his lonely home, and the rest slowly faded away much as Ramie less than twenty-four hours earlier.

Agent Faith broke the silence while her partner, Agent Noah, followed them inside.

"Mr. Childs, I know this can't be easy for you." Alyssa Faith was a veteran FBI agent. She'd started out as a police officer shortly after she turned twenty-two, worked homicide and special victims for several years, and now at age forty, she was a seasoned veteran. Agent Lucas Noah had taken a similar path as his partner, though he was two years younger, and his father previously served as an agent with the FBI, as well. "Agent Noah and I are here today because there's a possibility that your wife's disappearance is linked to a string of missing women cases across the area. Over the past eight months, there have been eight other women who've been reported missing that we think are being abducted by the same man." Agent Faith got right to the point, though she didn't come across as crass or insensitive.

"What do you mean by abducted?" He didn't understand how they could think this so quickly. A full day hadn't even passed.

"We don't know, for sure." Agent Noah stepped in to try and calm the distraught husband. "We've been working this case for the previous three months now. Over the past six weeks, three of the eight women have gone missing in the metro Atlanta area. The reason we suspect it might be the same man is because all of the other women were runners, all the women were white, and all the other victims were about the same height as your wife, between four-ten and five-three."

At least they don't suspect me, Isaac thought. He would never say those words out loud, but he had been scared they would try to blame him. They'd just said what he feared most, though – that word 'victim' pierced his heart.

"Okay, I see. Have you found any of those women?" Isaac could not recall hearing anything about a series of missing runners prior to right now. He kept up with the national and local news. How could there be eight missing women, yet he'd seen nothing about it on the news?

"No, Mr. Childs," said Agent Faith. "We haven't been able to locate any of the women up to this point. That's a good thing. I'll be honest with you, too. You're going to want to focus on anything positive that you can. Find the silver lining in what is a horrible situation, because hope is a powerful thing. We are closing in on a suspect. We feel like we are turning a corner when it comes to finding him and the missing women."

"I'm sorry, but I don't see how any of that is good news."

"We've been straight up and direct with you so far, and we're not going to change," Agent Faith said. "That's just our style. No matter how uncomfortable or troubling something might be, we're going to tell it to you like it is. Is that okay with you?"

"Yes, I apologize. I'm just out of my mind right now thinking of what might have happened to my wife. Men who kidnap women ... they don't do –"

"There's no use in speculating as to what may or may not have happened to Ramie," Agent Faith interjected. "That won't do you any good. That is our job, to figure out what this man is not only doing, but what he wants, and what his endgame is. We are close to figuring that out. I know that doesn't help you right now, but the silver lining is that we haven't found any bodies. That means there is real hope, and reason to think that your wife is still alive."

Of course she was still alive. Isaac had a hard time remembering life before Ramie. Like any couple, they'd had their struggles. They'd gone through phases of their marriage where they considered separating, though it never came to that. They always worked through their issues, and, over the past five or six years, they rarely argued anymore. It was true they'd come as close as ever to splitting up only a year ago, but they'd fought past it and grew closer together instead. It's just what Isaac and Ramie Childs did.

Agent Noah spoke gently, and with compassion. "We need to ask you some questions to figure out exactly when her disappearance might have occurred, and if this is indeed related to our case. Were either of you having an affair?"

"No, I already told the officers last night. I mean, I can't say one hundred percent that Ramie wasn't cheating on me, but I really don't think she was. We love each other."

Agent Faith stepped forward. "We're going to need to go through your computers and phones. Do you have a problem with us checking your phone and any computers you have, as well as your work computer?"

"No, that's fine. It's just my phone, and we have two laptops here at the house. Well, plus Ramie's phone but that's... well, that's not here. Take them, please. Search them and see if you can find anything that might help find my wife."

"What do you do for a living, Mr. Childs?" Agent Faith asked, still seated next to her partner across from Isaac.

"I work from home, but I'm semi-retired."

"That must be nice," Agent Noah jeered, not without some jealousy in his tone.

"I was lucky with a business I started after college. I sold it a year after its launch and did well." Isaac didn't enjoy talking about money.

He and Ramie both came from middle class families. His dad owned a modest tax business, and his mom stayed home, though she did teach a few years at Chapman Elementary. Ramie's dad had been a Lutheran pastor for thirty years and her mom had helped him in the church.

The whole sale of his company, as well as the twenty-million-dollar price tag, had felt quite surreal. Isaac had saved the majority of his money, invested some, and made sure not to splurge. He understood how difficult it was to earn money, that money could evaporate as quickly as it was made.

"That is nice," Agent Faith chimed in. She seemed to also be a tad jealous of him, though he wasn't sure. "What do you do from home?"

"I buy and sell stocks, but not for huge amounts. I know it might sound like an oxymoron, but I'm not a big risk-taker when it comes to money."

Agent Noah asked the questions that needed to be asked. "Would there be anyone you've had a business dealing with that went sideways? Is there anyone who would want to hurt you or your wife? Is it possible someone is holding her for ransom?"

"Nothing like that. Everybody loves Ramie, and I haven't made any enemies. I really have been fortunate when it comes to money. I haven't worked a real day in my life in over ten years. Like I said, I buy and sell some stocks, but I'm talking about a few thousand dollars here and maybe a few more there. I'm not in the millions or even the hundreds of thousands. We live modestly, and most people don't even know we have a lot of money, besides our immediate family. We kept it pretty hush hush when I sold my company, because Ramie and I have always watched crime shows and read those types of books as well. We didn't want someone coming after us. I know it sounds paranoid, but we always thought that one of those shows would come true for us. I guess we were right."

Suddenly, it truly sank in: Ramie might never be coming home. Eight other woman had been abducted. They had not found any of those women, and this was an actual FBI case. This was the real deal.

Isaac gestured toward the kitchen. "Please, let me get you two a drink. Would you like a water or tea? I have milk and probably some juice as well."

"No, thank you," Agent Faith said, speaking for both.

Isaac poured himself a glass of ice water in the kitchen.

"How sure are you of the timeline," Agent Faith asked, "that she went for her run at five PM?"

"Pretty sure. I wasn't here, but both Carter and Olivia said she left around five. That's the time she usually goes for her runs, unless it's incredibly hot or something."

"Does she always take the same route?" Agent Noah asked as Isaac sat back down in his recliner, water in hand.

"Almost always. She's a creature of habit. I would tease her and try to get her to go run at different parks or new trails. She liked the consistency, not having to drive anywhere. She enjoyed knowing how far along she was in her run when she passed certain streets or homes that she ran by each time."

"And where were you between four and six PM?" Agent Faith spoke with bona fide kindness. She didn't come off as accusatory or judgmental. Isaac felt safe with them both.

"I was playing disc golf down in Marietta, at Oregon Park. I play a few times a week, especially when I want to clear my head."

"Disc golf?" Agent Noah chuckled. "Is that like ultimate frisbee?"

"No, it's basically like golf, but you throw a disc that's kind of like a frisbee. It's fun. Ramie always made fun of me because I take it so seriously when I play."

"Sounds like a real golfer then," Agent Faith joked, all three of them smiling now, albeit awkwardly. "Is there anyone who can verify that's where you were? Also, what time did you get home?"

"I played by myself, but Ramie knew that's where I was going, the kids too. I got home a little before six, I think. I'm pretty sure I posted a picture on Facebook and Instagram after I finished playing, so that will probably show the time and my location. I shot a three under par, so I was happy."

"And what time did you begin to sense that something was wrong?" Agent Noah asked.

"I'd say close to seven is when I started to get nervous. She normally only runs for an hour or so. I checked with Carter and Olivia, and they both said she left right at five. By seven-thirty, I was beyond worried since she wasn't answering any calls or texts."

"You told the officers that the calls were going straight to voicemail," Agent Noah continued. "Was that the case from the first time you called, or did it happen as the night progressed?"

"I guess from the first time I called, but I'm not sure, to be honest. I'm sorry, I should have paid more attention. Have you guys tried to track her phone?"

Agent Faith looked Isaac directly in the eyes. He could see that she truly cared about finding Ramie, that this was not just another case to her. "We have tried to locate her phone, but it must be turned off. We've not been able to get a signal from it.

"One last thing for the time being, Mr. Childs. We noticed that she posted on Facebook and Instagram that she was going for a run. After browsing through her pages, it seems as if she did that most days. This has been a common theme with the other missing women, in addition to the physical attributes they all share. It's most likely going to come out in the news, and I have a feeling that this is going to be national news, Mr. Childs. Please advise your daughter to be careful with what she posts online. I'm not blaming your wife, not by any means. I just want to make sure you knew that, so you could warn your daughter."

"Warn my daughter?" Isaac asked, though he didn't expect a response. "Warn my daughter to always look over her shoulder so she's not kidnapped like her mother?"

After a few more questions, the agents left, taking Isaac's two laptops with them. They'd searched his cell records while they were at the house, but found nothing of value. Isaac was willing to sign his rights away, to obliterate his own privacy. Search thoroughly, he told them. Maybe this guy was stalking Ramie online, and they could catch him through her social media.

Isaac watched the agents drive off in their black SUV. *FBI agents always drove a car like that,* he thought. He looked all around him, but there was no one in sight. Everyone was still out searching for Ramie. He didn't know anything, and he had given them no useful information. He let his wife get abducted while he was off playing disc golf. Isaac sat down on the wicker chair and held Rylee in his lap. The pug licked his hand, something he rarely allowed her to do.

Isaac waited on his comforting porch until his friends, family, and the police returned. They didn't have to say anything. He could tell by their faces that the search was unsuccessful.

"I'm sorry, Dad." Olivia hugged her father, now back inside their home. Isaac thanked them all for their efforts and filled them in with vague details from his discussion with the FBI.

And now the three remained; Isaac and his two nearly-grown kids, plus the dog. They were still a family, just not as complete as they were yesterday this time.

"It's okay, baby," Isaac said to Olivia. "It's all going to be okay."

He tried his best to protect his kids, but knew that all of the details would be on the news shortly. The FBI was closing in on a suspect. They'd prepared him for the possibility of this story going nationwide. He asked Olivia not to post her location online anymore, to be careful with selfies and things like that. He told Carter the same.

"I just need to prepare you both," Isaac told them, trying to figure out what he should say and what he should keep to himself. "It's just that you're both older now. Carter, you're an adult, and Olivia, you are close. I want you two to stick together, support each other, and keep hoping for the best. They haven't found any bodies. That means there's a chance she's still alive. We have to believe that. There's also a chance that this psycho isn't the same man who took your mother. We still don't know what happened. All we know is that she's gone. But you're both old enough now." Isaac had taught his kids to ignore everything someone says before they said 'but,' yet he said it anyway. "You're old enough to know that it doesn't look good. Let's hope for the best and prepare for, well, I don't know exactly what. We simply prepare."

"Please don't talk like that, Daddy," Olivia said with tears flowing down her cheeks. "Mom's going to come home, and everything is going to go back to normal. It has to. She has to."

"Yeah, Mom is a fighter." Carter softly stroked the snoring dog. "I know it looks bad, but she's gonna find her way home, and we're gonna make it through this."

Dear God, his kids were better people than he. He raised them right, at least, but it didn't make him feel any better for trying to be realistic while his children spoke so optimistically.

"I'm sorry, guys. You're both right. We're going to get through this."

Isaac spent the rest of the day driving around Woodstock and going to different parts of Allatoona Lake. He hoped that he might see a piece of her clothing, or spot her phone discarded on the side of the road or in the woods somewhere. Instead, he found nothing but empty beer cans and old trash discarded what must have been years ago. He returned home and opened a beer from the back of the fridge. He'd quit drinking, mostly, over the past few years. He had to.

Tonight was quite different.

He only found a six pack of light beer in there, but it did the job. Six beers and ninety minutes later allowed Isaac to fall into a deep sleep and dream about his Ramie. He replayed their life together and fell in love all over again.

"Hey, are you new here?" Isaac said to Ramie the second day of school. It was their freshman year at Etowah High School, and Ramie had just moved to Woodstock from Minneapolis, Minnesota. Her dad took a position at an ELCA Lutheran church in Towne Lake, and she didn't know anyone yet.

"Yeah, I just moved here," Ramie responded quietly as she never liked to disrupt a teacher. "Are you from here?"

"Yeah, born and raised. Why?"

"You don't sound like you're from the South," Ramie teased the young boy, though she was serious. Isaac didn't exactly carry the southern twang that so many of his friends were proud of.

"What do I sound like then?" Isaac wanted to know, curious as to what the newcomer thought.

"I don't know, normal, I guess." She smiled at the handsome boy. As soon as she did, Isaac knew he was talking to someone special. Ramie spoke without any discernible accent. She nearly picked up the distinct sound that emanates from Minnesota, and did in fact pronounce counties as conies, mainly for fun, but she hadn't spent enough time in any one place to truly sound like one of their own.

Just as he was about to kiss her again for the very first time, Isaac shot straight up in bed.

"She's not coming home," Isaac whispered. He downed a glass of water from the nightstand and took four ibuprofen to ease the headache from the liquor. "I'm so sorry." Isaac fell back asleep, this time with dreams he did not wish to dream.

Someone had her, he believed this, and it was all his fault. He should have been there for her. This was happening because of his sins. Surely someone would find out shortly.

CHAPTER 3
Semantics

THE SECOND DAY PASSED WITHOUT ANY new leads or updates from the police. The FBI didn't contact Isaac, either, and neither returned his phone calls. He continued to call Ramie's phone, just in case, but it still went straight to voicemail.

At this point, he'd played out all the possible scenarios in his mind. As the third day rolled around, he was convinced that she'd either been kidnapped, or someone had struck her with their car, gotten scared and dumped her body. That sounded rather fantastical, but all of this seemed unbelievable to Isaac.

More and more, he realized with dread that this guy the FBI was searching for was probably the man that had his Ramie.

He rarely prayed, but he began to pray that God would somehow bring her home. If not for him, then for Carter and Olivia. Even Rylee moped around the house missing Ramie. The dog loved her more than anyone else in the Childs family.

Isaac stepped off the front porch with Carter and prepared to say goodbye.

"Goodbye, son. I'm sorry I can't go with you, but I have to stay here, in case." Isaac stopped there. Carter tried to stay at home and wait a semester to begin classes at Auburn, but Isaac insisted he go. They'd already made all his arrangements, from payments to student housing. It was too late to drop out or postpone college life.

"No, Dad," Carter said. "I'm sorry. I should be here with you and Liv. School can wait."

"Please, Carter, I need you to go. I know that nothing feels normal right now, but we need to keep living our lives while they search for Mom."

Isaac hoped he didn't sound callous. He didn't mean to. He knew that Ramie would want Carter to go to school. She wouldn't be happy with him simply waiting around the house for her to return home.

Isaac hugged his firstborn and cried weighty tears. He cried tears that held the memories of their happy family and still held onto a future of something yet to come. Carter sobbed, lightly at first, but he couldn't hold it in any longer. He let out his pain and heartache. Olivia rested her head on her father's shoulder while Rylee panted below, blissfully unaware of the tangible pain they all tried to push down. Isaac and Olivia waved as Carter drove away from their home on Bethel Drive, taking his five-year-old Lexus with him.

"It's just the two of us now, Daddy." Olivia held his hand as they walked back into the place they used to call home. Now, he wasn't so sure. Ramie was gone, and Carter too, though for entirely different reasons.

The week went by without any developments until finally, something happened. Isaac glanced at his phone and saw the missed call from Agent Faith. This was it. This was the moment he'd been dreading since he first peered through his living room blinds, waiting for Ramie to run by.

"Hi, Mr. Childs," Agent Faith said. "Thank you for calling me back. Can you meet with us later today? We have a few things we need to go over with you."

"Of course. Where should I meet you?"

"We've been stationed at the Marietta police station on Lemon Street. I know that's about a thirty or forty-minute drive for you. Do you think you could be down here in the next couple of hours?"

"I'm leaving right now." Isaac ended the phone call and kissed Olivia on the forehead. "I'll be back. The FBI has a few things to go over with me, and I have to go meet them in Marietta."

"Can I go too?"

"No, I better go alone. I don't know what they have to say, and the dog is still acting weird. She knows something is up; she's been sad since your mom went missing. Stay here with Rylee, please, and I'll be back as soon as I can."

"Okay but call me as soon as you know something," Olivia said as she walked up to her room.

Isaac drove down 75 South and worked his way to the police station on Lemon Street, a place he'd never been to previously. Until now, he hadn't even known it existed. He assumed they'd be waiting for him in the lobby, but they were not. The officer working the front desk had no idea who he was and had never heard of Agent Faith or Agent Noah. He called to the back, and Agent Noah came up right away to escort Isaac to their space in the back of the station.

"Thanks for coming down, Mr. Childs. I know this hasn't been an easy week for you."

"It's no problem. Agent Faith said there was something you needed to tell me. Did you find her? Did you find Ramie?"

"Here." Agent Noah stretched his hand toward the room that resembled so many he'd seen on TV. This room appeared to be a bit smaller, though newer than Isaac would have expected. "Let's go in and have a seat before we get started."

"Hello, Mr. Childs," Agent Faith spoke with more authority than when they first met, though she was still welcoming. She seemed focused, ready to get to the point. "We called you down here because something came up when we went through your laptops."

"Did she have a stalker?" Isaac interrupted.

"No, we didn't uncover anything like that, Mr. Childs. What we did discover is something entirely different. It's something we're going to need your help with."

"Anything. What is it?" Isaac was a bit puzzled now by Agent Faith's approach, and her shift in tone.

"We asked you if you were having an affair, and you told us that you were not." She leaned forward as she questioned Isaac, who sat at the metal table across from the agents. "When we searched your online history and phone records, we found something else."

Isaac's heart sank. He knew he'd been caught, though he didn't exactly mean for it to be a lie. The truth can be stranger than fiction, and this truth was something he wished were fiction.

"Let me explain."

"Yes, please do," Agent Noah said, "because right now all we have is a missing wife, paired with a husband who lied to us about sleeping with a seventeen-year-old girl. And from what we found while we were digging, she appears to be a friend or a girlfriend of your son. What in God's name have you been up to, Mr. Childs? Did Ramie find out about your affair? Is that what happened?" Agent Noah slammed his fist onto the table, unleashing far more emotion than Isaac might ever have expected of him. "Did you kill your wife and dump her body somewhere? You're a coward, aren't you Isaac? You think you've got all this money, and you can go around and screw any pretty girl you want without any consequences. How many other girls have there been? Does your son know? How's he going to feel when he finds out that his dad banged his girlfriend? You're in a lot of trouble, Mr. Childs."

Isaac's heart began to race at a thousand miles per hour. It was bad, but it wasn't as bad as the agents thought.

"It's not what you think. Yes, I made a mistake. I slept with that girl, Nicole, but it was only one time."

Agent Faith jumped in. "You're lucky the age of consent is sixteen in the state of Georgia. But I don't think that's going to matter too much to the girl's father."

"I know, it's horrible. I'm a terrible person. But you can't tell anyone. I was drunk, and Ramie and I were going through a really tough stretch."

"I thought you said you guys had a great marriage?" Agent Noah's voice shifted upward sarcastically.

"We do, besides that one time, and it was nearly a year ago. Nicole isn't my son's girlfriend. She graduated with him this year, but they are just friends. Still, you can't tell him. He'd never forgive me if he found out that I cheated on his mother. Olivia either. Please, I'm begging you. I know it looks like I'm just a liar and a cheater, but you have to know from my messages that it was only a one-time thing. I broke it off with her right away, and it's the biggest regret of my life."

"Not to mention the ten thousand dollars you paid her to keep her from saying anything," Agent Noah added. He appeared to take some joy in Isaac's previous mishap.

"My hands were tied," Isaac admitted. "After I slept with her, I told her that it could never happen again. I told her I was happily married, and she was my son's age, that it just couldn't work. She didn't like that, and she felt used, which I understood. I offered her the money so she wouldn't say anything because it would have ruined my life. That's part of the reason I've tried to quit drinking, and why I rarely drink anymore. I make bad decisions when I drink but never anything like this."

"What other bad decisions do you make when you drink, Mr. Childs?" Agent Faith asked in a tone that presumed the worst. "Do you start arguments with your wife and get violent? That would be a bad decision, wouldn't it?"

"Listen, I am not a violent person, and I barely drink anymore. I used to drink and drive a lot and almost got into an accident about five years ago. It scared me to death, and I swore I'd never do that again. I don't drink and drive anymore, but every once in a while I give in and drink. When Ramie and I were going through that rough patch, I gave in and got really drunk one night. That's when I started messaging Nicole, and we got together one night. That's it; it was one night. We weren't having an affair. It was the biggest mistake of my life but not an affair, and certainly not a reason to do anything to Ramie. I know that's what you're thinking, but I swear I didn't do anything."

"Did you get drunk a week ago, say a little before five PM?" Agent Noah asked.

Noah was getting under his skin - precisely the agent's intention, as Isaac presumed.

"Tell us about the rough patch you were going through," Agent Faith said, this time in a calmer voice. "What was so bad that you cheated on your wife with a kid?"

"She's not a kid, she's seventeen, and she looks much older." The moment the words left his mouth, Isaac heard them, heard how they sounded.

"Much better," Agent Noah said with a dark grin. "I bet Nicole's father will feel the same way, don't you? I'm sure your kids will understand that their dad just couldn't help himself. Nicole is just too damn hot. Anyone else would do the same thing that you did."

"So," Agent Faith persisted, "tell us about the rough patch."

"I'd really rather not get into it." Isaac shifted in his chair. It felt as if they'd given him an unbalanced chair on purpose. He glanced around to see if a light was flickering but saw none.

"You don't have a choice," Agent Noah reminded his suspect. "Your wife is missing, and you lied to us about having an affair."

"I didn't lie," Isaac said, firmer this time. "An affair is an ongoing relationship, not a one-night stand. I didn't have an affair. The one-night stand was almost a year ago. I didn't lie. Go check your notes."

"Check my what?" Agent Noah puffed his chest out in protest, staring Isaac down like he wanted to move the conversation to the sidewalk out front.

"You heard me. I didn't lie, and I won't sit here and let you try to pin this on me."

"Pin what, Mr. Childs?" Agent Faith asked, her tone now that of a teacher who assumed she'd caught her student in a lie. She was offering faux forgiveness in exchange for truth. "You seem to be hung up on semantics, and you still haven't told us about that rough patch."

"This entire disappearance. I didn't do anything. I'll take a lie detector test or anything else you want to give me. I swear on my life that I didn't have a thing to do with Ramie's disappearance, and I don't know who did. I love my wife, despite my mistake with Nicole. Our rough patch was over the fact that I found out Ramie had been talking to her old high school boyfriend on Facebook. I got pissed off, and after we argued the first day, I didn't talk to her for at least a week. Then I got even angrier and more jealous. I figured if she were doing that behind my back, who knew what else she was doing. So, I got wasted one night and jumped online and started scrolling through some of my old girlfriends. I only dated like three other girls my entire life and that was in high school. Ramie and I were high school sweethearts, together since our freshman year. The only times we ever dated anyone else were the two times we broke up. I stumbled across Nicole and started messaging her. She came over to our house all the time, so I already knew her. One thing led to another, and we hooked up. That was it. Ramie and I worked through it, and we stayed together."

"So, this is Ramie's fault?" Agent Noah asked. "Is that what you're saying?"

"No, I'm just trying to explain the rough patch that your partner asked about." The tension rose to a level Isaac had not anticipated.

"And Ramie knows about your little mishap?" Agent Faith suspected that she did not.

"No, I never told her."

"Why didn't you tell her?" Agent Noah interjected. "I thought you said you guys worked through it?"

"We did, but I think some things are better left unsaid. We've been married for nineteen years now. It was eighteen years into our marriage when this happened. In my mind, she did start it by talking to her old boyfriend. She said nothing happened, and after we made up a couple of weeks later, she promised me that she stopped talking to him. I believed her. I didn't think it would help anyone to tell her that I slept with one of our son's friends. That's the kind of stuff you see on *Jerry Springer*. That's not the sort of thing that healthy couples work through and make it past. Worst case scenario, if Ramie did sleep with him, I figured I could forgive her since I messed up too. Truth be told, I didn't actually want to know because I didn't want to deal with it."

Isaac made logical points, in his own mind at least. The agents never honestly considered him as their prime suspect, or even a viable suspect, but they had to work this affair angle, and make sure there wasn't more there. They gave him a lie detector test, two as a matter of fact, and Isaac passed them both. They interviewed Nicole, and she confirmed Isaac's version of events. They slept together the one night, and he paid her ten thousand dollars not to tell anyone. She was scared they were going to tell her parents, and she would get in trouble. But she was eighteen now, and the agents weren't interested in causing unnecessary family drama. As unsavory as it sounded, especially when spoken aloud, nothing illegal had taken place. Plus, the agents hadn't uncovered anything else from Isaac's phone or computers. He'd walked a fine line between the truth and fabrication, and both agents now looked at him differently.

It's true they'd both been involved in affairs of their own over the years, but still, the girl was seventeen, and he'd paid her all that money to remain silent. As far as they could tell, Ramie only messaged an old boyfriend back and forth. They found flirty messages and a few risque pictures, but no evidence they'd ever met up in person. They tracked down the ex-boyfriend, who lived south of Atlanta, in Macon, and he said what they already suspected. They didn't take the relationship any further, and he hadn't spoken with Ramie in nearly a year. She'd blocked him on all social media, he admitted.

"Please don't tell my kids," Isaac pleaded with the agents during their next meeting, two days after they followed up on his story.

"We're not going to tell your kids," Agent Noah said, "that's between you and your wife. I have kids of my own, so I understand. Still, I know kids. Kids don't keep secrets particularly well. I'm surprised that the girl has kept it quiet this long. It seems to me that someone who would pay ten thousand dollars would be willing to pay even more."

"How do you think I feel? I've had to live with this guilt, this shame over what I did for the past year. And now, my wife is missing. I feel like it's my fault. Like it's karma."

Isaac left the station for the second time in three days and thought about everything the agents said. He felt their judgment and knew that he deserved it. He debated whether to tell his kids or not about the one-night stand. If it came out from Nicole or one of her friends, they'd be crushed. He couldn't lose his wife and his kids. Maybe the best course of action was to get in front of this and come clean. They'd be angry with him, yes, but in time they would surely forgive him.

Isaac drove home and called Carter as he passed through the city of Kennesaw. If anyone would understand, it would be his son.

"Hey, buddy, how are you liking it so far?" He'd never felt so awful in all his life. He betrayed his children's trust and the trust of his wife. There was no way he could tell him what he'd done with Nicole.

"Hey, Dad, I'm doing great. You were right, I've met so many people already." Carter told his dad all about his new friends, including someone else from Woodstock who he'd never met before, and about life in the dorm. Isaac listened, eyes moistening.

He pulled up to their house on Bethel Drive, went in and laid down on the couch. Rylee jumped up and licked his chin before settling in a cushioned spot between his legs. He told Olivia they had more questions about the timeline from that dreadful day, but did not even consider telling her about his transgression. That secret would go with him to the grave.

CHAPTER 4
Monsters Hide under the Bed

"HEY, THANKS FOR MEETING WITH ME." Isaac looked around, nervously, though they were the only two people on the lower end of Hobgood Park after nine PM. Three weeks had passed since Ramie's disappearance, and he wanted to make sure his secret would remain hidden. He took in the baseball fields and tennis courts he'd once played on as a kid. He used to bring Carter here often to hit fly balls and pitch and play tennis. Olivia would join them sometimes, but she never cared too much for sports. She was the writer, the artist, and the creative one. Though Carter had his share of creativity, too.

"I know this is weird, and we haven't talked since that night," Isaac began.

Not the night we slept together, Isaac thought, *but the night I paid you ten thousand dollars in one hundred dollar bills to keep our deep, dark secret.*

"I just wanted to say that I'm sorry... again."

"There's nothing for you to be sorry about." Nicole spoke words that flowed like music to Isaac's ears. She'd grown even more stunning since they took part in that one forbidden night, a year prior.

"I took advantage of you, Nicole. I cheated on my wife, and I paid you to not say anything. I'd say that I did many things wrong." Isaac said these things as if he were at confessional, though he was not Catholic. He attended the Lutheran church that Ramie's dad pastored, fairly regularly, but he didn't consider himself to be a religious man. He wasn't sure what he believed or didn't believe and found himself content with not knowing what was true or what was a lie when it came to religious matters. He assumed, however, that God did not approve of his act with Nicole.

"You didn't take advantage of me. I'm not a child. I wanted to sleep with you, and I didn't want your money. I wasn't going to tell anyone even without the money." Nicole sported long legs, a youthful-yet-mature frame, and a river of rich black hair. She looked at least five years her senior. "We had fun, didn't we?"

Isaac had brought twenty-five thousand dollars in cash with him, in anticipation of keeping her even more quiet.

"I don't want to talk about that; I'm sorry. My wife is missing, and I love her. Plus, how would it look if I cheated on her so soon after her disappearance?" Isaac tried to take the words back as soon as they left his mouth. "I didn't mean it that way. Look, Nicole, you are beautiful, obviously. But you're only eighteen, and I'm thirty-seven. This could never work. You're friends with Carter, and he can't ever find out about us."

"I'm not going to tell anyone." Nicole moved a bit closer to Isaac. "And I am really sorry about your wife. It's just awful. You didn't have anything to do with it, did you?"

"No, why would you ask me that?" Any lustful feelings that Isaac tried to hide evaporated with this question. "I would never hurt my wife or anyone else for that matter."

"I don't think you did. It's just that I've heard a few rumors, and since no one else will ask you, I'm asking. Don't be upset, I didn't mean to upset you, Isaac."

Nicole weaved her words with precision, calming Isaac just as quickly as she initially shook him with the unthinkable question. It unnerved him how much she understood her power with words.

"I asked you to meet me here tonight because I need to make sure you're never going to say anything." Isaac reached into the back seat of the truck and grabbed his old, adidas gym bag, full of one-hundred dollar bills. "It sounds bad to say it out loud, but I've brought you more money. I know you said you won't say anything, and you haven't yet, but I just want to make sure you understand how big of a deal this is. If people find out about us, they will think I'm guilty, and my kids will never forgive me." Isaac handed her the bag and watched her face fill with disappointment.

"I don't want your money." He understood that Nicole Emerson still had a crush on him. She'd texted him periodically, but Isaac never responded out of fear he'd give into the temptation once again. "I don't know what I want," she finally said, after a deafening pause.

"Take the money. You can put it to good use, and it will help you with college. If things were different, I could see myself with you. You are smart, gorgeous, and you have your entire life ahead of you." Isaac couldn't understand why he kept saying things like this. Just give her the money and leave, said a voice. "But I do love Ramie, and I have to focus on finding her, as well as taking care of Olivia."

"I understand." Nicole held the gym bag full of money. Isaac was surprised at how much more it weighed than the first payment. She prepared to leave Isaac's truck, but before she did, she leaned over and gave him a friendly kiss on the cheek.

Isaac froze.

His lips wanted so badly to turn toward hers. He kept his eyes focused on the batting cages that stood fifty yards away, between the parking lot and the ball fields. He remembered all the times he took batting practice there as a kid before a baseball game, the days he pitched to Carter when he was younger. He breathed in Nicole's lavender scent and the smell of her freshly-washed hair. Nicole moved her lips around his troubled face and nibbled on his bottom lip. Isaac pressed his lips against hers, tears bubbling in his cheeks.

"I can't do this." He wrenched away. "Please leave."

Nicole opened the door and stepped out, her new gym bag in hand. Isaac watched her walk away, perhaps a touch longer than he should have. Her shorts barely covered her young backside, and Isaac stared, shamefully. She drove away, and he prayed she would not tell anyone. He also prayed for forgiveness once again.

What kind of a husband am I? He thought as he pulled out of the park and headed back to his once-happy home. He couldn't see the color in the leaves, but he knew they had already begun to change. Early October was a nice time in North Georgia. It didn't compare to the Northeast, but still, the air was finally willing to cool down after the year's brutally humid summer.

He turned the wrong way on Towne Lake Parkway and spotted Donovan's Irish Pub, all lit up and waiting for him. They stayed open late, probably the only bar in Woodstock that kept its doors unlocked until two AM. It was only ten, and Isaac just needed a couple of beers to help him sleep, to dull the memory of having nearly cheated on his wife again. This incident, however, made him feel even more despicable than the first time. He'd grown used to blaming alcohol for the biggest mistakes in his life, but that was probably just an excuse. It was him.

Isaac sat on the far end of the oversized wooden bar and ordered a local IPA. He drank it slowly, his eyes locked on the small, flat screen TV above him. He chose not to make any conversation with the few people around him. Several men laughed and joked with one another, while two college-aged girls talked at the other end of the bar. Isaac had not visited a bar in over a year, and he hadn't been in this particular pub in a few years. He drank his second beer quicker and his third in less than ten minutes. Isaac worked his way through six IPAs before the clock struck midnight. The bartender nodded as he left the bar, and he struggled to keep his heavy eyes open.

Isaac put the key in the ignition, but only after missing twice and stabbing the steering column instead. He turned all the way around to make sure there weren't any cops hiding in one of the connecting parking lots. They'd been known to watch people leave this bar, stopping them as soon as they pulled out. Isaac considered himself to be a great buzzed driver and a good drunk driver, despite his past faults. He squinted his eyes and focused on the white lines. He maneuvered through the parking lot, turned out onto the street. He drove exactly thirty-five miles per hour, not wanting to give a cop any reason to pull him over.

He noticed his brights were on, somehow. "Shit," he muttered, and switched them off.

He made it through Towne Lake and turned right onto Bells Ferry Road, still several miles and a good ten minutes from his home in Victoria Landing. He spotted a police car across the street from the front side of Hobgood Park, lights off and tucked away in the back corner of the parking lot. Isaac gripped the steering wheel even tighter and checked to make sure he was in between the lines. He checked his speed. He forced himself to keep his eyes averted from the car that could ruin his life even more. *Thank God,* Isaac thought as he peeked in the rearview mirror and made it out of sight of the police car. God, if you let me get home, I promise I'll never drink again.

He believed that he meant this.

He took the curves slowly, not wanting to hit a deer or swerve across the double yellow lines. Isaac turned right into Victoria Landing and felt his eyes begin to close. Nope, he whispered and slapped himself across the cheek, the same spot where Nicole had kissed him only a few hours ago.

At last, he pulled into his driveway, safe from the world around him. He stumbled toward the front porch. He'd become a lightweight now, compared to several years back when six beers would have barely given him a buzz. "Dammit." Isaac tripped on the second step, striking his shin on the painful wood. He finally reached the top of the porch and placed the key inside the deadbolt on the first try.

Olivia met her father in the entryway.

"Hey, Dad, I was worried about you," she said. "Have you been drinking? And you've been driving?" Her words flew out quicker than Isaac would have liked.

"No, I haven't been drinking. Why would you think that?"

"Because you smell like beer, and because I heard you fall on the steps. I'm assuming that was the loud noise I heard."

"Okay, I've been drinking a little, but I'm fine, I promise." Isaac walked over to his favorite recliner. It held his body's indentation. "I just needed to clear my mind and get something to help me sleep."

"That's fine, Daddy." Olivia sat back down on the couch and calmed Rylee. She was startled by the commotion so late at night. The pug slept more than any other dog alive. A ten-minute walk would knock her out for a couple of hours. If it was any later than ten, she was sound asleep for sure. "If you want to drink, then drink here. It's not safe, and you've always told me to never drink and drive. Why is it okay for you, but it's not for me?"

"It's not, baby, I'm sorry. Can we talk about this tomorrow?" Isaac closed his eyes and the only thing he saw was Nicole and her lips pressed against his. He didn't want to see that. He wanted to see Ramie, but she was never coming home.

He fell asleep in his chair, and Olivia covered him with a blanket. She turned out the lights and gathered the dog in her arms.

"Goodnight, Daddy." Olivia kissed him on the forehead and carried Rylee upstairs with her to bed.

It was already twelve-thirty AM, and Olivia had to be up by six-thirty for school. She fell asleep almost immediately, thanks to the Oxy she took earlier that night. She'd begun taking them six months ago, after first trying one at a party. Normally, she wasn't into any drugs. Seven months past her sixteenth birthday, she had yet to consume any type of alcohol. *There was something about a pill,* she thought, *that was different.* How bad could it be if it came from a doctor? She kept her habit in check, only using it a few days per week, though sometimes more than once on the weekends.

Ever since Mom had gone missing, however, Olivia had started using daily, morning and night. Sometimes, she took an extra pill during lunch as well. She bought them from a friend at school who dealt to only a select group of students, but whose main customer base were the fake-boobed, wealthy, overly-made-up moms.

Olivia had found her mother's stash of Oxy and Percocet, along with Vicodin and others she'd never heard of. She knew her mom took pills now and then, but it wasn't an addiction. "You know I have back pain from the accident," Ramie would tell her. "I only take what I need." That may have been true, Olivia didn't know, but based on what she'd discovered in her mother's bathroom and closet, Mom had collected bottles full of pills. Olivia had them now stored safely under her bed.

Five years ago, the pill addiction had started for Ramie Childs. Olivia was only eleven and Carter had just turned thirteen. Neither of the kids knew the truth of what happened in that accident. Isaac and Ramie told them that Mom swerved to miss a deer, lost control of the car, and crashed it into a tree. That's what they told everyone, including the insurance company. This actual accident is the near accident Isaac alluded to when he spoke with the FBI agents earlier. The truth is that Isaac used to have a real problem with drinking and driving, taking part in the deadly behavior since his sophomore year at Auburn. He'd never been caught, though he was pulled over one time, but he kept his composure and did not slur his words. The officer let him go with a warning, and Isaac left with his heart beating faster than ever before. He swore he'd never drink and drive again. He never could keep that promise.

Five years ago, Isaac and Ramie went out for a date night. They still enjoyed going to movies and out to dinner at least once a month when they could. Over the past few years, they missed a month now and then. They liked to take walks together and on that particular night, Isaac took a shot of vodka prior to leaving the house. At dinner, he drank two 7.0% IPAs, and he finished the meal with another straight shot of vodka. He tried to sober up during the movie and found some success, until they hit the Applebee's in Kennesaw after watching Argo at the AMC theater near the mall. Five margaritas and two beers later, Isaac drove his love home just before midnight.

"Please let me drive." Ramie place her hand on Isaac's arm before he backed out of the parking space in the Applebee's parking lot.

"I'm fine; I barely have a buzz." Isaac always insisted on driving. Ramie didn't usually mind. She preferred that Isaac drive, except for when he'd been drinking heavily. They'd experienced a few close calls before, but she agreed with Isaac; he was a good driver. She'd grown numb to his drinking and driving just like he had.

Isaac made it to 575 North and all the way to the Towne Lake exit without any problems. He turned and drove exactly the speed limit, something he'd mastered quite well over the years. As he neared the center of Towne Lake, he glanced down at his phone for just a split second. When he looked up, he saw his car drift over the double yellow lines. Isaac jerked the car back to the right, but he turned the wheel too hard and raced over the shoulder. The car tumbled down a small hill and crashed head on into a strong-willed tree at forty miles per hour. The airbag deployed and pushed Isaac back against his seat.

Ramie's airbag, however, failed to open. She flew forward and her head slammed against the dash. As she did, the lower part of the seatbelt squeezed her waist a little too tightly.

"Are you okay?" Isaac asked in full panic mode. "Oh my God, I'm so sorry. Ramie, are you okay?"

"I'm fine, but my back hurts." Ramie unfastened her seatbelt and stepped gingerly out of the car. She walked around and opened Isaac's driver side door.

"What are you doing?"

"We have to switch sides." Ramie pressed the button on his seatbelt as Isaac pushed the airbag in and slid over to the passenger's side of the car. "You're drunk. If the police find out you were driving, you're going to get a DUI and go to jail."

Ramie leaned delicately into the car while they discussed their story to make sure they were on the same page. Ramie swerved to miss a deer, something fairly common around Towne Lake. And of course she was driving; she was the sober one. The tow truck carried their car away, totaled as the frame was bent, while an ambulance transported them both to Northside Hospital. Isaac did not sustain any injuries, save a mild headache, most likely from the heavy drinking. Ramie displayed a red circle on her forehead which was caused by the steering wheel. She told the story to the nurses and doctor, and she suffered moderate nerve damage in her lower back. They referred her to a spine specialist in Marietta, and Ramie underwent several sessions where they burned the nerves to try and relieve the pain. It worked initially, but the pain always came back. They also prescribed her Oxy, Percocet, Vicodin, and a mixture of other pills to help with the pain. They tried one, then another, and then combinations of them all. By the third year after the accident, Ramie's back still hurt, and the pills were the only thing that made her feel better. She would have never been able to run without them. She reminded herself of this whenever she considered flushing them down the toilet.

"At least I'm not a drunk," Ramie told Isaac, a few weeks prior to their big argument and his mortal transgression. He was the one who'd started it, according to Ramie. She told him that he spent more time playing disc golf than he did with her. They seemed happy, and they were in fact happy, but not as happy as they should have been. Their love had grown from a puppy love to a young love. It then evolved into a deep love, and over time it grew stagnant. There wasn't any one thing they could point to, until Isaac found out that Ramie had been talking to her ex-boyfriend.

"I'd rather be a drunk than a pill popper," Isaac responded.

"The only reason I take these pills is because you wrecked the car and messed up my back, remember?" Ramie's voice rose at this point in the disagreement, but not enough to alarm the kids. "If it weren't for you, I'd be just fine. Sometimes I wish..."

"Go on, say it. Sometimes you wish what?"

"I wish things were different." She strayed from telling him that she was talking to her ex at this point. Isaac found that out a few weeks later when he walked past her phone and hit the home button. Still, that short sequence of words carried enough pain to crush him.

"I'm sorry I'm not good enough for you," he said. He hurried over and grabbed his wallet and keys.

"Where are you going? Don't leave like this."

"You know where I'm going."

Isaac would go where he always went after an argument, or to destress: A bar to where he could drink away his pain.

What couple went without ever arguing? he thought. *What grown adult goes through their life without at least one demon to fight?*

"Love you," Ramie whispered. She watched from the front door as Isaac strode to his truck, his every step weighed with purpose. He climbed into the truck, pulled out of the lengthy driveway, and left without saying a word.

CHAPTER 5
Atlanta Traffic

MORE THAN A MONTH PASSED WITHOUT any updates regarding his wife's whereabouts.

Late October in North Georgia could bring a winter chill that sometimes crept in early. This was one of those times. Isaac turned out of Victoria Landing as he'd yet to visit Carter over in Auburn.

He set out on the two hour and fifteen-minute drive southwest. Olivia stayed behind, mature enough to stay home alone by any metric Isaac could measure. He needed to see his son, to let Carter know that he was still there for him. It was strange to not have his kids around. They had always been a close family. Isaac and Ramie had grown up in similar families, with parents involved as much as they could be.

He managed to avoid all Atlanta traffic by leaving late in the morning. Surprisingly enough, encountered no accidents or road construction along 85 South. Isaac received the welcome from the Sweet Home Alabama sign and cruised into the college town he once lived in and still loved. This was the place he'd started his life with Ramie, after leaving Georgia as man and wife, and, during their first year in Auburn, where they welcomed Carter into the world. This is where he started and sold his business, before they moved back to Georgia in 2003.

Auburn greeted Isaac with more than nostalgia. It offered hope and redemption, neither of which he understood right now.

"Hey, buddy." Isaac hugged his son. "I've missed you so much." Isaac wondered if he'd grown another inch already. It felt as if he'd put on a bit of muscle in the month he'd been away.

"I've missed you too. Thanks for coming, Dad." Carter ushered his father into his dorm and pulled out a chair for him, as he sat on the edge of the bed.

"So, you really do have the place to yourself."

"Yeah, the other guy never showed up, and they haven't filled his spot yet. I'm not complaining. I like the peace and quiet."

"How are your grades so far? I know you said you were having a tough time in math."

"They're good, and I've got a low B now in Math 201," Carter said. He knew that he always wanted to please him, and that he was hurting from all the not knowing, as was Carter.

"That's great," Isaac said. "I always did well in Math, but I had to work hard at it, especially once I reached the higher levels." Isaac paused, trying to withhold the moisture gathering in his eyes. "I'm proud of you. You're a good man."

Carter averted his eyes, as if hoping to opt out of the palpable sadness in the air. Isaac didn't even understand why he was crying. There was something about seeing his son for the first time in a month that made him miss Ramie even more. It forced him to face the reality of an incomplete family. It left him distraught, wrapped up in his transgressions, his problems with drink. He suddenly felt like the worst father and husband in the world.

"Guess what," Carter said.

"What's that?"

"I've kind of started seeing someone."

Carter blushed. They'd always been close, but neither one of Isaac's kids had a lot of experience with dating. Olivia was even less patient with the whole scene.

Isaac smiled. "What's her name?"

"You'll see. I'm coming home for Thanksgiving in a few weeks, and I thought I could bring her over to the house then."

"I'd love that. You can't even tell me her name?" Isaac jabbed a soft, cajoling elbow in his son's direction. "Is it one of your professors?"

"Very funny. No, she's not a professor. You'll see."

"Okay, okay." Isaac didn't press the issue. He was so happy to see Carter that the kid could have told him pretty much anything right then. "Let's go get some lunch. I'm starving. My treat?"

"Of course."

As Carter donned his jacket over his broad shoulders, Isaac noticed a bottle of vodka and a bottle of whiskey in the corner of the closet. He feared that his demons were following his son. He didn't smell any alcohol, so maybe he was being paranoid. Carter was in college, after all, and drinking was hardly unheard of.

Isaac followed his son down the hallway and out of the four-story dorm. Carter's room sat on the first floor, so their walk was an easy one to Isaac's comforting pickup truck.

His phone rang and Isaac answered it. "Hello?"

"Mr. Childs."

Isaac froze. It was Agent Faith. They hadn't spoken in weeks.

"We need to talk with you as soon as possible," Faith said. "Can you come down to the station?"

"I'm actually in Auburn visiting my son. What's going on? Did you find Ramie?"

"I'd rather speak in person. How long until you can get here?"

"I wasn't coming back until tonight." Isaac started the truck and drove away from his alma mater.

"That's fine. We're actually in Atlanta now, just north, to be exact. There's been a major break in the case. I would advise you not to turn the radio or TV news on until we speak tonight. I'd like to give you the most accurate information there is, and from what I've seen on TV thus far, it's mixed, at best."

Isaac's heart sank. He looked over at his son and realized they were embarking on their last supper of sorts. In just a few hours, he'd be for sure without a wife.

"Thank you. I'll call when I'm on my way home."

"Who was that?' Carter asked tentatively. "Is it Mom? Did they find her?"

"That was the FBI. I need to call your sister. They've had a major break in the case, but they wouldn't tell me anymore over the phone." Isaac called his daughter and made her promise not to turn the news on. "Please, just stay in the house with the dog," he pleaded. "I'll be home tonight, and I'll tell you everything then."

Carter asked again, "Dad, what's going on? Just tell me."

"I don't know." Isaac turned the truck around and headed back for the dormitory parking lot. They'd only made it a half mile or so down the road. "I have to go back and find out, son. I'm sorry. I promise I'll call you right away and let you know what they found, and I'll be back soon. I'm sorry."

Isaac stepped out of the truck and wrapped his arms tightly around Carter before driving back to Georgia. Atlanta was a bit closer than Woodstock, but still nearly a two-hour drive without traffic. He drove as fast as he could, his stomach as light as the first time freshman year when he'd asked Ramie if he could kiss her.

"God, if you're real," he muttered, "please bring Ramie back to me, to us."

Though Isaac prayed aloud, it made him feel like the prayer had a better chance of coming true.

A couple hours later, Isaac pulled into the police station on Paces Ferry Road. This time, Agent Faith and Agent Noah stood outside the front doors, waiting for him. Both agents shook his hand as they met him at the edge of the sidewalk. Everything about their greeting felt awkward and wrong to Isaac. His stomach knotted tighter, and he considered throwing up to see if that might take away the nervousness. Ramie surely was not waiting inside for him. If she were, they would have hugged him or smiled. They would not have shaken his hand, like this was some uncomfortable business meeting. This was not going to be good news.

They made their way through the lobby. The room the agents led Isaac to seemed more welcoming, though that diminished little of the anxiety. Both agents sat down on the far side of the table. Isaac took the seat across from them. Agent Noah looked softly at Isaac, nearly eye level, while Agent Faith stared at him.

"This isn't easy," Agent Faith spoke faintly at first. She reminded Isaac of his wife a bit, though Agent Faith stood a few inches taller, and she looked her age. Ramie still looked like she could pass for a woman in her upper-twenties or early-thirties, at the most. "We believe we caught the man who abducted Ramie. A man named Charles Haney wrecked his car earlier this morning, around nine AM, just north of Atlanta. He was driving south on Highway 75 when someone rear ended him just before the Highway 285 interchange. He lost control of his vehicle and crashed into a concrete barrier. The accident knocked him unconscious and left the front of his vehicle smashed in. Several bystanders rushed over to rescue him, and were successful. By the time paramedics and police arrived, Haney was conscious again, but on his way to the hospital with a broken leg and a severe concussion. The officers on the scene noticed a distinct smell coming from the vehicle, and when they opened the trunk, they found the remains of a female body. Now, we know that it was *not* Ramie, but once we interrogated the suspect at the hospital, we quickly discovered that he was our guy."

"So, she's dead too then, isn't she?" Isaac asked, though he already knew the answer.

"We believe so, Mr. Childs." Agent Noah crossed his arms and straightened his mustache. His black hair began to show a touch of white, though it hadn't spread to his mustache yet. "We can't be completely sure, but Charles Haney is a sick man, and it took all of thirty minutes for us to get a confession from that spineless coward. As soon as he heard the death penalty would be his fate, he begged us to cut him a deal. We're going to have to search his residence and belongings better before we agree to a deal, but as of now, we only have the confession for the murder of this one woman. If it means finding out what happened to your wife, how would you feel about him receiving life without parole, as opposed to the death penalty?"

How would I feel? Isaac expected to receive terrible news, but this all hit him heavier than he anticipated. Of course he wanted to know what happened to his Ramie. It wasn't just a want; he *needed* to know. He didn't think he could go on living without knowing. They found a woman's dead body in the trunk, and they only caught him because of a random car accident? Isaac hated everything about this. This was not how the story was supposed to end.

"I have to know what happened to her and where she is. If she is gone, I want to be able to give her a proper burial. I can't not know where she is. I just can't."

"We have the suspect in custody. He's still at the hospital, and we are searching his home as we speak. He lives in Acworth, about fifteen miles from your house." Agent Faith spoke in a tone that made Isaac feel like they had everything under control, yet there were still nine other women out there, missing, probably dead. "We've recovered some physical evidence from his car that will help lead us to your wife and the other missing women. So, even if he doesn't admit to all of the abductions, we feel confident that we are on the right track."

"This guy is willing to confess right now," Isaac said. "Why would you gamble and allow him to lawyer up? I don't want to tell you how to do your job, but I want to know where my wife is. If he's willing to tell you that right now, then do whatever you have to, and go find my wife."

Isaac left the Atlanta police station on Paces Ferry Road and made the most depressing phone calls of his life. He called Carter first, then, once he made it back to their home on Bethel Drive, told Olivia in person, He spent the next hour calling their parents, his brother, and Ramie's sister. He had news, he told them. It most definitely was not good news. It was the reality that everyone in the family had dreaded.

"So, they found a body in the trunk?" Olivia held the dog closely. "That doesn't mean that Mom is dead, does it?"

"It doesn't mean that she's dead for sure, but they think this woman was abducted after your mother. If she's dead, the odds aren't good for your mother. They have already searched his residence and all his vehicles. Agent Faith actually just texted me that they still haven't found your mother."

"How did he kill the woman?" Olivia asked, though Isaac didn't want his daughter to know what her mom most likely went through as well.

"You don't want to know, baby. I wish I didn't know, to be honest." He couldn't get the mental picture out of his head. Thank God the agents didn't show him an actual picture of the victim. They wouldn't, of course, but he feared he might have to identify Ramie's body whenever they found her remains. That was a task he could not prepare himself for.

"Just tell me. I'm not a kid." She loosened Rylee's collar a bit as the sleepy pug needed more room to breathe. "It can't be that bad, if they told you."

Isaac needed a drink more than anything right now. "I'm sorry, Liv, but I can't tell you."

"I swear to God, if you don't tell me, I'm going to my room, and I'm going to kill myself." Olivia crossed her arms, and he could see the worry on his daughter's face.

They both stared at each other. Isaac was stunned by his daughter's sudden and overdramatic response. He could sense that she regretted her words, though he understood she had every right to be emotional. His daughter never spoke like this. She was the sweetest girl in the world. She did not make threats, nor had she ever talked about suicide in the past.

"Please don't say something like that," Isaac said. "I love you with all of my heart."

"I'm sorry, Daddy, I didn't mean it," she said as she straightened her shirt and appeared to ready herself for the details. "I just really want to know. I don't know why, and I can't explain it. I don't care how bad it is. I can take it, but I need to know, so I can stop going over all these different scenarios in my mind. I am literally driving myself insane."

"Okay. The woman they found in the trunk of his car... what they found was..." Isaac struggled to get the words out. "They found her cut up in pieces. He cut her arms and legs off and other body parts. He'd tied her up in black garbage bags. They only found parts of her body, not her entire body."

Silence.

He was right - she did not want to know. Neither said another word for what seemed like a lifetime. The only noise was that of Rylee's snoring, unaware that her favorite person in the world would never be coming home.

Olivia carried Rylee upstairs where she curled up beneath her quilted, patchwork blanket, crying. She reached for one of the bottles hidden under her bed and took one more pill, though she didn't know what that pill was. She opened the drawer of her nightstand and took a swig of nighttime medicine to wash it down. She watched her tears stream down her cheeks and rest on the pillow. Her eyes closed, and she drifted off to somewhere new.

Meanwhile, Isaac grabbed the keys to the truck and left. He pulled out of the driveway and raced down Bethel Drive, going much too fast for a residential neighborhood. He sped out of the subdivision and watched the speedometer to see if he could get it to seventy miles per hour before he reached the stop sign across from the church, at the end of the road.

Isaac screamed at the top of his lungs and pounded the steering wheel repeatedly with the palm of his hand. "Why are you *doing* this to me?"

He cried for the loss of Ramie. He cried because he knew he was going to get drunk again. He cried because he knew he was going to text Nicole, and that made him a pathetic piece of shit. He waited until he reached Donovan's Irish Pub, took his seat at the far end of the bar, and quickly downed a bitter IPA.

"Hey," he texted.

Moments later, he got a response.

"Hey, you. What's up?"

"Just thinking about you. I know I shouldn't be, but I am."

"I'm always thinking about you :)"

Within fifteen minutes of arriving, Isaac finished his second beer and followed it up with a straight shot of vodka. He chased the shot with a half glass of light beer, then drank another IPA as they continued to text back and forth.

"You wanna get together?" Isaac finally texted. The guilt grew in his stomach.

"Yeah :) Same place as last time?"

"Thirty minutes?"

Isaac chugged the IPA and left two twenties on the bar. "I'll text you the room number when I get there," he wrote. "Maybe give me forty-five minutes."

Nicole texted back with a topless selfie. It didn't seem so wrong this time since she was eighteen. Now, he was grieving. It sounded horrible when spoken out loud, but it was easier for Isaac to rationalize, silently, privately, in his own head.

He made the troubling drive to the motel across town, just off Highway 92. He booked a room and texted Nicole the room number. He tried not to cry while he waited for her to arrive.

I can still leave, he thought, contemplating whether to put his shoes back on and go home. He could even go back to the bar. That would be better than what he was about to do.

Nicole knocked on the door. He let her in. It was too late for him to choose anything else.

CHAPTER 6
B.B.

AGENTS ALYSSA FAITH AND LUCAS NOAH made it to Biloxi, Mississippi, the week before Thanksgiving. They finally finished searching everything that belonged to Charles Haney, including a second home he had farther north, in Cartersville, Georgia. To call it a home would be generous. It was a run-down, mildew-spotted trailer with a blue tarp filling in for half the roof, and it sat on a secluded piece of land outside town, several hundred yards away from the closest neighbor.

While they found plenty of evidence tying Haney to the abductions, they failed to locate any bodies. Haney had become proficient in his crimes, disposing thoroughly of the bodies. In exchange for the D.A. taking the death penalty off the table, he'd confessed to the murders of all ten women, counting Ramie Childs. He would show the FBI where he dumped the bodies, but recovering the bodies would not be easy, if at all possible. The agents accepted this as the unfortunate reality. They had no other reasonable choice.

They took in the beauty on both sides of the bridge that carried them from Ocean Springs into the Biloxi strip. Parking in the dockside garage of the Golden Nugget Casino, Agent Noah opened the door and led Charles Haney to his own boat, bobbing lonely on the water and covered in police tape. The letters B.B. were painted across the starboard side of the twenty-foot vessel. The media had taken this acronym and run with it, dubbing Haney the Biloxi Butcher.

Recovering the bodies from the unforgiving depths proved an obstacle for the FBI. They had only the remains of the latest victim, thanks to the dumb luck of a bad fender-bender. This seemed to please the Biloxi Butcher. The agents were all too familiar with men like him. The Butcher's crimes were more gruesome than most, however, and his body count was higher as well.

They searched his boat thoroughly, while the local police guarded Haney. When they finished, the agents and two dive teams sailed out past the sandbar to where Haney claimed he'd dumped the bodies. Even if he were telling the truth, there was no guarantee that the bodies would still be there. The elements may well have made off with any remains. Two hurricanes had worked their way through the area over the past year. When they finally reached the area that Haney said he disposed of the bodies, they anchored and began, search-and-rescue divers descending from two boats spaced a hundred yards apart.

The search and rescue team dove into the sea from each of the boats, which were spread about a hundred yards apart. Agent Faith studied Charles Haney, wondering if they were truly in the right location, or if this might be a game.

After a few moments, she leaned in toward him.

"What made you do it?" she asked.

"Do what?" Charles Haney resembled a slightly older version of George Costanza. He stood a bit taller than the Seinfeld character, except he weighed a few pounds more than George did in his prime.

"Abduct and kill all those women," she said. "As far as I could tell, you've never been in trouble with the law before this. Had it not been for that accident, we may have never found you." She tried to stroke his ego, to make him feel like he'd accomplished something great.

With a fairly calm demeanor, Haney replied, "Nothing made me do it. I just did it."

On being caught, he'd been scared, even panicked. Since then, however, he'd relaxed a bit. He seemed to relish his burgeoning fame, his growing fanbase.

"I understand that, but most people don't abduct and kill women. I'd just like to know what made you decide to start doing this."

"Most people don't play professional sports either. What made those athletes start playing?"

"They possessed natural talent, and they worked hard at it," Agent Faith replied. She watched his face intently as the water rippled lightly in the background.

"Exactly."

"Exactly what, Mr. Haney?"

"I'm good at my sport." The Butcher appeared to have no problem talking about what he did or how he did it. He carried no qualms with discussing his suddenly infamous crimes.

"I'll give you that much, Mr. Haney. You were very good at what you did. You destroyed a lot of lives in the process, but you accomplished what you set out to accomplish, didn't you?"

"What do you mean?"

"You made a plan to abduct and kill all of those women. You succeeded. You killed ten women and nearly got away with it."

This'll be one of his last days outside of a prison, thought Agent Faith, *and certainly his last ever on the open sea.*

"Sort of. If that dumb bitch hadn't rear-ended me, I'd still be hunting. I'd be up to at least twelve women by now. I would have set records that this pathetic world has never seen, or dreamed possible."

"So you failed then?"

"How did I fail? I killed ten women, and there's nothing you can do about it. You can't even kill me."

"You set out to kill many more. I'd say that you fell just short. That's probably not the first time you've fell short though, is it, Mr. Haney?"

After a short staring contest, Haney lunged at Agent Faith. Hands cuffed behind his back, he tried to headbutt her with his hands, but she caught him in a headlock yet in his momentum they couldn't stop their plunge off the portside edge of the boat.

The Butcher slipped out of her arms a little, but Agent Faith held onto his torso and pressed her fists tightly into his stomach. Agent Noah rushed over to help and grabbed the Butcher's legs, but they both held him in the water for another twenty seconds or so. This didn't compare to the pain that Haney inflicted on those women, but it made her feel a little better.

"You stupid bitch!" Haney coughed up water and spat toward Agent Faith, missing her by a few inches.

"Would you like to go back in the water?" Agent Faith asked, only half-joking. "We'd be happy to reunite you with your victims."

"I'd love to be alone with you for a few hours. You wouldn't be talking this much if I didn't have these handcuffs on. You wouldn't be talking at all after I cut that tongue out of your pretty little face." The Butcher stepped toward Agent Faith. Agent Faith fixed her gaze on the monster and kneed him with a sufficient amount of force in the groin. Haney fell to his knees and grunted like a boy who'd just been punched in the gut without any warning.

"Why'd you do that?" he cried out. His tears fell and mixed with the ocean water on his face. He cried out, buckling. Tears sprang to his eyes. Agent Faith and Agent Noah leaned down and picked Haney up by the arms. Agent Faith kneed him one more time. They held him up so he couldn't fall down, and they shoved him over the edge of the boat once more. Agent Noah held his head in the water while Agent Faith clutched his legs. They brought him back to his feet and promptly knocked him to the ground.

"It doesn't feel so good to be someone's prisoner, does it?" Agent Noah crouched down in front of the grown man, who sat there crying like a child. "You better get used to pain like this. I hear they don't exactly like rapists and serial killers in prison."

"Well, that's not completely true," Agent Faith intervened, "you're going to be very popular with some of the men, I'm sure."

About fifty yards out, a diver signaled for them.

They weren't typically the kind of agents who would treat a suspect like this. The Biloxi Butcher, however, was not the same as any other suspect. They certainly held no sympathy for him, and with no one else watching, they took a bit of pleasure in roughing up the monster. They received more joy when he cried like a little girl.

"They found something." Agent Noah, pointing. The second boat made it to the diver and helped him aboard. They lifted the black garbage bag he'd discovered on the ocean floor and carried it toward the middle of the boat. The agent's boat pulled up alongside so they could hop over and examine the bag's contents.

"I told you," the Butcher said from the empty boat. He sat next to the two rescue divers now guarding him. "I'm a man of my word."

"You're not a man at all," Agent Faith argued. "You are nothing."

Agent Faith donned a surgical mask and latex gloves. She opened the bag and was greeted by one of those oversized, clear storage bags. She lifted the storage bag out of the garbage bag and counted the body parts: one arm, seven fingers, one ear, fourteen inches of darker hair from the victim's head, and eight bricks that the Butcher added to weigh the bags down.

There were no means of identifying the body out there on the boat. They would need to bring her back to the lab for testing.

"Where's the rest of her?" Agent Noah called out to the other boat. Haney stood watching them with relish.

"The rest of who, or is it whom? I never can remember which one is the right one to use. Can you remember?"

"Shut the hell up! Do you know which victim this is?" Agent Noah asked again, more sternly than before.

"You'd have to let me come over and look more closely," said Haney. "I can't be sure from where I'm standing."

"Fine." Agent Noah motioned toward the search and rescue divers who stood with the Butcher. "Bring him over, carefully."

Agent Noah took control of the Butcher and guided him over to the boat with the woman's deteriorating remains. Charles Haney smiled wide.

"Do you know who she is?" Agent Faith now stood less than a foot from the Butcher.

"How do you know it's a she?"

"This is a game to you?" Agent Noah asked. "Do you need more help remembering?"

"Are you going to hold my head under the water again, or is that bitch going to knee me in the balls one more time?" His hands remained cuffed behind his back, but he turned his body away from her as if she might knee him again.

"Whatever it takes." Agent Noah stepped closer to the Butcher. He stood between the monster and the sea. "We have no sympathy for you. If I have to hold your head under the water until you pass out, I will. If I have to throw you over the edge of this boat, I will. If I have to cut your balls off, I will."

Haney lunged at Noah and slammed his forehead into the agent's face. Blood instantly flowed from Noah's nose. Agent Faith tackled the Butcher to the ground, and two of the divers held his legs down. Agent Noah kicked Haney in the ribs, forcing a high-pitched scream. Agent Faith pressed her knee into the back of his neck, then pushed all one hundred and forty pounds of her body into his fat head.

Haney curled up into a fetal position and cried.

"This is police brutality!" Haney shouted. "I'm going to sue you and the entire FBI!" He spoke through the tears that would not stop flowing. Snot ran down his face as he continued to blubber and threaten the agents and the divers alike.

"Go ahead, dumbass," Agent Noah said. "You headbutted me and broke my nose." He wiped some of the blood out of his mustache and spread it across the front of his shirt. "You're lucky you're still able to speak."

They took the Butcher back to the other boat and locked him to one of the rails, away from the edge. He cried actual tears as the dive team continued their search for several more hours, until the sun began to drift away for the night. No more remains turned up.

They transported Haney back to Atlanta while they searched for six more days in the unforgiving Atlantic Ocean. Though they managed to find partial remains that first day, they did not have any further success the following days. Still nothing.

Their case was solid, however. They had the remains of the last victim from the accident, and now, partial remains of another victim. They had the Butcher's confession and signed agreement for him to receive life in prison without the possibility of parole.

Yet there were still victims out there. Agent Faith couldn't imagine how the families must feel, knowing that their wife, their mother, their sister, their daughter was lying at the bottom of the ocean. Closure is a key part of the grieving process, and the Childs family would not be receiving their relief anytime soon.

CHAPTER 7
Disc Golf at Your Own Risk

ISAAC SWORE THAT HE WOULD NEVER drink again.

He'd made that promise a hundred times before, sure, but this time he meant it - again. He slept with Nicole after his last night of drinking, and he vowed to stop that as well. He received the updates from the agents in Biloxi, though it was not what he had hoped for. He wanted to lay her to rest, to somehow try to move on. They found one victim, but it was not his Ramie.

Was she still his Ramie, though? The fears raced through his mind. She'd been missing for just over two months now. Most likely, she'd never be found. Even if it were recovered, ocean scavengers would surely have destroyed her body by then. Best he could hope for now would be for divers to find her bones.

Thanksgiving was this weekend. Carter had arrived home yesterday, and would be bringing his girlfriend to dinner. So there was that to look forward to.

Isaac just needed to clear his head. He managed to resist drinking since his last mishap with Nicole, but he hadn't played disc golf since the day Ramie disappeared. He filled his days with trading stocks, morning runs, evening walks, and daily phone calls to Carter. He spent as much time as he could with Olivia, and the two grew closer together with no one else around. He even bonded more with Rylee, taking her for walks each day. Now that the air had finally cooled down for the year, the lovable pug looked forward to their afternoon strolls. She still panted like it was ninety degrees outside, but it only took her a few minutes to settle down after they'd made it back to the house. Many times, she would stop at the bottom of the steps, and force Isaac to carry her the rest of the way.

Isaac left his home on Wednesday, the day before Thanksgiving and made it to Oregon Park, his favorite place to play disc golf.

Tomorrow they would go to his parent's house in the morning, then to Ramie's in the afternoon. The afternoon visit would be difficult. While he still got along just fine with her parents and her sister, it was not easy for either side since Ramie's disappearance.

Now that the Butcher had confessed to her murder, it felt more finite than simply a missing person's case. But without Ramie's body, there would always remain a sense of uneasiness. Many nights, Isaac woke to frightening dreams where he would see Ramie. Sometimes she was happy, other times she wasn't breathing.

Seeing her family only sharpened his guilt and deepened his loss.

Isaac parked on the right side of the building and stretched behind his truck. He never did anything anymore without stretching. He even stretched before taking the dog for a walk. Several years back, he took Carter and Olivia out to play disc golf with him. They began by throwing the frisbee around before actually playing disc golf. Carter threw it to him, and Isaac lightly jogged to catch the frisbee. He caught the frisbee, and as he did, his right calf muscle popped. He knew immediately that an audible pop coming from his leg could not be a good thing. He fell to the ground and tried his best to stand back up. His calf still held an indention in it from that tear all those years ago.

After stretching, Isaac took a few practice throws at the front basket. He then decided to play the silver to silver course. This was one of the nicer parks around. It offered gold and silver tee pads and baskets to choose from. Isaac got in his stance and threw a beautiful, two-hundred-and-seventy-foot throw that landed about fifteen feet to the left, just short of the silver basket. This was going to be a good round, he could tell.

After the ninth hole, he was two under par, nicely set up for a strong finish. His record was five under, but as long as he shot under par, he would leave happy. He teed off on the tenth hole and let go of the disc just a little late. The mid-range disc skated along the treeline off to his right, barely managing to curve back into play and avoid the woods. The disc curved a bit too much, actually, threatening to land close to the group up ahead of him.

"Fore!" Isaac yelled, probably a second or two late. The group consisted of three women, which is not something he saw everyday out here. He noticed women out there all the time, but rarely groups.

The girls turned, all but one ducking. Instead, she turned at the wrong moment - right into the path of the careering disc which struck the side of her head and sent her to the ground. Isaac took off running, tripping down the slight incline that led from the tee-pad to the middle of the course. He leapt up and continued on.

"Oh my God, I'm so sorry! I yelled fore. I know that's not an excuse..."

The woman sat up and rubbed her head. A golfball-sized lump swelled up on her temple. She touched it and flinched, which made him feel even worse.

"I don't know what to say," Isaac stammered. "I feel awful."

He took notice of this woman's natural beauty. She looked about his age, and wore very little makeup. He glanced at her pair of black yoga leggings and her vintage, 90s *Simpsons* t-shirt featuring Homer strangling Bart. Isaac and his kids always loved *The Simpsons*. It was their family show.

The woman was not skinny, per se, but certainly not fat. She carried her weight well, and Isaac was awestruck. Nicole was pretty, yes, but this woman was gorgeous. It reminded him of the first time he'd met Ramie, even though they looked nothing like one another. She had a Téa Leoni look to her, but this woman was thicker, and her hair blonder than the hair of the actress.

He instantly felt an immense amount of guilt for having these feelings so soon after Ramie's death. He didn't know when the appropriate time would be to meet someone, but surely this was too soon. It had only been a couple months. They hadn't even held a memorial service yet.

Isaac crouched down, dribbling apologies. Her friends helped her up and tried to assure him that it was okay, that they should have been paying more attention.

"No, it's my fault," he insisted. "I threw my disc when you guys were still on the course. I didn't see you around the corner. I am so sorry."

"It's okay, honestly." The woman finally spoke. Once she stood up and looked Isaac in the eyes, he felt actual butterflies in his stomach.

"I'm Isaac, by the way." He reached out and shook the remarkable woman's delicate hand. He greeted the two other women, then focused his attention back on her. He saw her ring finger sat empty with no signs of life. Isaac still wore his ring. It seemed like the right thing to do.

"I'm Julia." The woman smiled and twisted her left leg behind the right.

"Let me make it up to you ladies and buy you lunch after we're done playing," Isaac said. "Also, there's only three of you playing. Would you like a fourth?"

"I don't know," Julia said as she picked up his disc and threw his second shot for him. "We don't really know you. You could be a psycho or something."

"How'd you know?" Isaac watched his disc land less than ten feet from the basket, an impressive throw for sure. "That is my ruse. I hit beautiful women in the head with my discs, then I try to win them over."

"Well, you're very good at it – the first part, anyway." She felt her bump again, as the four of them walked back to get Isaac's bag full of discs.

"Thank you. I've had a lot of practice."

"So, I'm not the first girl you've hit in the head with a disc?"

Isaac laughed. This was somewhat ironic, as Olivia once hit him in the head from about twenty feet away when she was only ten or eleven-years-old. That might have been the first time he dropped an f-bomb in front of his kids. He knew how much one of those discs hurt when it connected with the head.

"Well, you certainly are the best-looking girl I've ever hit in the head." Her friends giggled and lagged behind a foot or two.

"So, tell me about yourself, Isaac." Julia carried a bounce in her step, much like an energetic child, full of life, ready for adventure. "You look like you're married."

"Well, I kind of am." Isaac wasn't sure how to respond to her. Except for two drunken nights with Nicole, he hadn't talked to a woman like this in his entire life. That wasn't really the same thing either. His relationship with Nicole had been purely physical. They didn't spend time talking or getting to know each other like a potential couple would. He wasn't used to flirting, and had no idea how to really approach it in this post-Ramie era of his life. "What I mean is... it's complicated."

"It's not complicated," Julia said, visibly turned off by the suddenly not-so-charming man. "You're either married, or you're not. Go home to your wife, Isaac."

Julia began to walk away toward the eleventh hole while Isaac gathered his thoughts. Should I tell her or just leave it be and go home? It's not like I can have a relationship yet anyway. What would be the point in explaining anything to this woman?

"Wait, let me explain." He jogged and caught up with Julia and her friends. "You may have heard about it on the news, but there was this guy, the...Biloxi Butcher? He kidnapped and killed ten women. My wife was one of the women. So that's why I said I'm kind of married. She's only been gone for a couple of months, so I don't really know what I am."

The group looked at Isaac, stunned, before the friends quietly walked away. Julia remained there, speechless.

"I didn't know; I'm sorry," Julia said. "I can't even imagine what you're going through right now."

"Thank you," Isaac responded. They strolled up behind her friends and sat down at a nearby bench. "This is my first time playing since she went missing. I haven't got out much since everything happened, except for spending time with my kids and running. Besides that, I haven't really wanted to be around other people. It's even tough to see family, you know, 'cause it reminds me of Ramie. That was her name, Ramie. I'm sorry. You don't want to hear about all this."

"No, you're fine. I do remember hearing about that case on the news. I couldn't believe how sick that guy was. I am so sorry for your loss. I'm sure that's what everyone says, but still..."

"Thanks. I'm sorry too."

"How are your kids doing? Are they little or big?"

"They are doing okay. My oldest is Carter. He's eighteen and goes to Auburn. He just came home yesterday for Thanksgiving, so it's great to have him back. He's adjusted, I think. It's hard to know for sure, but we talk every day. And Olivia is sixteen. She's a junior at Etowah, and she is perfect. She's been fighting off depression since the guy confessed, but she is strong. I think she's dealing with it the best that she can."

"And what about you? How are you dealing with it?" Julia talked to Isaac like an old friend. Even more, she listened more intently than Isaac could ever remember someone listening to him.

"It's weird, you know? I'm thirty-seven now. We married at eighteen; were high school sweethearts. I've been with her my whole life except for a few short times in high school. It feels strange to be alone. I'm thankful I still have my kids. I don't know what I would do without them." He paused. "What about you, Julia? Are you married? Do you have any kids?"

"I'm divorced. It was an unhealthy marriage, to say the least. Ended about five years ago. We were married for twenty years but no kids. We were never able to have any."

"I'm sorry to hear that, but I'm glad you're out of it. It sounds like it's for the best. Still, twenty years is a long time. I'm sure that wasn't easy for you." He didn't want this conversation to end. Already he felt a deep connection with her. They'd gone from zero to eighty instantly, discussing their lives like old friends during their most difficult times. "But twenty years? There's no way you were married for twenty years. I thought that I got married young. You can't be any older than me. I would have guessed thirty-five, to be honest."

"That's sweet of you to say, but I am older than you. I think I'm going to make you guess how old I am." Julia brushed his arm, and Isaac felt light and warm.

"That doesn't sound like a fun game," he said. "I already guessed anyway. I'll stick with that guess. You're thirty-five." Isaac allowed his leg to rest against hers. It felt like he was in high school again. The blood rushed through his body, made him feel incredibly alive.

"Fine, I won't make you guess." She kept her hand in her lap this time. "I'm forty-four."

"Forty-four?" Isaac asked, surprised.

"Is that too old for you?" Julia said, with a note of impending disappointment.

"No, it's not that, I just can't believe you're that old. I didn't mean it like that. You're *not* old. What I mean is that you look incredible for your age. Okay, *that* didn't sound right either. You look amazing, period. You look much younger than forty-four, so good job. You are honestly one of the most beautiful women I've ever seen." Isaac looked at her with what he hoped she perceived as tenderness. He couldn't kiss her just yet, but everything in him wanted to hold this woman tight and never let her go.

"Thank you, you are sweet. You're not so bad yourself, Isaac." He loved the sound of his name when it fell from her luscious lips.

Isaac hesitated. He wanted to do something, but his nerves were stopping him from being too forward. He battled himself for what seemed like an eternity and finally built up the courage to ask her what he considered to be the bare minimum.

"Can I get your number? I don't know what I'm ready for, or if I'm ready for anything, but you are too perfect to let go and never see again."

"I'm not perfect, believe me, but I don't know. What would your kids think?"

"I don't know. I haven't even thought about it. I didn't think I'd meet someone so quickly, much less you." He handed her his phone so she could input her number. He noticed a slight blush in Julia's cheeks. "I'm not asking you to marry me, just for your number. I really don't know what I want. Let's just talk and go from there. Deal?"

"Deal." Julia grinned and entered her number into his phone, before handing it back to Isaac. "What about lunch? I thought you said you were going to buy us lunch for nearly knocking me unconscious? I could have a concussion, you know."

"You're right, I do owe you ladies a meal. Do you want to play the rest of the course?"

Isaac and Julia finished the course, then caught up with her friends after the last hole. He treated them to pizza at the Marietta Pizza Kitchen. He wasn't even tempted to order a drink, which was a pleasant surprise. They talked all about their past lives and current endeavors. Julia was an author. She'd written seven novels and two novellas. She mainly wrote crime novels. This intrigued Isaac, seeing as how he and Ramie had been into all those crime documentary shows. She'd grown up in Kennesaw and went to Harrison High School. She finished her undergrad at the University of Georgia and earned her masters from the University of Tennessee.

"What do you do when Georgia and Tennessee play each other in football?" Isaac asked as they left the restaurant, while Julia's friends waited for them in the car.

"I win either way." She exuded something so adorable with everything she said. Isaac thought she might be too good to be true.

"Yeah, you technically win, but you also lose."

"I never lose, Isaac. I always win."

"Either way, Auburn is better than both of your schools. When was your last championship by the way?" He softly needled her as the Georgia and Tennessee programs were always competitive, but it had been quite some time since they were dominant in any major sport, particularly football.

Julia raised an eyebrow. "What year did you play football for Auburn?"

"Very funny."

"Oh, was it basketball that you played then? Did you play with Charles Barkley?"

They both smiled. At the car, they gave each other a friendly hug before Julia climbed in and drove off with her friends. Isaac adjourned to his truck and sat for a minute. He glanced in the rearview mirror and grinned at himself. A good day today.

Arriving home, he noticed a familiar car in the parking lot.

Nicole's.

Isaac's heart sank. *Do they know?* he thought.

He stepped out of the truck and slowly walked into the house. He felt like a kid coming home from school with a note from the principal. He knew he was in trouble, and there were only two options: turn and run, or go inside and get it over with.

Opening the front door, he saw Olivia near the kitchen, Carter seated on the big couch, and Nicole right next to him.

"Hey, Daddy, how was your day?" Olivia skipped over and gave her father a hug.

"It was good. What are you guys up to?" This certainly didn't seem as if he'd been found out. This felt like friends hanging out, thankfully.

"Hey, Dad," Carter said. "This is my girlfriend. I think you know, Nicole."

It was meant to be funny, surely, as Nicole had spent many days at their house throughout high school. She and Carter had always remained just friends, however. Whenever Isaac or Ramie would ask Carter about her, he'd always say that he didn't like her like that, that she was just a friend. That was part of the reason Isaac initially rationalized his original transgression. At Carter's insistence.

"This is the girl you were telling me about?" Isaac smiled awkwardly at Nicole and walked over to the kitchen, farther away from the couch.

In a flash, he realized that his second transgression with Nicole had occurred while she was dating Carter. He felt sick.

"Yeah, I thought it would be a good surprise. We started talking more after I got to Auburn, and one thing led to another."

"Hi, Mr. Childs." Nicole waved, smiling longer than necessary. "It's good to see you again."

Isaac didn't know how to process any of this. This was not real life. This could not be happening.

"It's nice to see you too, Nicole." Isaac rubbed his forehead. "I'm going to go lay down. I'm not feeling too well."

"What's wrong, Daddy?" Olivia asked, sounding genuinely concerned.

"I think I was outside too long, and the cold air kind of got to me today. It's no big deal. I'm going to go take a nap and see if that helps."

Isaac trudged up the stairs and locked the door behind him. He crawled under the covers and closed his eyes, hoping this would all just go away. Before he pulled into the driveway, he was on top of the world. Now, he guessed that his world would be crashing down at any moment. He wanted a drink ... no, he needed one. Thankfully he didn't have any alcohol at the house, and he wasn't about to go back downstairs and deal with this again. Maybe this was punishment for meeting someone he liked so quickly after Ramie's death.

A text popped onto his phone. It was from Nicole: "Don't worry... I didn't tell anyone. I promised I wouldn't."

He deleted it. As soon as he did, another text came through, this time from Julia.

"Hey, it was really nice to meet you today, even if you did knock me to the ground. That wasn't very nice, you know :)"

"It was great to meet you too." Isaac quickly texted back. "Don't think of it as me knocking you to the ground... think of it as me sweeping you off your feet."

"Very well, thank you then... My Prince Charming."

Isaac fell asleep, replete with mixed emotions, though the warmer thoughts began, slowly, to outweigh the troubling ones.

CHAPTER 8
The Chicken and the Egg

NICOLE KEPT HER WORD, AND THANKSGIVING passed with tearful, yet happy times together. They watched football and visited both sides of the family. The following week, they held a memorial service.

They didn't have a body to bury, so they each put something special inside the empty casket. Olivia brought an Auburn t-shirt that her mother had given her, but she kept the sweatshirt Ramie used to wear all the time around the house. Carter wrote her a letter that he did not let anyone else read. He sealed it in an envelope before setting it inside the lonesome box. Her sister placed a single white rose inside, Ramie's favorite, and her parents put their favorite childhood photos of Ramie atop the t-shirt that Olivia laid across the bottom. The kids also included an old water bowl of Rylee's.

Finally, Isaac placed down a card for their final anniversary. Ramie saved every card he'd given her. He read it to himself one last time before gently giving the card away. Inside he'd written:

Ramie,

I love you more than anything, and am so thankful to have spent the last 19 years married to you. I can't wait to see what the next 19 have in store for us, & of course, all the places we will go :)

Love, Isaac

He let go of the card, and they all held hands around the casket. They said their goodbyes and left before it was lowered into the ground. Even though Ramie's body was not inside, it still felt like it was.

Isaac desperately wanted to be a better man. He'd failed with his drinking, and with his unforgivable sin. Now, he felt like he had a second chance at life. This time, he would do it right. He would be the man he should have always been. and spend the second half of his life as an honorable man. Sure, he'd accomplished many great things and raised two wonderful children, but he should have done better. He could have done more.

Isaac had not drunk since his mishap with Nicole. Carter and Nicole seemed happy together, which made Isaac feel even worse. He prayed they would break up. *What if they got married?* he thought. He couldn't let his son marry a girl he'd slept with. That was just too unnatural. Plus, she'd slept with him while they were together, and it didn't seem to bother her one bit. She was poised to break Carter's heart, acting like that. If he'd known they were a couple, he never would have texted her.

He continued texting Julia, and they spoke on the phone as well. He let the holidays run their course and just after the new year, he felt comfortable enough to ask her out on a date.

"What, like dinner and a movie?" Julia asked on the other end.

"You don't like dinner and movies?"

"I like both, but are you sure you're ready? Have you told your kids yet?"

"I think I'm ready." Isaac liked how Julia showed concern for his kids. "I know it's still soon, I guess. I actually don't really know. What is the appropriate amount of time? It seems that it will always feel too soon, and you are too special to pass up."

"Thank you, but I can wait. I like you too, Isaac. I just don't want to hurt your kids, and I don't want to rush you either."

"I haven't told the kids yet. Let's go out, and as long as we don't hate each other afterwards, I'll tell them, and then I'll introduce you to them. If they aren't okay with it, we'll figure it out at that point."

"Sounds good. See you in a few hours?"

"Yep, see you then." Isaac hung up the phone. He was struggling to not get ahead of himself. She seemed perfect, but it felt too good to be true. He'd begun reflecting on his life more since Ramie's death, finding much of it too good to be true. He'd married young, and it had lasted. He'd started a business and become a multi-millionaire in his early twenties. His kids were nearly perfect.

Now, he'd met this new woman, and she fit like his other half.

He agreed to pick Julia up from her home in Kennesaw. They would head down to Marietta for their night out. He wanted to avoid places he'd gone with Ramie, not sure how he'd deal with seeing a movie at their movie theater or eating at a restaurant they used to frequent. Nearly four months had passed since her disappearance, a seeming lifetime. He didn't know whether that feeling made him a bad person, or if it was just how time worked. Either way, he didn't tell anyone. All these feelings were new to him. He simply tried to work through them and love his kids the best he could.

At the same time, he believed he was meant to be with Julia now. He still loved Ramie, but his feelings toward Julia provided him with hope and made it easier for him not to drink or succumb to his other weakness again. Now that Nicole was with Carter, he felt disgust at the mere thought of being with her.

"You look nice tonight," he said, eyeballing her leather jacket and the crimson dress that fell just below her knees. Julia dressed with the perfect mixture of class and cuteness. Tonight, he would have guessed she were closer to thirty, definitely not above forty.

"You look okay yourself, Isaac." There it was; his name falling from her lips again. That was the sound he missed so dearly since they met that day on the disc golf course. They hadn't seen each other in person since, and she was every bit as beautiful as he remembered. He'd begun to worry that he had possibly misremembered her beauty. Maybe, he debated on more than one occasion, it was merely a temporary crush, and it would fade. He feared that the next time he saw her he wouldn't experience the same sentiments.

He was wrong. He stood here now, fairly confident that he already loved this new woman.

"I hope I look better than okay." He brushed the side of her head, the spot he hit her in with the disc. "I see you healed up nicely." Julia reached for his hand and held it tenderly. Tingles coursed through Isaac. She probably didn't mean for it to happen that way, but sparks undoubtedly flew when her fingers mixed with his. She held onto his fingers, and they lowered their arms together. They walked from her front porch to his truck, hand-in-hand, like a couple who's made that walk a thousand times before.

"Is this okay?" Julia broke the silence as he opened the truck door for her, still holding onto each other's hands.

"It's more than okay." Isaac leaned in and kissed her lips softly. It was not a passionate kiss nor was it a long kiss. It did not shake the earth beneath them or stop the wind around them. It was, however, a kiss meant to be. They held their lips together for several seconds and rested their foreheads against one another. They did not get carried away or move in for anything more. They simply stared at each other and continued to hold hands.

"We better get going," she finally said, their heads still touching each other.

"Yes, we better." Isaac pecked her on the cheek and closed the door gingerly before making his way to the driver's side of the truck.

They arrived at the Chicken and the Egg restaurant on Whitlock Avenue, a place neither of them had ever eaten. They shared pimento cheese fritters. Both drank ice water.

"You can order a soda, you know," Isaac said. "Or a beer or wine."

"Well thank you, sir," Julia teased. "Am I allowed to use the restroom as well?"

"Very funny. I just meant that..."

"If I need to use the phone, am I allowed to do that, or should I ask for permission first?"

"Okay, okay, I'm sorry. I just meant that I want you to be comfortable. Order whatever you want. Or don't. You're a big girl."

"Oh, I'm a big girl, am I? You haven't dated much, have you?"

"I didn't mean it that way. I'm sorry; I sometimes speak before I think. You are not a big girl. You are an astonishing woman, even if you did go to Georgia and Tennessee. It hurts just to say that out loud, you know."

"And just what does War Eagle mean anyway?" Julia smirked and took a drink of her water. "Your mascot is a tiger, yet you've got this strange eagle as well? It sounds like you attended a school with an identity crisis."

"Really? The Tennessee Volunteers?" He proudly smirked back at his beautiful dinner date. "Your mascot is a dog, and you guys are a bunch of volunteers. How about we agree that we both have schools with an identity crisis?"

"Fair enough, except that my Bulldogs don't have an identity crisis."

"No, they don't have an identity crisis." Isaac pushed the last cheese fritter over to Julia's side of the plate. "But they still haven't won anything in a generation." Julia smiled toward Isaac. Her joy rushed upon him like a breath of fresh air, one he never wanted to stop breathing.

"So, tell me about your marriage." Isaac took a bite of his New York strip steak, the same dish that Julia ordered, both medium-well. "If you want to, that is. You don't have to talk about it if you don't want to. I'm not one of those guys."

"One of what guys?" Isaac could see that she enjoyed teasing him, and he liked it as well.

"I just mean that I'm not this super jealous guy who has to know everything about you. Whatever is in your past, it's your past. There's nothing I can do about it anyway. I guess that's how I look at it. Thanks, by the way, you've got me rambling again."

"I like it." Julia dipped her steak into the mashed potatoes and took another bite. "I don't mind talking about it, but it's not the best story. We got married at nineteen, and things were good at first. He treated me well except for when he drank, but even then, he was just verbally mean to me, not completely abusive. I don't know when things changed really. I guess it was after my first book was published. He didn't like that I got my master's degree or that my book was published. He was insecure. Eventually, he started hitting me whenever he was drunk, which started to happen regularly. He cheated on me with more women than I care to know. And eventually, I had enough, and I filed for divorce."

Isaac wasn't quite sure what to say. "I'm sorry. You don't deserve that."

"Thank you, but I let it go on too long. I should have left him after ten years, yet I stayed married for twenty." Julia chuckled. "Probably because I'm Catholic,"

"Divorce is a pretty big deal for you guys, huh?"

"Yeah, more so than beating your wife and cheating on her, apparently. I went to my priest, and he advised me to work things out. He said that God could save our marriage. He didn't."

"You tried. That's more than most these days." He didn't know if he believed this or not. It seemed like the correct sentiment to offer, however.

"Yeah, and look where it got me. I'm forty-four with no kids. I always wanted kids, but he wasn't able to have any. I guess that's actually a good thing, now that I think about it.

"I think you're pretty great." Isaac blushed. He felt like a mushy boy, but with every word Julia spoke he was falling harder for her. "Did the marriage at least end on okay terms?"

"Literally the opposite." She set her knife and fork down before proceeding. "I hope you're ready for the finale."

"Uh oh."

"He held me at gunpoint and threatened to kill me. He said he'd never let me leave him, that he'd kill me before I could. I thought that was the end, honestly. He shot me in the stomach, and then he turned the gun on himself. He shot himself in the head, but the bullet missed his brain and really just grazed his skin. Still, blood went everywhere, and he hit the ground. I thought he was dead. I called 911 and, long story short, he'd basically passed out from the wound. They said he had a heart attack, the stupid bastard. It took me a couple of weeks to recover and a few months to get back to normal. He's in prison now for attempted murder and kidnapping. I bet you're glad you asked me." She shook her head as she lifted more food to her mouth. "This is such wonderful dinner conversation and first date discussion."

"No, I'm glad I'm getting to know you," Isaac said. "I'm sorry if this is uncomfortable..."

"Don't worry about it."

"I'm certainly glad you're alive to be here with me now."

"I'm happy that I'm alive as well." Julia smiled again. Isaac guessed he would never grow tired of seeing her flawless smile.

"Do you think you'd ever consider getting married again?" Isaac asked. "Is it something you've thought about?"

"You're cute. Honestly, at the time I didn't think I'd ever get married again. Now, I'm not so sure." They both glanced down at their nearly-empty plates, then looked back up at the same time. "There are a few things I'd have to be sure of before ever getting married again. First, he would have to know that my ex-husband promised to kill me when he gets released from prison. That's going to be another five years, at least, probably more, but still..."

"He? Is there another guy you have in mind?"

"You're the first man I've dated since my divorce." She looked at Isaac, waiting for him to speak. There was an alluring unreality to the moment. It surrounded them as they shared their stories.

"I appreciate you telling me. That can't be an easy thing to talk about."

"You're in a similar boat," Julia admitted.

"Yes, yes I am."

"The other thing has to do with honesty. I spent so many years being lied to; I just can't take that anymore. I know it's soon, and forgive me if it's inappropriate for me to ask, but did you ever cheat on your wife?"

Nicole's image raced to his mind's eye. He tried to push it out, but she would not leave. He could not tell Julia that he slept with a seventeen-year-old girl, then once again when she was eighteen, not to mention the fact that she was now dating his son. He'd hid it from Ramie, then from his kids, and now he had no other choice except to keep it from Julia. After all, it wasn't an affair. It was just the one drunken time when Ramie was still alive, and that was in response to her flirty messages with her ex. The time after she went missing didn't count as far as Isaac was concerned.

"No, I never cheated on my wife," he said. "Did you ever cheat on your husband?"

"Yes, I did." Julia admitted this easily. Isaac was taken aback. "It was after I found out about my husband's affairs, but still, I did cheat. I'm not proud of it, and I would never do it again. I was a different person then. I try my best to be honest, though I'm not always successful."

"Thank you for being honest with me. I appreciate it." Isaac debated whether or not to tell her about Nicole. He could admit he lied, explain why he did so, and surely she would understand. Or, she might leave, and he'd lose any chance at being with her. "I try to be honest as well, but I guess I'm like you. A liar, that is."

"Very clever." Julia wiped her mouth and drank the last of her water. "Since we're being honest, can I tell you something?"

"If I say no, are you going to tell me anyway?"

"Never mind, I think I'll just keep it to myself."

"I'm kidding, tell me." Isaac studied her face, found her every subtle expression endearing. Her right cheek offered a dimple when she smiled, and light freckles raced underneath her eyes, as well as a few more scattered across her forehead. She was a stunning woman.

"No, you had your chance, Isaac. Now you'll just have to spend the rest of the night wondering what I was going to tell you."

"Okay, okay, I'm sorry. Please tell me, and I won't make you pay for dinner."

"Well, aren't you the perfect gentleman. You're from the South, I would have expected better manners." She rested her foot atop Isaac's. The simple motion electrified him.

"All right, I'll pick up the check this time. But you owe me."

"Fine, I'll tell you since you're basically paying me to do so. I know we were supposed to go to the movies, but I thought maybe we could go to a park and walk around for a bit."

"That sounds good to me." Isaac couldn't think of a better way to spend the rest of their night together. He remembered going on walks with Ramie, but it had been many years since they'd done so. He felt guilty for comparing the two women, but figured that was only inevitable. He assumed other people would do the same thing in his situation, but it wasn't like there was anyone he could talk to about it. He'd actually considered looking for a group of other widowers to join, but he decided against it since he was only thirty-seven, and he figured everyone else would be much older. "Did you have a park in mind?"

"Well, there's always Oregon Park, but I'm afraid you might hit me with a disc again."

"Very funny."

Isaac took her hand as they left the Chicken and the Egg.

"There's not really a good place to walk there anyway. There's another park I enjoy going to sometimes. You know Adams Park?"

"Oh yeah, off Highway 41, right? My brother and I used to play baseball there when we were kids."

"Adams Park it is then."

They climbed into the car and began driving, and Julia reached over and took Isaac's hand once more. "I like places that have people names. Don't judge me; I know it's weird."

"As long as you don't judge me for my strange habits. Plus, our pug's name is Rylee. I like pets with human names."

"I can't promise not to judge you if I don't know what these habits are. I mean, are you out stalking women, or do you count the steps when you're walking up a flight of stairs?" She grinned when she spoke, and brushed her fingers back and forth over his, like they were created for each other.

"I haven't stalked a woman in many years." He squeezed her hand. "I can't say I've ever counted steps before, but now I'm pretty sure I will the next time I'm faced with a set of stairs."

"Oh, you should try it. It's surprisingly fun, and addictive."

"I'd say my weirdest habit is that I enjoy watching the local news when I'm out of town." Isaac gently braced for the joke surely to come.

"That's not strange."

"No? I gotta say that I'm surprised. I figured you'd have some sort of jab for me." They pulled into the Adams Park lot and sat for a second.

"I don't make jokes," she joked, grinning, "I make observations. I apologize if you feel like these observations are at your expense."

Julia hopped out of the truck and ran around to the driver's side. She opened the door for Isaac, and their hands slid back together. "But that's not strange at all. It's more than that. It's borderline insane, if I'm being completely honest."

Isaac squeezed her sides just enough to make her jump and quickly rejoined his hand with hers. "It's a guilty habit of mine. I don't know what it is, but the worse the news is, the more I enjoy watching it."

"Any favorites? Any cities in particular that stand out as being truly awful?" They walked over to the playground, and Julia sat on the swings. Isaac positioned himself behind her and pushed her on the swing like they were kids. She pumped her legs, both goosepimpled from the winter chill.

"Cincinnati was particularly bad. I think it's because of the commercials. I never watch commercials at home, but I like them when I'm on the road. Commercials in other cities are terrible, but I suppose I'm biased. Cincinnati aired commercials from Ohio and Kentucky, so they were destined to be bad with two states battling each other. It was a double-up of badness."

"So, you're saying you like bad local news broadcasts from other cities, and that you enjoy their awful commercials as well?" She jumped off the swing and nailed the landing, even with her Toms and no socks on. "There might not be any help for you, you know. I think you better take me home, Isaac."

"You are hilarious. I guess it's a good thing I found you then, since you are perfect and all." He took hold of her hand once again, and they walked around the playground. Only a handful of lights shone down, and they enjoyed the park to themselves.

"I am pretty amazing." She brought another dimple to her face.

"Can I tell you something now?" Isaac turned and locked eyes with Julia.

"Please do."

"I think I'm falling for you. Actually, that's a lie..."

He leaned in and kissed her, this time a bit deeper and more passionately.

"...I've already fallen for you," he said, when they pulled softly away. His hands remained locked onto her hips and her left hand held the back of his neck.

"I've fallen for you too, Isaac. I didn't want to, if I'm being completely truthful. I tried to make myself forget about you, but you won't go away."

"Thanks," he said sarcastically as they continued wandering around the peaceful park. "So I'm like a jingle? I get in your head and then you can't get rid of me."

"I'm sure that's it." Her voice lowered. "I just don't want to get hurt. And I don't want to cause any pain to you or your family either. We both have such strange stories, such painful pasts. Maybe that's why we're meant for each other."

"I agree." He stopped walking and took half a step back from Julia. "I think that this, what we have here, is more than special. I try not to even think about how I got here, about what happened to Ramie. And I hate that you've had to live through such heartache and tragedy as well. I know it's not the same, but ...hey, I need to tell you something. Admit something, really."

"Okay." Julia said, and Isaac knew he was about to tell her something that she did not want to hear. "If you want to."

"No, I don't want to, but I feel like I need to. You asked me earlier if I'd ever cheated on my wife, and I said that I hadn't. That was only partially true." Isaac's heart sank, but the words were already out his mouth. "It was about a year and a half ago, and it was only a one night stand. I found out that Ramie had been reconnecting with a boyfriend from high school. We were high school sweethearts. This was the only other guy she'd ever dated, and that was just on one of our little breaks. After I found out she'd been talking to him, we argued for a while, then we didn't talk to each other, and then I got super drunk one night, and I hooked up with this girl. It wasn't an affair, but it was still wrong, regardless of whether Ramie started it or not. I took it to a whole other level, and I was wrong. I never told her about it, and I could never tell my kids. It would crush them. I didn't plan on telling you either, but there's this bond between us. I just felt like I needed to tell you and clear the air."

"That must have been tough for you to admit." Julia took his hand back in hers. "This is our first date, Isaac. Do you realize that this is our first time out together since we met? Well, since you knocked me out, really. Anyway, we may have talked a lot, and we've shared years' worth of information tonight, but we are still getting to know each other."

"I don't want to stop getting to know you." He leaned in and gently kissed her full lips.

"I don't either. I'm just saying that neither of us are obliged to confess anything to the other." She placed her hands on his deceivingly-firm chest. "We aren't even a couple yet. We are... I'm not sure what we are."

"What do you want us to be?"

"I want the same thing as you," she admitted.

"Good. You make me happy, Julia. Does it sound strange for me to say your name?"

"No, I like it. Why do you ask? Is it strange for you to say it?"

"No, I like your name. It's just that I love to hear you say my name. Every time you do, my heart flutters. I know, I sound like a girl, but still."

"Yeah, you do sound like a girl." She kissed him on the cheek, and the scruff of his beard rubbed against her lips. "We have to take this slow. I don't know how, or what's right, or when is the proper time. I just feel like we need to take it one day at a time and pick the appropriate moment to tell your kids."

They walked back to his truck, and Isaac drove her home. On reflection, it was one of the best nights of his life. They'd spent nearly two hours talking at dinner and another two hours at the park. More than anything, the night had given him hope that there might be a joyful ending within reach. He hoped and believed that she felt the same way.

CHAPTER 9
Chalkboards Are Forever

ISAAC AND JULIA SPENT THE REST of the winter discretely talking and dating. They partook in lunch or dinner nearly every day of the week, or Isaac would go to her house and spend time there. They went to the movies, visited parks, enjoyed short hikes together, indulged whatever moments they could together. Isaac found pleasure in the simple things, and he could see that Julia adored him for it. They even snuck off for a weekend getaway to the North Georgia mountains. When May arrived, they agreed that it was time to tell the kids and the rest of his family.

"I just think it's best that we tell them now," Isaac said as they sat on Julia's screened-in back porch. She had a large back yard with two pear trees and a peach tree that highlighted the splendor of the yard. They both savored many days and nights on the porch, watching the birds race by and the squirrels climb one of the many trees. "It's been eight months since Ramie went missing and more than six months since she passed away. It feels right now, I guess. I take that back. It doesn't feel right, but it does feel necessary."

"I'm nervous. What if they don't like me?" Julia stirred her coffee with her pinky finger and licked the foam from the end of her finger.

"They're going to love you. I love you. They want me to be happy, and it's not like they're little kids. They know that life moves on. Don't take that the wrong way. I don't mean to sound insensitive. I just mean that Carter has been with his girlfriend since before the holidays, and Olivia is doing great in school, and she's about to finish her junior year. They've done well with moving on and continuing their lives, like their mom would have wanted them to do."

"I hope you're right, and I love you too." Julia leaned over and kissed Isaac on the lips. "What are you going to tell them, that we're a couple, or that we've been talking, or what?"

"I don't want to lie to them, but I'm not sure it's the best thing to tell them we've been seeing each other for the past five months. We'll tell them the truth, how and when we met, that we've been talking ever since, and that we recently started dating. We don't have to go into all the details or tell them that we said, 'I love you' on our third date." He chuckled a bit.

"I trust you, but I'm still nervous. Do you want to tell them by yourself, or do you want me there with you?"

"I need you there with me. I'm scared too. Plus, you'll get to meet Rylee and see my home."

"I do want to meet Rylee, and I can't wait to see a millionaire's home." Julia threw him a teasing smirk.

"You'll just have to be careful around the house. The railings are made of gold, and the toilets were sculpted from pure silver."

"What? No golden thrones?"

"No, I thought it would be over the top. Silver was a practical compromise."

They agreed to wait the rest of the month until school was out, when Carter returned home for the summer, to sit down and tell the kids. Isaac decided to tell them by himself that he'd met someone, and then bring Julia over later that day so they could meet her. He just hoped that Nicole would not be there. She and Carter were still together, and she'd practically moved to Auburn with him. She stayed with him many nights, even though that was a violation of his dorm rules.

Either way, Isaac had not drunk since November. This was the longest he'd ever gone without a drink since he was eighteen. Meeting Julia had pretty much absolved him of the temptation.

It was now the first day of June, the kids were home and Isaac sat down with Carter and Olivia in their living room. This was the place where Carter told them he'd been accepted to Auburn, the room they told the kids about Ramie's miscarriage all those years ago, and where they last saw their mother before that fateful run. It was a space they filled with memories pleasant and painful. Isaac hoped that this would be a happy moment to remember.

"I'm just going to get right to the point." He tried to keep the tremble from his voice. "I've met someone."

"You met someone?" Carter sounded betrayed, even shocked. "How could you have met someone? Mom has barely been dead for what, like eight months?"

"I'm sorry, I didn't mean for it to happen."

"Yeah, I accidentally meet people all the time." Carter crossed his arms.

"Please, just hear me out, and then you can be angry if you still feel the same way." Isaac continued as Olivia sat quietly and listened, while Carter teared up. Isaac assumed it would have been the other way around, though he didn't truly know how they would react to the news. He was glad that Nicole was not here for this. "Her name is Julia. She's a wonderful woman, and we did meet by accident. I hit her in the head with my disc while playing disc golf, last November."

"You've known her since November?" Olivia's voice cracked. "Were you ever going to tell us?"

"Yes, just let me explain. We met then, but obviously it was too soon for me. I love your mother. I still love your mother. This isn't about me forgetting your mom or falling out of love with her, but it is about me moving on with my life. I'm still a young man, and I don't want to be alone. I didn't expect to meet anyone this quickly, but there was a connection there from the moment we met. We started out by texting and talking some, and we went on our first date in January. I didn't say anything because if it didn't work out, I didn't want to have this conversation for no reason. I love you guys, and I don't want to cause you any more pain that you've already endured."

"Do you love her?" Carter asked, calmer than his initial reaction.

"Yes, son, I love her. I love her dearly. She is a special woman, and you two are going to love her as well. I know it's hard, but don't compare her to your mother. She is not your mother. She knows that, and I know that. But this is our life now. It's all new to me, and it's new to you as well."

"I can't say I'm happy," Olivia admitted, "but I'm happy for you. I want you to be happy, Daddy."

Carter's crossed arms loosened. "Yeah, plus aren't you like forty-five already?"

"Very funny. I'm only thirty-eight. You sent me thirty-eight dollars for my birthday last month, remember?"

"How old is she?" Olivia asked. "Please tell me she's not like twenty-two, and this is some sort of mid-life crisis."

"No, she's not twenty-two. She's older than me. She's fifty-nine."

"Fifty-nine?" Carter gasped. "Is she super rich or something? But we're rich, that doesn't make any sense."

"I'm teasing so it wouldn't seem so bad. She's forty-four, almost forty-five actually. She doesn't look her age though; she looks younger than me, to be honest."

"When do we get to meet her?" Olivia asked with a slight grin on her face.

"I'd like to introduce you guys to her today. I thought she could come over and get to know you, and the dog. I thought it might be nice for her to see our home for once."

"I don't know that I'm ready for another woman to come to our home," Olivia said. "And what do you mean for once? How often do you go to her house?"

"I go there regularly for lunch or dinner, just to talk, really. And that's fine, I'm sure she wouldn't mind us coming over to her house."

"What's her name again?" Carter asked sarcastically.

"Julia."

"Like Drew Barrymore in *The Wedding Singer*," Carter laughed. "Julia Goolia."

All three laughed, and Isaac stood from his recliner and reached for his kids. He embraced them, and they squeezed each other. He understood that, above all else, they were a family. They were there for each other, and they loved one another.

"Let me call her and see if we can head over there now, if that's okay with you guys. Rylee can come too. You know how excited she gets when I let her ride in my truck."

They piled into Isaac's truck, and Carter held Rylee in his lap, covered in a blanket so she wouldn't get hair all over the seats. She panted for the first ten minutes before she finally laid down and fell into a deep sleep for the final fifteen minutes of the drive. When they pulled into Julia's oversized driveway, Isaac immediately spotted his new love and looked over at his kids to see if they approved. She waited on the front porch steps and greeted them with a smile. They stepped out of the truck in unison, and Rylee ran in excited circles.

"Hello!" Julia called from the steps. "It's so nice to meet you both. I'm Julia." She reached out her hand and shook Olivia's first, then Carter's.

"You too," Carter said, "thanks for having us over."

They followed her up the steps and took in the charming, brick home Julia had purchased after the incident with her ex-husband. It sat nestled in the back of an established neighborhood with other homes that told stories of perfect families having lived and loved within their walls. The home was much too spacious for her, but she told Isaac that she liked the storage and the extra rooms. One room she used only for writing. Another, she turned into her mug collection room. She had collected more than five hundred vintage and collectible coffee mugs from all over the world. She loved to go to thrift stores and bought most of the mugs for a dollar or less. That room, the one past her bedroom upstairs, displayed mugs on shelves and in glass cabinets all over the room. It was quite the spectacle, and just one of the quirky things that Isaac loved about her.

"Thank you, Carter," she said. "I bought this place about five years ago, but I feel like I've lived here forever." She welcomed them into the living room and sat down next to Isaac. He nearly grabbed her hand out of habit.

"So, it's just you here?" Olivia asked as she looked around at the raised ceilings and the ornate staircase that led to the mysterious upstairs. "It's a pretty big house."

"I know it is. It's really too large for me, but I got a great deal on it, and it felt like home from the first time I walked inside. As soon as I laid eyes on the back yard, I knew this was where I was meant to live. Let me show you two around."

Julia led them to the kitchen first and insisted they drink something. Everyone chose a glass of water that Julia poured for them, and they followed her throughout the house. Carter commented on how cool the mugs were, and Olivia on how much she loved her writing room.

"Did you make the walls like this, or were they like this when you bought the house?" Olivia's face lit up when she saw the room. The walls in Julia's writing room were not walls at all. They were floor-to-ceiling chalkboards. Olivia and Carter perused the different quotes and ideas that Julia had written across the once-black chalkboards. They now displayed as much white and colorful chalk as they did blank space.

"I had these put in a few months after I moved in." Julia struggled to hide her excitement. Isaac split his time observing her and his kids to see their reactions to everything.

"They are awesome." Olivia stared, wide-eyed and childlike. "I've never seen anything like it."

"Thank you, I love them too. I saw a picture on the internet, and I didn't know if it was real or not, but I figured, why not? So, I called my dad. He owned a construction business all of my life, and a few weeks later, there they were."

"This is almost better than your mug collection," Carter joked.

Rylee followed Julia around as well, staying close to her leg and begging for attention from the new friend.

"I don't know about that," Julia said. "I do love my mugs. But I think I love this room more than anything else in the house, even the back yard. I don't know if your father told you or not, but I'm a writer. The walls help to inspire me. It sounds weird, I know, but I am a bit strange sometimes."

They all looked at the walls, and Olivia read some of the quotes out loud. Much of the wall displayed Julia's thoughts and ideas, but a few of the quotes stood out to her.

"You must be the change you wish to see in the world." - Gandhi

"Love your enemies." - Jesus

"There is nothing permanent except change." - Heraclitus

"It doesn't sound weird." Olivia smiled. "I can see how this would inspire you. I want my walls like this. Dad?"

"We'll see." Isaac wanted to cry. He felt such joy that his kids seemed to genuinely like Julia. He was beyond scared that they were not going to accept her or that something would go wrong. Instead, they acted like they'd known each other forever. This was just one more thing that seemed too good to be true.

"The back yard is great, isn't it?" Isaac asked.

"It's really nice," Olivia agreed.

"It really is nice to meet you both," Julia spoke softly. "I know this can't be easy for either of you. Thank you for being so kind to me and giving me a chance."

The four of them sat inside that screened-in porch and enjoyed the subtle, late-spring breeze as it warmed their skin. Isaac wished for this day never to end. The conversation started out shaky back at his house but quickly turned into something that resembled normality. Julia looked happy, as well - and relieved.

"I really like her, Dad," Carter said as they closed the doors on the truck, and he tried to calm Rylee in the back seat.

"Yeah, I didn't want to at first, but she's really sweet," Olivia said. "I wasn't sure what I wanted to be when I grow up, but after I saw her chalkboard walls, I think I might want to be a writer."

"You guys have no idea how happy that makes me. Love you."

They drove home as a family, and Isaac's heart felt complete for the first time in what seemed like ages.

CHAPTER 10
Hangman's Curse

"WHAT DO YOU THINK THIS MEANS?" Agent Noah looked all around the floor. He and his partner were trying to make sense of why the Butcher chose this day to send a message. He'd confessed almost immediately, so that he would avoid the death penalty. Now, eleven months later, he'd chosen to do something this drastic.

"I think it means that we need to search the waters down south again."

Agent Faith stared at the deceased body of Charles Haney. The Biloxi Butcher had hung himself the night before, and his cold body still dangled in his cell.

"We've searched three separate times," Agent Noah said as he scanned the note that the Butcher left behind for at least the tenth time. "We've only been able to find three portions of the missing women's remains. I doubt we're going to be able to find more after all this time."

"We have to try." Agent Faith studied the note from the Butcher, though it wasn't exactly a note. It was more a poem of sorts.

They counted the women one by one,
They searched the water just for fun.
The only one who truly knows,
Might just tell a living soul.
Follow me, and you will see,
The numbers drown out the harrowing sea.
One, two, three, four,
So many bodies on the floor.
Five, six, seven, eight,
A work of art some choose to hate.
Triple that number and make it wide,
They lived, they died, my love, she tried.

"It has to mean that he had more victims," Agent Noah said. "Eight times three is twenty-four."

"At least," she agreed. "There has to be something we're missing. There's no way he disposed of every victim in Biloxi." The body in the man's trunk had been a Jane Doe for so long: No fingers or teeth to help them figure out who she was. It took several months before they definitively identified her. When they did, they were shocked to discover that she was the fifth victim, not the tenth victim, as was originally believed to be the case.

"We searched his homes." Agent Noah led the way out of the cell. "There were no bodies there. The dogs picked up scents on his tools, but nowhere else on the properties."

"I don't know," said Agent Faith. They were overlooking something crucial, she was sure of it. "Maybe he dumped some of them in a lake. Maybe he buried them in the woods. Maybe we failed to see something at his house or at the trailer. We need to go back and start over with fresh eyes. We also have to be absolutely sure that he didn't have another property somewhere else."

Agent Noah glanced back at the cell. "I still don't understand why he killed himself. It doesn't make any sense. What changed in the past year that made him go from begging for his life, to killing himself in his cell?"

"And what made him keep the woman we found in his trunk longer?" Agent Faith said. "Or did he actually keep her longer? We need to search again to make sure there aren't bodies buried somewhere on those properties or in the surrounding areas. We were convinced he dumped them all in Biloxi. What if we were wrong? What if he just wanted us to think that so that the families couldn't get closure?"

"They certainly don't have closure right now," Agent Noah said.

The FBI had not completely closed the case, but it was no longer active, either. With the suicide of the Butcher, though, and this ominous "poem", they'd need to take a closer look.

CHAPTER 11
Two for One

ISAAC COULDN'T BELIEVE HOW SUPPORTIVE HIS kids were regarding Julia. They welcomed her into their home, and while it was weird at first, they quickly got used to having her around. She never stayed the night, but she came over regularly throughout the summer until Carter went back to Auburn in September - shortly after the one-year anniversary of Ramie's disappearance.

They couldn't be sure when she passed away, of course, so they marked that fateful day in September as her last one alive. Julia didn't mind seeing pictures of Ramie, and the kids grew comfortable with pictures of Julia added around the house. Isaac's family was incredibly supportive, as was Ramie's. Her sister even took Julia out for coffee on more than one occasion and seemed to really like her. Ramie's parents still treated Isaac like their son, and they were fond of Julia as well, as strange as that seemed to Isaac. He was grateful not to lose Ramie's side of the family.

The agents informed Isaac about the Butcher's suicide after it happened last month, and he in turn told the family. That did not feel real, either, nor did it make him angry or mad. Part of Isaac wanted him to rot in prison for the rest of his life; another part was glad no more money or time would be wasted on his pathetic life. Unfortunately, the agents told him they would be investigating the case more as they received new information, though they would not tell him what it was. More importantly, Isaac had not drank in nearly a full year, since his last mishap with Nicole, who was still with Carter. If he could somehow convince Carter to break things off with Nicole, life would truly be perfect.

Isaac did not focus on anyone else now. Yes, he helped Olivia fill out college applications, though he kept nudging her toward Auburn, and he still talked to Carter on the phone each day. He enjoyed the close relationship with his son, the type of relationship that is normally reserved for a mother and her daughter, rather than for a father and his son. He made sure they were taken care of and that they remained a priority in his life. But now that a year had passed, it felt like an eternity to Isaac and his kids. He spent the past nine months getting to know Julia, and his kids took the past four months and made them feel like four years.

"I'm the luckiest man in the world." Isaac kissed the scar on Julia's stomach, the wound that her ex-husband placed on her for the rest of her life. "How on earth did I find you?"

"You hit me in the head when you were playing disc golf, remember?"

"I remember. Do you remember?" He nibbled her smooth, perfectly aged stomach. She'd added a few pounds since they met, but Isaac enjoyed her deceptively thick body. She was not big by any means, but she wasn't exactly skinny either. She held just the right amount of life on her skin and exuded a sexy confidence that made him happy.

"Barely." She stroked his hair like she was trying to calm a scared child after a bad dream. She gazed at his head and teased him for his slightly receding hairline as she counted the follicles that were attempting to retreat from his forehead. "I'd say you are incredibly lucky that I gave you the time of day, seeing as how you nearly killed me."

"Okay, Ms. Drama Queen. Let's not go overboard." Isaac savored the taste of her skin. "You taste good today. Oatmeal and apple?"

"What, I don't taste good everyday? I taste better than you, I'm sure, and it does smell like oatmeal and apple, doesn't it? That's funny because I was reading the box that the bar of soap came in today, and it said oatmeal and lavender, but when I smelled it, I thought of oatmeal and apple. And hey, head injuries are no laughing matter." She tugged at his hair and quickly straightened it back out, then wrapped her legs around his waist and placed her other hand on his cheek, which encouraged him to kiss her stomach one more time.

"Maybe that hit did mess with your head a little," Isaac said. "You kind of rambled on a bit back there. Anyway, what do you want to do today?"

"I'm up for anything. I'm going to write for a couple of hours, and I wanted to go for a walk, but I didn't have any plans. What did you have in mind?"

"I thought we could grab lunch at the Chicken and the Egg, and then maybe go to Adams Park. You know, relive our first date?"

"That was a fun night, and it will be even better in the daytime. Let's go now. I'm starving."

Isaac kissed her scar again, then rose and scooped her up from the bed and twirled her around before falling back onto the bed, dizzier than expected.

"Easy there," Julia teased. "I'm a big girl, you know."

"You are absolutely perfect." He nibbled her neck since he fell back on top of her anyway. "I love you."

He felt like a kid again, and had made up his mind that she was the woman he wanted to spend the rest of his life with. He felt guilty for not just moving on so quickly, but for falling so deeply in love with this new woman. He loved her as much as he ever loved Ramie, possibly more.

They ate at the Chicken and the Egg for the first time since that January night, and they walked around Adams Park once again. Accompanied by the daylight and the warm September air, this time they ventured deeper into the park. Isaac held her hand and stopped on the far side of the baseball fields.

"Julia," he said as he got down on one knee just like in the movies, "I knew you were special from the first time I laid eyes on you. I believed that I wanted to be with you from the moment I watched the bump swell up on your head." He withheld the chuckle. "I tried not to, but I fell madly in love with you on our first date, and even more each day since. You are beyond perfect, and you make me a better man. Will you make me the happiest man in the world and marry me?"

Julia thought for just a split second. "Yes, of course I'll marry you. But are you sure you want to marry an old woman?"

"Very funny." Isaac kissed her passionately after sharing their common response to the other's sarcastic joke. "You still look younger than me. That's all that matters. Did you hear me? THAT'S ALL THAT MATTERS!" He'd raised his voice just shy of yelling, which forced her to smile and hug him tight.

"I do love you, Isaac. I'll always love you." She rested her head on his shoulder and began to cry.

"Don't cry." He kissed her tears and lifted her head so that their cheeks were pressed together. "Are you sure this is what you want? You can tell me anything, you know."

"I know. I'm crying because I'm happy. I didn't think I'd ever be this happy again or in love, much less madly in love. I'm also sad for your kids and for your wife's parents. This won't be easy for them."

"The kids love you and so does everyone else in the family. Ramie is gone. Nothing is going to change that. You and I were made for each other. You know that. I know that. Anyone who's seen us together knows that."

Isaac once thought the same thing about him and Ramie. Even when they went through their rough stretches, they kept their love public, front and center for the world to behold. He wondered if people would think that about them if Ramie were still alive. He questioned whether or not he would still love her if she were. He also considered the alternate path his life would have traveled, seeing as how he never would have hit Julia in the head with the disc since he would not have been playing at that exact moment in time. Something in the universe meant for them to be together. Some supernatural force or maybe even God took Ramie's tragic death and gave him a second chance at life. He lived each day on purpose now, bound to do life the right way this time around.

"I do know that. I suppose I just need to hear you say it sometimes. I am an old woman, remember?"

"I think we both remember." He kissed her forehead and dried her tears with the backs of his hands. "But I can't always be sure with you." They strolled around the park, their hands locked with a loose yet confident bond that promised each other happy and secure moments still to come. "How does a Christmas wedding sound to you?"

"This Christmas?" Julia said. "That's only a few months away. And we can't get married on Jesus' birthday. I'm pretty sure he frowns on things like that."

"I didn't mean Christmas day exactly. I just thought that it would be really pretty around Christmas with all of the lights and decorations." Christmas had always been Isaac's favorite holiday. When he was a kid, he would open one present on Christmas Eve, and then he woke up incredibly early on Christmas morning. He would drag his parents out of bed, grab his brother, and run downstairs to wait for his parents to get up and join them to open up their presents. They would sit in a circle, pass out the presents, and each person opened one gift at a time. It was a tradition that he and Ramie continued with Carter and Olivia, though this past Christmas proved difficult to do anything according to tradition, as it was Ramie's first Christmas not there. This year could be different. He could spend this Christmas with his new wife and continue the pastime with the kids.

"There's my girl." Julia pressed her thumb and index finger into his side and forced him to squirm. They were both ticklish, but she could tickle him with little effort. One time when they were watching TV in her bed, she got up to get them a drink. When she came back, she handed him his glass of water and proceeded to slide her fingers across his bare foot. As she did, Isaac jumped up, tossing his water all over the pillows and blankets. They both burst out laughing. Water covered everything, and he threw his arms around her before tossing her onto the soaked covers. They enjoyed many memories like this, most of which ended with their arms wrapped tightly around each other.

"I can't wait to tell the kids." He beamed as they prepared to leave the park. "They are going to be so excited."

"I hope so, but before we leave, there's something I need to tell you."

Isaac shifted the truck back into park and turned to face his bride-to-be. "Sure, what's up?" he asked, casually. He'd grown accustomed to shifting tones over the past year. This felt like a significant shift.

"I didn't know when would be the right time to tell you, and I'm sorry for not telling you right away." She spoke hesitantly, not like her usually confident and spunky self.

"You're not having an affair, are you?"

"No, nothing like that. I love you, Isaac. I would never cheat on you."

"Okay then, what is it? As long as it's not something like that, I can handle it."

She hesitated for another brief moment before she revealed her news. "I'm pregnant." She paused for only a second, then rubbed her belly.

"But I thought... I mean, how? I thought you weren't able to get pregnant?" Isaac's body flooded with emotion, and he began to shake. He wasn't sure how to process this, even as he'd done it twice before.

However, this time was different.

"My ex was unable to have kids," Julia said. "I suppose I always could, but I just assumed I was too old now. They say that forty is the new thirty, so I guess that makes me the new thirty-five."

"This is the best news you could have ever given me." Isaac tried to stop the tears from streaming down his face, but the overwhelming joy beat out his self-control.

"Even better than me saying yes?"

"Well, it's not a competition, but I suppose so. I am so happy." He leaned over and kissed his love with tenderness and reassurance, a kiss that let her know that everything would be okay.

"I'm so relieved. I was nervous you wouldn't be excited about the baby."

"Why wouldn't I be excited? This is amazing news."

"Because we're so old, and you were almost done with the kid phase of your life. I ruined that."

"I'm pretty sure I had something to do with that as well. You didn't ruin anything. I love babies, and I get to raise one with you now. This is perfect."

"I'm going to be sixty-four-years-old when he or she graduates from high school. Everyone will think I'm their grandma, not their mother. What will the other mothers think?"

"Forget about them. Who cares what they think? Plus, you still look like you're in your early thirties. By the time you're sixty, I bet you'll still look like you're in your forties."

"That's not exactly young, you know." She grinned. "I took three pregnancy tests before I finally went to the doctor to get confirmation."

"If it makes you feel better, I'll always be younger than you." Isaac couldn't help but tease his love whenever he got the chance.

She playfully slapped his arm. "Why would that make me feel better?"

"Because it's funny to me, and you always want me to be happy, right?"

"Yes, I want you to be happy. I want *us* to be happy."

"When did you find out?"

"A week ago. I wanted to be absolutely sure before I told you."

"And when are we due?"

"We? I didn't realize you were going to be giving birth as well." She returned his sarcasm with a hint of her own. "The doctor said I'm about eight weeks along now. The due date is May 2."

"It is we. I mean, you'll be doing all the hard work, but I am going to be there every step of the way. I'll go with you to buy everything we need, to pick out a crib, and to choose paint colors once we find out if we're having a boy or a girl. Do you want a boy or a girl?"

"Honestly, either one is fine with me," she said. "I just want a healthy baby. I know that everyone says that, but at my age, that really is all that matters."

"I know it's easier said than done," he said. He knew that she worried about many things in life, and he wanted her to know that he was truly excited about the unexpected news. "But you have to work on being positive. Stress isn't good for the baby, and it's not healthy for you either. This is a good day. We're getting married, and we're going to have a baby."

CHAPTER 12
Cross Country

"I DON'T UNDERSTAND... HOW COULD YOU do this?"

"Answer me. You owe me that much..."

Silence. He let the time pass by, though a few seconds dragged on, painstakingly.

"We can't have this conversation. I thought we moved past this?" Isaac finally texted back. He grew increasingly nervous that Nicole would expose their secret if he didn't respond. It had been an entire year since their second mishap, but she had never completely gone away. She'd broken up with Carter after Isaac and Julia announced their engagement. Carter took the breakup hard. He began drinking more heavily with a morning glass of Monster and vodka, followed by steady self-medication throughout the day. He spent each night sipping Jack and Coke in between his dozen beers or so. Isaac lived somewhat unaware of his son's struggle. His focus shifted to the love for his new bride, whose adorable belly began to pop out.

They moved the wedding up to the end of October, because Julia didn't want to be showing too much on their wedding day. They held a small ceremony with immediate family and close friends. Isaac and Julia both wanted something intimate and low key, and that's exactly what it turned out to be. Ramie's parents and her sister attended the wedding. They wanted to show their support for Isaac and make it known that they didn't begrudge Isaac for moving on with his life. Julia found it strange, but she didn't want to make things awkward, though it should have already been awkward, by telling them they could not come. They made special disc golf discs as a funny, yet memorable gift, to tell the story of how they met. Isaac and Julia both received a disc that they wrote their vows on, and they made a tiny one as well for the new baby they would welcome in the spring.

"I get it," Nicole texted "You're married now, but you were married before. Are you saying you don't want to be with me? We could meet right now. No one has to know. I swear I won't tell anyone. I haven't told anyone yet, have I?"

Isaac felt nothing in the way of temptation. All he wanted was Julia.

"I'm sorry," he texted. "There's nothing I can say to make this better, but I am happy now. I wish you all the best, but please, you can't text me anymore."

She did not text him back.

Isaac and Olivia moved into Julia's house. It served as the only condition for Olivia and Carter to offer their approval of the marriage, primarily Olivia. She was happy for them, but she made it clear that she did not want to see another woman live in her mother's home. Carter would be at Auburn for the next three years, but he agreed with his sister.

Olivia seemed to adjust well in the new home. She made the drive to Etowah each day, as she was not willing to switch schools her senior year. Isaac did not want her to change schools either. She also joined in their excitement for the arrival of the new baby. She always wanted a baby brother or sister, preferably a sister, and Isaac remembered their immense sadness when he and Ramie had told her their new baby was in Heaven now. He prayed that Julia would not have any problems in her pregnancy. The third time was supposed to be the charm. For Isaac and Ramie Childs, it was anything but.

"Bye, Daddy," Olivia called out as she left the house. She told her father that it didn't quite feel like home yet, but it also didn't feel like someone else's home. She thanked him for not selling their home in Woodstock. It made the transition easier for all of them. With their comfortable financial situation, he decided to keep their house and all of their furniture in it, while moving his everyday items to Julia's, and they would adjust to her home. Within just a few weeks, Julia's home seemed more like hers and Isaac's home. Olivia appeared to know that she was welcome, but Isaac could see that she still missed something in her life.

"Bye, sweetheart," Isaac said, "have a great day at school." Isaac caught her at the door and kissed her on the cheek. He often stared at his seventeen-year-old beauty, in awe of the woman she was quickly becoming. Julia called out too, wishing her a wonderful day.

Isaac turned to his wife. "And what do you want to do today, tubby?"

"Who are you calling tubby?" Julia smiled and patted his slight belly in return.

"I've gained a few pounds, but they are sympathy pounds. You see, I care about you." He leaned forward and kissed her pooch, lifting her oversized t-shirt before he did.

"Well, aren't you sweet." She nudged his head away from her. "I need to finish some editing in my book, but I'm free in the afternoon. What did you have in mind?"

"Tell me what your book is about again? A killer kid or something like that?" Isaac remembered what the book was about, but he liked to mess with her, and he enjoyed hearing her describe it even more. Julia exuded a passion for her writing that Isaac typically only saw at sporting events or political rallies.

"Very funny. The kid is not a killer, at least we don't think he is. His father is being investigated for the murder of his father, the kid's grandfather. The police look into the wife as well, since it seems like she knows more than she is willing to admit. During the investigation, the grandmother goes missing too and after she does, the son and the father are at odds. The police focus on the father, the son, and even the mother, as they have reason to suspect all three might be guilty. In the end, the son attacks the father just before the father is about to go on trial for the murder of the grandfather and the disappearance of the grandmother. When he does, it becomes the son versus his parents, and only one side walks away alive."

"Remind me to stay on your good side."

"Like this?" Julia smacked his butt and quickly jumped back herself, to avoid his imminent revenge.

"That's not my good side." Isaac squeezed her backside cheeks with a playful force. "*That* is your good side." They finished their back and forth with a kiss.

"How about we go thrifting today. I know, I know, you hate it, but I really need some new mugs. The baby needs new mugs. Don't you want to make the baby happy?" Julia looked up at Isaac with puppy dog eyes. As she did, Rylee stared at him too, though she just wanted more water in her bowl. Nevertheless, both girls would be successful in getting what they wanted.

"Fine, as long as you promise not to shop too long," Isaac said. "I like looking too, but not for hours."

"I promise." Julia lifted her leg and pecked him on the cheek. "I'll go get ready."

Isaac followed her upstairs and changed into more comfortable shoes. He enjoyed the thrill of the hunt, though not nearly as much as Julia. She viewed it as a mini treasure hunt. He loved that she found so much joy in something so simple.

They left their home in Kennesaw and drove to one of Julia's favorite thrift stores in Smyrna, just outside of Marietta. She had received a coupon for fifty percent off, so she was in prime position to explore.

They made it to a shelf lined with mugs, and Julia picked one out.

"Here it is." She held it out, a vintage *Simpsons* mug with a picture of Ralph Wiggum counting to blue. "I knew we were meant to come here today. One, two, tricycle, blue." She read it aloud loud to Isaac with her best imitation of the dimwitted character. She looked at the bottom and read the date, *1995*. After tax, her new, favorite mug would cost a mere ninety-eight cents.

"It was fitting that you wore your *Simpsons* shirt today. You won't be able to wear it much longer, you know. At least not for a while." Isaac took the mug from her delicate hands and placed it carefully into the shopping cart. The shopping cart they chose originally came from a Sports Authority. This thrift store did not own any carts with their name on it, save a handful that only offered three working wheels. Most of the carts worked that way, and Isaac possessed a special knack for finding the most damaged cart on his first, and even sometimes his second try.

"I wonder if they make pregnancy *Simpsons* shirts." She continued to browse through the shelves full of mugs. "I bet they don't make any vintage ones." Julia frowned a bit, though her dimple still managed to shine through.

"I'm sure they don't make vintage ones, but I bet there are repops." Isaac spotted a large Auburn stein and quickly grabbed the glass mug before she could beat him to it. "Look at this, and it's only a dollar fifty after your little discount."

"That's cute, but you know it can't go in my mug room, right?"

"How presumptuous of you, Mrs. Childs." It felt strange to call her that since Ramie had always been Mrs. Childs. "This is going in the living room. Maybe I'll build a shelf just for it."

"You're going to build a shelf?" She asked this, sure, but they both knew the answer.

"Okay, I'll call your dad, but still, I can get a shelf for it." Isaac never was much of a handyman. He could change a turn signal bulb, but could not do much else under the hood of a car. He painted a wall with the best of them, but framing one would be a different story altogether. He turned a lawn or a garden into something absolutely gorgeous, but if he needed to fix a mower or anything of the sort, he would be calling someone else for help.

"I'm sure you can." She poked his tummy and rescued another cup that rested on the top shelf, lonely and in desperate need of relocation. She snickered. It was a teal green colored mug with a fish that said, *Sometimes it's hard to get your bass in gear.*

"That's the perfect mug for you." Isaac snatched it from her hands and looked it over carefully to make sure it did not have any cracks or crazing. She had trained him well on what to look for and the right way to pull on the handle to see if it was in good shape. The double-sided design from the 1980s still held its color surprisingly well.

"You're hilarious. Now please give me my mug back, as long as it passed your detailed inspection, sir."

"It does, and you are welcome."

They browsed the store for another forty-five minutes until her feet could not take it any longer. She left with four new-to-her mugs, and he kept the Auburn stein, though he would not drink from it. Julia also picked a pair of pregnancy pants, as well as two cute maternity tops. They stopped for fast food and visited two more thrift stores as the afternoon progressed. Isaac finally convinced Julia that she needed to get home and write, and they headed home with the back seat full of new treasures.

On the way back, his phone rang.

"Hello?" Isaac said. It was a number he did not recognize. "Yes, this is him... Oh my God... Is she okay? Where is she? Okay, I'll be there in like thirty minutes. Thank you."

"Who was that?" Julia's mood changed immediately. "What's the matter?"

"I don't know." Isaac made a u-turn at the light and headed toward Woodstock. "It's Olivia. She was hit by a car. They wouldn't tell me anything else over the phone."

"Oh, sweetie, I'm so sorry. It's going to be okay." She reached over and took Isaac's hand and put it back together with hers, where it assuredly belonged. This was its permanent resting place. Any chance they had, they made sure to hold hands and feel their all-consuming love for each other.

Isaac pulled into the parking lot of Northside Hospital, a place he'd been a handful of times over the years. This is where they took him and

Ramie after their car accident, where Ramie went following her miscarriage, and the place he called the night she went missing.

They hurried into the hospital and located Olivia's room on the ninth floor.

"Oh, Liv. Are you okay?" Isaac gingerly hugged his daughter. "What happened?"

"Hey, Daddy. Thanks for coming. I'm so sorry." Olivia lay in her hospital bed with her head wrapped. She had a few light cuts, bruises, and some swelling on her face and arms. Isaac couldn't tell with the sheets covering her, but the car had struck her in the right hip and broken her pelvis.

"Why would you be sorry? You got hit by a car. I'm just relieved that you're not hurt too badly." Isaac teared up as he spoke. All his adult life, he'd cried only one or two times. In the past fifteen months since Ramie disappeared, he shed more tears than all those years combined.

"I'm sorry too." Julia placed her hand on Olivia's. "How much does it hurt?"

"Well, they have me on a lot of medicine right now, but it still hurts a little. The doctor said I have a concussion, in addition to the hip stuff and other bruises. I should be fine in a month or so. It's not a big deal."

"How did it happen? And it *is* a big deal, you could have been hurt much worse. Head injuries are a serious thing. I want to talk to the doctor and make sure they are running all the right tests on you, and then a few more to be safe. Where did you get hit at?"

Isaac moved a chair to one side of the bed for Julia, then another for himself on the opposite side.

"The doctor wants to talk with you as well," Olivia said bleakly. "We were just running during cross country practice, at the school, and this car pulled onto that little side road by the baseball fields. They didn't see me as I was running by, and they just ran right into me."

"Were they texting and driving?" Isaac asked.

"I don't know; no one told me. I didn't see it happen, and I barely remember it. They weren't driving that fast, but when the car hit me, my head struck the pavement pretty hard. Apparently I passed out."

"I'm so glad you're okay," Isaac said. "Do you want anything? Are you hungry? How about ice cream or maybe some chicken tenders with honey mustard? I know those are your favorite. I can run to Chick-fil-A really quick for you." Isaac wanted desperately to comfort his daughter and simply be there for her. There was nothing he could actually do for her, except sit beside her and feed his baby girl.

"Mmmm, some Reese's ice cream sounds great right now. Could you get me some from Bruster's, please?"

"Of course." Isaac and Julia left the room to get Olivia some ice cream, as well as a snack for Julia. He started to call Carter when the doctor caught him just before he reached the elevators.

"Mr. Childs." The doctor wore a light blue shirt and khaki pants, not scrubs or a white coat as Isaac imagined he would. "Can I have a word with you please?"

"Sure thing, Doctor." He and Julia followed the doctor down the hall and into his office, where the doctor shut the door behind them. "How is she? I mean I know about the injuries, but how is her head? Is there any brain damage or long-term concern with the concussion?"

"Olivia is going to be just fine." The doctor carried an air of confidence that put Isaac at ease. "She's going to need about four to six weeks to recover from the broken pelvis. The concussion doesn't seem to be too serious either, but we're going to continue to monitor her closely for the next week or so, just to be sure."

"That's good news then. I'm just glad she's okay."

"There is one more thing, Mr. Childs. We've come to learn that your daughter had been taking quite a few different medications, medications that were not prescribed to her."

"What do you mean? What kind of medications?"

"She was pretty straightforward with us when she was admitted, possibly thanks to the concussion. Still, she confessed that she was on Oxy and Vicodin. Were you aware that your daughter has been taking these pills?"

Was he aware? Isaac felt incredible shame wash over him. He'd been so focused on Julia, and now the pregnancy, that he had not monitored Olivia as closely as he should have. He didn't think that he needed to. She was his good girl, but now he feared that Ramie's demons might have passed down to Olivia, like his possibly had with Carter. He blamed no one but himself.

"I was not aware. I'm terribly sorry, Doctor. We've gone through a lot over the past year plus."

"Yes, I'm familiar with your family situation. I empathize with you all, I truly do. Your daughter is only seventeen, and we need to find the proper treatment for her to get well so this does not take over her life."

"You aren't going to report her, are you?" Isaac instantly feared that the doctor might be required by law to report Olivia. He also considered that he might be bound by the Hippocratic oath to not say anything. He hoped for the latter.

"I am not going to report her. I'm only telling you because she technically is still a minor, plus she gave me permission to talk with you. I do have to note it in her records, but there is no need for the law to get involved. I want your daughter to get help, not punished. That does make this somewhat difficult, though, as she needs medicine right now for her pain. I've got her on morphine currently, but I will be transitioning her off that and onto Tramadol. Hopefully it helps with the pain. While it still can be addictive, the risk for long term dependence is lower than with opium-based pain medications."

"Thank you for your help, and I'm ... sorry again."

The doctor handed Isaac two different pamphlets for inbound treatment centers, as well as three counselors he could contact for Olivia to meet with.

Later, he and Julia brought Olivia her ice cream and some chicken tenders.

"Thank you for understanding, Daddy." Olivia licked the sides of the waffle cone as it arrived dripping. "I feel like such a failure."

"Hey, don't talk like that." He inched closer. "Look at me. We all struggle with our issues. You know I've had my problems with drinking." He tried not to look over at Julia. He hadn't exactly hidden it from her, but he'd never delved into all the specifics of his drinking struggles with her. She simply knew that it led to his one night stand a few years back, but she had yet to see him drink. He knew that it seemed more like a past life to her, not something that could possibly flare up again in their new life together. Isaac remained clean and sober for a full year at this point. "I'm going to get you whatever counseling and treatment that you need, and we will beat this together. I gave up drinking, and I know you can do this. You are strong... except for right now. You look pretty weak right now."

Olivia laughed and wiped a smidge of her melting ice cream onto her father's sleeve. This was merely one more trial for the Childs family.

CHAPTER 13
The Treehouse

THE FBI SEARCHED HANEY'S HOME AND property again in Acworth, combing the woods of his three-acre plot of land. They didn't locate anything new from their initial search the prior year, save a rusted chainsaw discarded underneath some brush. The house originally looked abandoned and now showed its age even more. It appeared kin to a run-down home from a horror movie. This was not a place in which any family would ever reside again. Once they completely closed the case, the city would most likely demolish it.

The FBI took the chainsaw back with them and sent it off for testing. While they knew the woman from the trunk and the other victim found in the ocean had not been dismembered with it, they still needed to check it for evidence.

"What are we missing?" Agent Faith asked her partner, as they left the house in Acworth and headed north to the Butcher's trailer in Cartersville. "Where did he cut and mutilate these women? The amount of blood and DNA, it would have been impossible for him to completely clean everything up. Why didn't we find more evidence before?"

"We found quite a bit, don't you think?" said Agent Noah, proceeding to remind his partner of a few of their discoveries from the initial investigation. They'd recovered three knives, a replica samurai sword, two machetes, one axe, and a shovel. They'd also found clothing and other personal items belonging to the victims, as well as another cell phone of the Butcher's. Each of the homes contained basic everyday items like food, clothing, and cheap furniture, but only the home in Acworth offered running water and electricity. The FBI had not been successful in finding any of the other missing women, on either of his properties.

"But where did he remove the arms and the legs from these women?" Agent Faith asked. "There's no way it was at the home we just left. It had to have been somewhere on his land in Cartersville."

Charles Haney owned both properties free and clear. Those, along with his two vehicles, were the only two items of significance registered to his name. He'd worked as an IT engineer and did not have any friends. He left behind no presence on social media, no wife, and no kids to aid the investigation. He appeared to be a loner who kept to himself and a man whom no one missed. In truth, the authorities had no idea how many women he'd abducted and killed, or when he'd even begun. Digging into his past, they'd found no siblings and learned his parents had passed away years ago. Everywhere brought them to a dead end.

Arriving at his deserted property in Cartersville, they were greeted by the eerie sight of the dilapidated single wide. The trailer sat on a little over thirty acres of land, also heavily wooded, and previously searched by the FBI. Agent Faith stepped out of the SUV convinced that they had missed something, that there was evidence hiding in either that tiny trailer or beneath the earth surrounding it. Agent Noah followed her toward the front door that still displayed the yellow tape and years of accumulated mildew, a sight that would most definitely stay that way for the rest of its existence.

They entered the aluminum structure and quickly exited, overcome by the stench within. After locating and securing their breathing masks from the vehicle, they attempted their search one more time. The place looked just as dark and depressing as it did a year ago. Cobwebs filled the corners and dust lined the window sills from the prolonged absence. The agents walked through the living room, took the few steps to pass through the kitchen and once more checked the only bedroom inside. They traveled back to the living room when Agent Faith noticed something strange in the corner, between the couch and the wall.

"What does that look like to you?" she asked her partner.

"I don't know. What the hell is that?"

They stepped over to the misshapen lump in the floor, and she crouched down to get a closer look.

"It feels like there's something underneath the flooring." Agent Faith didn't know if there might actually be a body stuffed below the flooring, and if so, how they might've missed it during the original search of the trailer. They hurried outside, and Agent Noah ran to the SUV to grab his flashlight. He rushed back to the far side of the trailer and crawled underneath the home, raised just high enough for him to do so. He shined his light in front of him and jumped back, striking his head on the floorboards.

"Shit!" he cried out as he slid backwards to get out of the suffocating space.

"Are you okay? What did you see?"

"Nothing, and I'm fine. I hit my freaking head after I found what we were looking for."

"You can say the real word, you know." Agent Faith tried not to smirk. "You just said, 'shit.' What was it?"

"Dead opossum." He rubbed the back of his head. "Looks like it crawled up there and got stuck. Just my luck. We think we've found something important, and it's a dead animal. I almost threw up down there. The smell was thick, and it scared the crap out of me. You know I hate stuff like that."

Despite her partner's solemn face, Agent Faith burst into laughter. She didn't care, however, she was just so incredibly grateful that she had not been the one who went underneath, only be greeted by a rotting opossum.

"I'm sorry," she said. "I'm not laughing at you. Well, I am, a little, but I'm not trying to. I can't help myself. Maybe it was playing dead. They like to do that, don't they?"

Agent Noah brushed himself off, and they located their backpack from the SUV so they could properly search the rest of the property. They decided to do what they'd done at the first location and search the entire property again, just the two of them. They carried gloves, evidence bags, two cameras, a video camera, and other essentials for bagging and identifying any evidence they might find. These woods would take them at least two days as they were not only larger but thicker and more difficult to penetrate.

They began their search on the east end of the property and stayed within ten yards of each other. They walked slowly as each of them followed their flashlights. The dense woods allowed little more than a sliver of sunshine. They bent over and moved leaves and twigs out of their way. They kicked branches and lifted logs together, hoping they might spot a hidden weapon or evidence of any kind. They searched for more than an hour when Agent Noah spotted the treehouse on the back side of the east end of the Butcher's land.

"Let's go look inside it again - maybe they missed something," he said as they moved their heads from left to right and then back again.

They climbed the treehouse ladder. Nothing remained at the top. A spider web stretched from one corner of the east window to the other corner. A smaller web hung on the opposite side, next to the coarse rope that stretched outside the window, all the way to the ground. It appeared to be about a fifteen-foot drop, and the rope was tied off as if it were there for structural support. Each side of the treehouse sported its own rope that connected from the side to a nearby tree, though they were all covered in camouflage. The agents couldn't see the rope until they walked right up on it.

"Why would he have a treehouse anyway?" Agent Noah asked. "He didn't have any kids. And why are these stupid ropes here? It's not like they're actually doing anything."

"Maybe it was here when he bought the property. I'm not sure."

Both agents peered through the window containing the only rope reaching inside. All that surrounded them was more trees. No nearby neighbors or roads. Agent Faith tugged on the rope. When she did, it moved ever so slightly.

"Check this out." She pulled a bit harder the second time, using her leverage to pull the rope down over the massive beam it had been tied around. As she did, something on the ground lifted toward them. "Dear God. Hurry down. I'll hold it up until you get down there."

Agent Noah carefully rushed down the steps. He jumped onto the stiff ground and looked into the space Faith had accidentally uncovered.

"Christ Almighty," he said. "How did they miss this?" He immediately asked God for forgiveness, out loud so that his partner could hear him, for taking His name in vain. He then performed the Sign of the Cross. "I don't know what to say. I've never seen anything like this. Can you tie the rope off and come down here?"

"I think so." She pulled some more, surprised at how much weight there was to lift, and gave herself more slack to tie a knot that would hold. Once she did, she joined her partner at the bottom and gazed upon their discovery. "This can't be... this can't be real." She repeated herself because she could not find any words suitable for what they were forced to fix their eyes upon.

CHAPTER 14
It Runs in the Family

ISAAC'S FOCUS SHIFTED TO HIS DAUGHTER, and of course, the growing belly of his new bride. Julia looked absolutely adorable as a pregnant woman, and at right around the midway point, everyone knew she was with child.

Olivia healed up quickly after being struck by the car. She missed the rest of the cross country season, but it didn't faze her much. She enjoyed running, but it wasn't a passion. She mainly ran cross country to stay in shape. Isaac took her entire stash of pills and disposed of them. He found her a local counselor for the pill addiction, and another to talk to about the loss of her mother. The doctor recommended giving both a try as the two were most likely connected.

He was right.

Olivia transitioned well to the Tramadol, and once it came time to quit, she quit. She was three weeks clean now and committed to her counseling sessions. In addition to the counseling, she started a daily walking routine at Hobgood Park. Isaac wouldn't let her go anywhere else to walk or run unless it was a fairly crowded place.

"You are a gorgeous young woman. You have to be careful. I know you're not a child, but you are my child, and you're my baby. Please, just trust me with this."

"I trust you, Daddy," she said. "Eventually, though, I have to live a normal life."

"And you will. Just give it some more time, please."

Olivia did trust her dad, and, while not admitting it, she remained somewhat paranoid herself. Yet she found peace in her walks around the park and in the counseling sessions, particularly with the therapist who helped her deal with the loss of her mother. In fact, she stopped seeing the counselor for the pills after only a few weeks.

"Any time you feel like using again," Ms. Brooks would remind Olivia, "think of yourself. Don't think about anyone else. You can't change for your father or for who you think your mother would want you to be. The only person you can change for is you. You have to be who you want to be. Do you want to be someone who needs these pills? Do you want to be a woman who depends on something smaller than your pinky finger in order to be happy?"

The way Ms. Brooks explained it made sense to Olivia. In overcoming her addiction, she felt like she'd reached a particularly grueling summit.

"You're right," Olivia said. She appreciated also how Ms. Brooks treated her with the respect of a grown woman, not just a kid or a teenager. "I don't need them. I can't even remember why I started in the first place. My mom apparently couldn't stop her habit, but my dad broke his addiction to alcohol. He drank for a long time, and he quit. If he can do it, so can I. And I agree with you. I'm going to do this for myself."

Olivia wanted to make her father proud, but she also wanted to improve, and every passing day made her feel more successful.

Carter, on the other hand, quietly drank through his days. At the tender age of nineteen, he'd begun to drink like a seasoned veteran. His habit continued to grow over the months following his separation from Nicole. He reached a point where he kept a bottle of vodka next to his bed, and every time he woke up during the night, he would take a drink. He hoped that might change once he came home for the holidays, but the opposite happened - it grew even worse. He wanted to quit, but the temptation was too great.

Isaac met Carter at Hobgood Park so they could play tennis together like they did when he was younger. As Carter progressed through his high school years, they didn't play as often. Carter stayed at their house in Woodstock when he visited. He liked sleeping in his own bed, and it made it easier for him to drink without anyone knowing. Carter arrived at the park with a steady buzz that only went away when he slept. He'd learned to hide it well from others, much like Isaac when he used to drink too much.

"You ready for your old man to beat you?" They walked to the tennis courts together from the same parking lot they'd visited so many times for running and baseball games; not to mention the night Isaac paid Nicole the twenty-five thousand dollars to remain silent. Hobgood Park was a place that held mostly happy memories for Isaac and Carter alike.

"I haven't played in over two years." Carter sipped his vodka-infused water. "You should be embarrassed if you don't beat me."

"I haven't played in the same amount of time. The last time I played was with you."

They battled across two-and-a-half sets of tennis, each man dripping with sweat. Isaac won the first set, while Carter prevailed in the second. Isaac finished ahead during their third set, up four games to Carter's two.

"You're lucky I agreed to stop playing," Carter teased, truly winded from the intense match. "I was just about to complete the comeback."

"Really? Is that what you call throwing up halfway through our game?"

Isaac had no idea his son threw up because of the alcohol. He just assumed that, now a sophomore, studies had forced Carter out of shape. He appeared heavier, as if it'd taken a little while for the "freshman fifteen" to catch up to him. He didn't smell any alcohol on him and had no reason to think otherwise. They said goodbye in the parking lot, and Carter returned to their home in Woodstock to shower and drink. He desperately craved water, which he inhaled when he walked into the kitchen, but then he settled in with a case of hoppy beer to wind down his day.

Isaac picked Olivia up from her counseling session and headed back to the new home in Kennesaw.

"How was it today?"

"Really good," said Olivia. "I like Lindsay so much better than the other counselor."

"You call her Lindsay? That's kind of weird. How old is she?"

"I don't know. She's older than me, but young for a counselor I suppose. She's probably like thirty or something." Olivia glanced toward the window, unsure what she might truly be feeling. She didn't think about love much, or feelings that might lead to love. She'd never had a real boyfriend, but her parents always attributed that to her dedication to school and having a good head on her shoulders. "Is that okay?"

"Yeah, I suppose it's okay. I guess I should have met the counselor. I just felt safe since it wasn't a man."

"Why couldn't I have met with a man?"

"Because you are too beautiful. I wouldn't trust a man to be alone with you like that." Olivia knew that her father only cared about her safety, and she didn't mind that he was acting so protective. It made sense given what happened to her mother.

"I'm about to turn eighteen, Daddy. You can't baby me forever."

"I know, and I'm sorry. I only act this way because I love you. And I do trust you. You're a good girl."

"Thank you. I trust you, too." Olivia chuckled, and turned back to thoughts of her counselor. She wondered if Lindsay might feel the same way as she did. She'd encountered a few crushes before, toward both boys and girls, but she never had a real boyfriend before, and she'd not exactly acted on those crushes, either. She "went out" with a boy in eighth grade for a few weeks, but they never actually went anywhere. Watching the round after round of break-ups in Carter's social circle destroyed her desire to really date in high school. She was willing to wait some time for that drama. Plus, she liked who she was—and she had a crush on Lindsay, though she had no idea what to do about it.

"Hilarious," Isaac said. "Does that mean that you're paying for lunch?"

"No way. You stink too bad, plus you gotta bring home food for Julia, right? She would make me go broke."

"I'm telling her you said that." They both laughed. "She wants fried chicken. Does that sound good to you?"

"Sure thing. I'm good with anything right now." Olivia liked being able to think with a clear mind again. Her pill-popping seemed like another lifetime, another existence.

Isaac and Olivia ate at the restaurant, then took food home to Julia, who met them at the bottom of the front porch.

"Thank you so much," Julia said. "You have no idea how hungry I am." She carried the small bucket of fried chicken into the dining room and began to eat. Rylee sat off to the side and stared with a desperate hope that Julia might drop something.

"I'm sorry it took so long." Isaac reached in for a drumstick even though he'd just eaten. Tennis had heightened his hunger, but Julia slapped his hand away. "Okay, okay, I won't take your food. Like I was saying, I'm sorry it took so long. Carter and I played longer than we expected, and then Liv and I ate at the restaurant so your food wouldn't get cold."

"You're fine." Julia smiled as she wiped the grease from her mouth. "Did you win?"

"We both agreed to stop playing, but I was ahead. Not that it matters, but I feel like you need to know that." Isaac worked his way upstairs to shower. Olivia followed her father upstairs and veered off to her bedroom, where she texted Lindsay.

"Hey," she wrote. "I just wanted to say thank you for all your help." She assumed it was inappropriate, but she needed to talk with her more, if only to confirm her feelings.

A moment later, Lindsay replied.

"Not a problem. You are a strong woman, and you are going to do amazing things in life."

"I appreciate that. It's been a tough year. It's nice to have someone who I can talk to."

"Of course. That's what I'm here for."

"How long have you been a counselor?" Olivia asked. She knew it was wrong to talk casually like this, via text. Even though neither woman had said or done anything improper, she could feel the slight change in tone.

"Five years now. I graduated from Mercer and went straight into my master's program there as well. I was lucky..."

"The Bears. I hear that's a good school. My dad went to Auburn. My mom did too for a year, and my brother goes there now."

"Auburn is a good school, except it's in my least favorite state."

"What? Lol." Olivia actually did laugh out loud a little. She sat up straight in her bed, her back leaned up against her cushioned headboard. "What do you have against Alabama? You don't want to Roll Tide, or whatever the hell that means?"

"No, I most definitely do not want to Roll Tide... I had a bad experience growing up in Alabama. I'm actually from Mobile, born and raised. I went to Mercer to get away from the state and be closer to a city like Atlanta."

"What do you mean? Why did you want to get away from Alabama? My parents loved it in Auburn, and Carter says he does too." The texting process didn't feel connected to real life, and Olivia could tell Lindsay liked it, too. She assumed that she would stop texting if she didn't want to talk.

"I like girls. I probably shouldn't be telling you all of this since you are my patient. This isn't exactly what we should be talking about."

"I don't care that you're a lesbian. I'm not judgmental."

"It's not that. It's just... it's hard to explain," Lindsay texted back the vague response. Olivia understood the age difference between them, but she didn't care. She didn't care that Lindsay was in a position of authority, or that she was older. She only knew that she liked her, and for her, that was rare.

"We're friends. There's nothing wrong with that. Is there?"

"No, there's nothing wrong with that." Lindsay responded with the only answer Olivia wanted to hear. They texted back and forth for the next three hours. Olivia grew absolutely giddy at the thought of her new friendship with the older woman, who, as she learned, was actually twenty-nine, which made it seem less taboo even if it was only a year's difference. By the time nighttime rolled around, the two had shared many secrets with each other, including Lindsay's past relationships. Olivia found it all so grown up and exciting. She'd only kissed a boy, one time, and that was in eighth grade. She knew very little about relationships, but she grew confident that they were both flirting back and forth, and that Lindsay held romantic feelings for her too.

"What would your family say about me being black?" Lindsay asked.

The two women looked completely different. Besides their age and racial differences, Lindsay stood about five inches shorter than Olivia. Lindsay's hair touched the bottom of her back, just above her complimentary bottom. It was a dark black that contrasted nicely against her medium-toned, black skin.

"I think they will care more that you were my counselor. But it won't be too bad. We just won't meet for a session again and then it won't be a problem."

"So the race thing isn't going to bother anyone?"

"No, of course not. Will it be a problem with your family?"

"It's just me, remember?"

"Sorry, I wasn't thinking." Olivia felt awful. No more than an hour had passed since Lindsay had told her about how she lost her parents in a fire when she was only twelve. She spent her last six years of childhood in foster care with no other family to turn to.

"Don't be sorry. I'm the one who should be sorry. You're only seventeen. I'm twelve years older than you. What will your family say about that?"

"I'm almost eighteen, and I don't know what they'll say. We've got plenty of time to figure it out though. We get to be super secretive for the next few months, and then after I turn eighteen, we can tell them. Or not... or we could just keep it a secret."

"You needed my help, and I've let you down. I'm so proud of you for not using. Promise me you're not going to use just because we won't be having our weekly meetings."

"I promise I'm not going to use. I don't even have that desire anymore. Plus, now I will get to see you more than just once a week."

The women kept texting until the night faded away, and Olivia drifted off to sleep around 1:00 AM. Shortly after she entered into the most wonderful dreams of her young life, she awoke to a knock at her door.

"Olivia, wake up."

"Daddy? What is it?"

"Something is wrong with Julia. I have to take her to the hospital. I just wanted to let you know. I'll call you as soon as I know something."

Olivia's heart raced a thousand miles per hour. The knock on the door startled her, and now that she sort of had something to hide, the adrenaline of somehow being found out rushed through her veins. The pill habit was easy for her to hide, and if it had not been for the accident, she figured she never would have been caught. This, whatever this was or was going to grow into, she was not sure. All she knew was that she liked it, and she wanted to protect what might become of her and Lindsay. She settled her body down and went back to sleep, concerned for Julia, but focused more on her own happiness, as cold-hearted as that sounded.

Isaac helped Julia down the stairs and out to his truck. She held both sides of her belly with trepidation. This was all new to her. She'd never experienced a pregnancy before, but at age forty-five, she'd lived long enough to know that something was not normal.

They checked into Kennestone Hospital, a place Isaac went to as a boy when he fell on a metal pipe trying to catch grasshoppers. The pipe went straight into his leg, and he left there with thirteen stitches. He still showed the scar today, shaped like a smiley face, a reminder of why he never cared much for bugs.

"Please, Doctor," Julia pleaded with the unknown man. She needed to hear something that would calm her nerves. She could not leave without knowing that the baby would be healthy. "Tell me that everything is okay."

The doctor instructed Isaac to sit down before he delivered the news. After he did, Isaac and Julia's world would never be the same. This proved to be the future for the Childs family.

CHAPTER 15
The End of the Rope

"THAT'S THE WORST THING I'VE EVER seen in my life." Agent Noah turned and walked away from the gruesome sight in the ground. When Agent Faith pulled on the rope, she accidentally lifted the camouflaged door that was completely indiscernible to the naked eye, connected to the similarly disguised rope.

The Butcher had constructed an oversized door, nearly twice the size of the front door to a house, and fitted the bottom side with approximately one hundred pounds of metal to keep it from moving if ever walked upon. The top lay covered in earth, leaves, twigs, and pine cones. Beneath that, he'd laid sod down on top of the door, then used an industrial strength glue to keep the natural decorations from blowing away. He'd placed compacted dirt and natural earth atop the door and joined it all together so it wouldn't be swept away. Underneath the door, the Butcher dug a hole about ten feet deep and as wide as the door.

"I've called in for help with bagging and identifying all of this, as well as a larger search team to see what else might be buried on the property." Agent Faith gazed down at the surreal discovery. "We need to wait until they arrive before we move anything, so we can place the arms in their own bags."

Once the rest of their team arrived, they lifted the arms out from the earth, one at a time. When they finished counting, they all stared at twenty-five severed arms that the Butcher had amputated from his victims. Each arm was a left arm, meaning that they had at least twenty-five women to identify.

"That's what he was saying in his suicide poem." Agent Noah broke the silence after everyone on the scene stood silent for what seemed like a lifetime. No one could blame them. The sight of twenty-five decaying arms would shock any normal human being, even if they did work for the FBI. The arms kept most of their normal characteristics as the Butcher wrapped each one in a clear storage bag, and then wrapped it in another bag, and finally he placed it in the ground. "But I wonder who was his love that he referred to."

"I doubt it was any of these women, God rest their souls." Agent Faith mourned for these women. She understood that they would be able to identify most of these women by their fingerprints shortly. This would give many of the families closure and peace, but it would also give a dozen or so families an ending to a story that they did not know anything about. Maybe they suspected that their loved one had been kidnapped, or it's possible they believed they had run off and started another life somewhere else. She had no idea.

They transported the arms back to their lab and ran the fingerprints for testing. While they waited for the results, they continued to search the property for more evidence. They hoped for another discovery like the one that had fallen from the treehouse, but they understood the odds of something like that were unlikely. They didn't want to find more bodies, but they did long for the missing pieces of evidence that stubbornly eluded them.

The search stretched into days, and then it grew into a full week without any other major discovery. They did not locate any more hidden doors or bodies buried on the property. They even examined larger trees to see if something might be hidden inside.

"Where are the bodies that belong to those arms?' Agent Noah asked, on returning to their headquarters in Marietta.

"If I had to guess, I'd say they are lost in the sea. But still, we are missing something. We haven't found the place where he removed the arms from the victims. We need to go through his life again. Let's start at the beginning and work our way back through the case." Agent Faith's frustration began to fester, to even cause her physical pain. She needed to find the place where he killed these women.

The agents interviewed his coworkers and boss again, as well as his past employers and old neighbors from twenty years back. The more people they spoke with, the less they felt like they were learning about Charles Haney. They even interviewed his mailmen, from both Acworth and Cartersville, but they'd never much interacted with him. They continued their search, and Agent Faith's vexation grew. The week of digging turned into weeks as Christmas loomed.

"The results are in on the fingerprints from the arms," Agent Noah told his partner.

"And? Were all of our victims identified?" Agent Faith guessed that they were. She assumed they now had twenty-five families to devastate.

The agents sat behind their desks and took a moment of silence. Agent Noah picked up his phone and prepared to make the worst phone calls of his life. One family at a time, they would schedule a meeting to sit with them, face-to-face, and deliver the news in person.

"Wait." Agent Faith stopped him before he could finish dialing the first number. "We can't call these families right before Christmas and tell them that we've found their loved one's arm. I know we're not supposed to, but let's wait until after Christmas and make the calls then."

Agent Noah hung up the phone. Faith could see his relief at being given more time. They left the station together and stopped at a bar for drinks.

CHAPTER 16
Keep Portland Weird

"ARE YOU SURE, DOCTOR?" ISAAC FELT lightheaded after hearing the news from the doctor. This all seemed like a dream. It couldn't possibly be real. "I mean, how did they miss this before?"

"I'm one hundred percent sure. See, look right here." The doctor pointed to the screen that displayed the baby. Isaac and Julia watched their baby girl, and they could make out so many of her features already. "Now look over here." He touched the space that displayed the second baby, also a girl. "It's likely the little girl was playing a game of hide-and-seek the other times they did an ultrasound. The good news is that they both appear to be healthy, Mr. and Mrs. Childs. You were probably feeling a leg or an arm poking at you because they don't have as much space as one baby would."

"Isaac, I'm scared." Julia smiled anyway. A calm washed over Isaac since hearing that the baby was healthy, but now he didn't quite know how to process the revelation of a second little person inside of his love. He took his initial emotions of fear that Julia shared, and he turned them into nothing short of pure joy.

"This is great news," Isaac said to Julia. "You went from not having any kids to having two kids. We're going to have two little girls. I can't wait to tell Liv. She's going to be ecstatic."

"Isaac, I'm scared. You don't think it's too much for us to handle?"

"Of course not. It's not like I won't be there. I'm going to change diapers and feed them. I'm going to hold them on my chest when they sleep and cherish every moment with them. Don't forget, I thought I was done with the baby portion of my life. This is the best news I could have ever received. I love you so much." Isaac leaned down and kissed her cheek. "And I love babies. They are so much fun."

"I love you too," she said with an innocent smile. "Promise me that everything will be okay." He knew that she needed to hear him say it one more time.

"I promise you. Everything is going to be just fine. The doctor said so himself. He said both of our girls look healthy. Our girls. That sounds so good to say."

"I just have a strange feeling, that's all." Julia always fancied herself as being in tune with upcoming events in her life. She'd told him before all this that something would be changing in the near future. He only prayed that their babies would be born without any complications and that Julia was simply being paranoid. What she wouldn't give for her to be a paranoid mother-to-be right now.

"You heard the doctor." Isaac tried his best to calm his new bride. The doctor had exited the room by this point in the conversation, so they could be alone with this unexpected news. "It's all of their little arms and legs kicking and punching you. I bet it's just one of them. I'm sure we'll find out one day which girl is the feisty one. Though if they're like you, they will both be feisty."

"Very funny."

Isaac took his wife home and waited until the morning to update Olivia on the extra baby. He called Carter afterwards, though his response came across as lackluster to Isaac.

"Aren't you excited?" Isaac asked his son.

"No, I am excited. I'm sorry, Dad; you just woke me up, that's all."

"It's noon."

"Yeah, but this is Christmas break. Can't I sleep in a little? I'm happy for you. That's awesome."

"You're right, I don't mean to make you feel bad. When are you coming over today?"

"I don't know. Was I supposed to come over?"

"It's Christmas Eve. I assumed we'd eat dinner together. Have you seen any of your grandparents since you got in?"

"That's right. I almost forgot that it was Christmas Eve. I'll swing by and say hi to them today, and I'll be there for dinner. Sorry, Dad. Love you."

Carter hung up the phone before Isaac could respond. He felt guilty for unintentionally shaming his son.

"Are you nervous about having twins, Daddy?" Olivia hopped around the house after her life-changing conversation with Lindsay the previous evening. "You're not exactly a spring chicken anymore. You do realize that, don't you?"

"You're hilarious. When is your next stand-up performance by the way? I want to make sure that I don't miss it because you are just that funny."

"Make sure you sit up front." Olivia finished putting on her shoes and prepared to leave the house to go and meet Lindsay for coffee. They decided on a random Starbucks in Marietta, since the odds of running into anyone they knew would be smaller there. Both girls knew too many people in Woodstock, and they each feared they might see Isaac or Julia if they met in Kennesaw. Marietta lay just down the road, but it offered more anonymity for the girls. "I want to make sure you can hear me, you know, with your old age and all."

"You better not let Julia hear you talking about old age like that." Rylee sat off in the corner of the dining room as Isaac ate his sandwich. She patiently waited for him to offer her a bite of his bread. "Where are you going anyway?"

"I'm going for a walk and then to write for a little bit."

"Look at you. You've been writing a lot lately. I guess you have taken after Julia after all."

"You know I like Julia, and yes, I have found writing to be a stress releaser for me."

"Stress? What stress do you have? You're only seventeen." He tossed a piece of bread to the dog, and she inhaled it as soon as it hit the floor.

"Where have you been, Daddy? I just got over a pill addiction, I was hit by a car, Mom died at the hands of a serial killer, and I'm trying to figure out where I'm going to go to college. Am I missing anything? I'd say I have a ton of stress." Olivia actually didn't feel all that stressed or worried anymore. Ever since the accident, she'd felt more like her regular self. She liked the woman she was becoming. Now, with her new friendship with Lindsay, life couldn't get any better. She still missed her mom, but she made peace with that the best she could.

"I guess I don't think before I speak sometimes. Forgive me, sweetie. I didn't mean to sound harsh or condescending. You've gone through a lot and sometimes I forget all that you've endured. Your brother too. I love you guys, and I'm thankful each day for you. Have fun on your walk and your time writing. You should tell Julia you've been writing. I'm sure it will make her happy. I'm proud of you."

Olivia left the house with those final words in the back of her mind, and Isaac gave Rylee the last of his sandwich and the few chips that remained. She was the perfect dog. She sat and stared while anyone ate, an act that usually annoyed Isaac, but even if he set food on the floor right in front of her, she wouldn't get up and eat it until he said, *Good girl.* It might have been her only trick, but it was a trick nevertheless, and one he enjoyed showing people when they came over to the house.

Isaac headed up the stairs and greeted his wife with a peck on the cheek, surprising her as she found herself deep in thought and writing as usual.

He smiled. "You take this writing thing seriously, don't you?"

"Someone's gotta make some money around here." She spun her chair around to face Isaac and rested her hands on her plump belly.

"Any pain today?" he asked. "Are the girls behaving?"

"No pain, thankfully, but what do you mean by behaving? Is that a passive aggressive sexism joke?"

"Stop it. I'm not even going to go down that road with you. You'd win anyway, I'm sure."

"I always win, Isaac."

"That's not entirely true. I won when I found you."

"You mean when you knocked me out? You seem to conveniently leave that part out of the story." She reached for his hands and placed them on her belly. He felt what he guessed was a foot and held his hand still as one girl or both stirred just under his palm.

"It really is a miracle that human life can live inside you. I'm just glad that miracle isn't offered to guys as well. I don't think I could handle a baby growing on the inside of me, not to mention the actual birthing process. Though I don't know how women handle it."

"What, you wouldn't want to gain fifty pounds and walk around like a weeble-wobble that doesn't come back up if knocked over?"

"No, I would not like that at all. I owe you one?"

"You owe me more than one, but some food would be a nice start."

"Fine, but then we're even. What would you like today, sweetheart?"

"Honey, we are never going to be even. You'll always owe me one. As for the more important matter at hand, what do I want to eat... Oooh, I know. How about that little pizza place off of Main Street. What's it called?"

"Pisano's?" Isaac loved this place as well. They served cheap beer and New York style pizza by the slice. He'd avoided the restaurant ever since he quit drinking.

"That's it. I'll take two slices of pepperoni, one of them with bacon, and one slice of cheese only."

"I know you're eating for three, but still." Isaac jumped back but not before she gave him a playful kick.

"I'll save one for dinner, Einstein."

"We've got the spiral ham and other festive sides for dinner, remember?"

"We can have both. It's okay, tomorrow is Jesus's birthday, remember? Since we moved our wedding up, I think he'll allow it."

"Yeah, but we did get pregnant out of wedlock, and ours wasn't an immaculate conception. I don't think He approves of that kind of stuff."

"I enjoyed our conception, though I'm starting to rethink things at this particular moment."

Julia kissed him on the lips and returned to her writing. Isaac left the house and hoped they would be open since it was a holiday. He assumed they most likely would be, though they would probably close early and stay closed tomorrow. He'd need to leave a good tip as no one enjoyed working on a holiday, and he did not want any special surprises in his pizza.

Meanwhile, Olivia pulled into the Starbucks parking lot to meet Lindsay, surprisingly nervous now that they were about to see each other after all their talking and flirting the night before. She stepped out of her car and went inside to wait for Lindsay to arrive. She ordered a salted caramel mocha with no whipped cream and slid into the corner comfy chairs. Once she sat down with her drink in hand, Lindsay walked in, and they were now at the point of no return. Or so it felt.

"Hey." Olivia broke the silence with an awkward wave as she stood to her feet.

"How are you?" Lindsay asked as she leaned in for a friendly hug.

"Nervous, honestly, but I'm starting to feel better now." The younger girl appeared less nervous than the older woman, though that made sense, given what Lindsay had to lose by starting a relationship with a patient.

"Same here. Let me go get a coffee and then maybe that will calm me down."

"So, caffeine is going to calm you down?" Olivia smiled as she teased, and Lindsay joined her. The caffeine might not calm her, but Olivia trusted that her wit surely would. She also knew that being able to hold something in her hands would ease her nerves. *She can start with the coffee,* Olivia thought as she watched Lindsay wait for her coffee, *and finish with my hands.* Lindsay returned to the oversized chair across from Olivia with a vanilla frappe.

"That looks really gross," Olivia joked. It didn't look gross to her, she just wanted to make her smile again.

It worked.

"And just what do you have to drink?"

"A salted caramel mocha."

"So you've mixed salt into your coffee, not to mention all of the sugar. Sounds like a healthy choice, Ms. Childs."

"Hey, I stay active. A little salt and sugar won't kill me. Well, at least not yet." Olivia grinned and crossed her legs as she sipped her coffee. She wore a plain white t-shirt and skinny jeans while Lindsay arrived in more casual clothes than she'd ever seen her in, wearing a Boston Red Sox tank top and khaki shorts down to her mid-thigh. She wore a pair of flip flops that completed her laid-back ensemble. Olivia found her stunning.

"Yes, I can see that you stay active," Lindsay said. "Have you started running again, or does it still hurt too much?"

"I've mainly been walking. It still hurts a little bit when I run, but I've been trying to mix in a touch of running here and there. How about you? Do you run? You look like you do, of course." Olivia blushed, unsure of why she suddenly began to ramble. She knew that she took after her father when it came to times like these.

"Thank you, and yes, I do run. I like to run two or three times a week, I ride a bike at least once a week, and I walk on the other days. I like to mix it up while still staying active."

"How about we go for a walk together right now?" Olivia forgot all about her previous rambling and decided to jump right in.

"I'd like that." Lindsay stood and led the way out of the coffee shop. "Let's take my car, if that's okay with you. It will save gas and the planet, I guess."

"Oh yes, I do care about the planet," Olivia said, with a smirk.

The girls drove away from the Starbucks and chatted about their Christmas plans. Olivia kept reminding herself that Lindsay had no family. She wished that she could invite her over, though she knew that was not a possibility.

"So, what do you do for Christmas?"

"Nothing really. I always watch *A Christmas Story* on Christmas Eve, and Christmas is just like any other day for me. I've been in relationships before, but I'm not right now, so no big plans."

"That sounds incredibly lonely." Olivia tried not to pity her, but she did feel sad for her. "I could sneak away tonight and come watch the movie with you, if you didn't mind."

"That sounds like fun," Lindsay said in an almost shy voice as they pulled into the parking lot of Oregon Park, a place too familiar for Olivia.

"I didn't know we were going here. I mean, it's probably not a big deal, but my dad comes here all the time to play disc golf."

"Is that what those baskets are for?"

"Yeah, he's a dork. But we should be okay today. He's at home with my stepmom and she's pregnant with twins, so I doubt she'll let him out to play disc golf on Christmas Eve."

"Okay, are you sure?" They stepped out of Lindsay's car and walked close to each other, conscious to maintain a buffer. "I don't want to get you in trouble, or me for that matter. I do not want to get in trouble."

"Why would we get in trouble?" Olivia raised her eyebrows as she spoke. "We're friends. Is there anything wrong with us being friends?"

"No, I suppose not. I just thought, well, never mind. Let's just enjoy our walk together."

"I plan on it." Olivia gave a gentle nudge to her new friend, pressing her shoulder against the shorter Lindsay. "If you can keep up with me, that is."

"Me keep up with you?" Lindsay looked both surprised and amused. "You're coming off a broken pelvis, and you're wearing jeans. I've at least dressed the part. My money is on me."

"You do look nice." Olivia ran her hands through her hair and tied it into a ponytail. "I'll give you that much."

"You look nice too." Lindsay beamed her a smile. "Can I ask you something?"

"Of course." Olivia braced herself for disappointment. She tried not to get her hopes too high, but she was beyond that point now, and there was no going back.

"I mean, we talked about it some yesterday, but that was just through texting. That's not the same as real-life talking, you know?"

"Yeah, I agree. Ask me anything."

"Okay, well I guess it's a couple of things. The first thing is more about you. Are you sure that you even like girls?"

"I like you." Olivia wasted no time with her response.

"Right, but you're so young and inexperienced."

"Thanks."

"No, don't take that the wrong way. It is the reality though. You're much younger than me, and you said yourself that you've never been in a real relationship. What if you just like the idea of being with me, rather than actually being with me?"

"I suppose I don't know for sure. I've never had a real boyfriend or girlfriend before. I've always been attracted to both sexes, like physically, but there aren't exactly a ton of lesbians in Woodstock you know."

"Believe me, I know," Lindsay said with a nervous laugh.

"And I realize that I'm young. I'm probably a bit naive as well. I haven't figured everything out yet; only that I like you, and that I want to spend more time with you." Olivia reached over and touched Lindsay's hand and held it there. She waited for Lindsay to either accept her hand or pull away if it were too soon.

"I like you too." She wrapped her fingers around Olivia's, and the two continued to walk along the trail that led through the woods, around the disc golf course. "You've been through a lot with your mom, and the pills, and your dad getting remarried. I want to make sure that you're not looking for a relationship, thinking that it will make everything better."

"That's not it at all. In fact, I'm thinking clearly for the first time since before my mom disappeared. I started using a few months before then, so really, now is the first time where I know what I actually want in life. I want to be a writer. I want to go to college. I want to challenge myself, and yes, I do want to find love. I'm not saying I love you, please, pretend that I didn't use that word. I'm saying that I like you."

"I want that too, but we have to wait until you're eighteen. That's only three months away, right?"

"A little less, but yeah, I can wait." Olivia pulled her hand away in slow motion, not truly wanting to let go. "Before we start waiting, can we try something?"

"Sure. What do you want to try?" Lindsay asked, though Olivia guessed that she already knew. She assumed that the older woman needed to hear her say it.

"Can I kiss you? I've only kissed that one boy before, and it was in eighth grade. I need to know that what I'm waiting for is something that truly feels right." Olivia had a way with words, also like her father. She knew how to spin a yarn that fell just right for whoever might be listening.

"Are you sure?" Lindsay stepped in closer to the young woman. She looked around first to make sure no one else was around. "We both probably have coffee breath."

"I've been chewing gum." Olivia smiled and threw her gum off to the side. Lindsay did the same and leaned upwards to kiss Olivia for the first time. Lindsay worked her flawless lips against Olivia's, and they both broke at the same moment, frozen, staring into each other's eyes.

Lindsay rubbed her thumb against Olivia's cheek. "Is that worth waiting for?"

Olivia kissed her again, full of joy and a sudden windfall of feelings she never knew existed before this singular moment in time. "Very much so. Am I?"

They continued to walk and hold hands while they did. That seemed innocent enough, so long as they didn't take it any further. *Parents hold hands with their kids every day all over the world,* Olivia thought. *How bad could it be?*

"What else did you want to ask me?" Olivia asked.

"There are a lot of things, but I guess you like men and women, right?"

"I suppose so. I don't know for sure. I find both attractive, like I said, but I like you. I know that."

"I only like women. I just wanted you to know that. But that's not the other thing I wanted to ask you. The other thing has to do with me being black and you being white. I know you said your family won't care, but we do live in Georgia. What are people going to say when they see two girls together, and two different races on top of that?"

"Screw them. Who cares what they think?"

"That's easier said than done, sweetie. I've been judged based on my race throughout my life and for my sexuality. When you combine the two, it can be tough to deal with at times."

"I hadn't really thought about it, to be honest. I don't think that it bothers me, but I won't actually know until I'm faced with the situation."

"I just want to prepare you that when we are a couple, if we hold hands or show affection in public, it can cause people to become uncomfortable. It can make some people mean and cruel. A few say or even do hateful things." Lindsay told her about the first time something like that happened to her. She was twenty-one and holding hands with a girlfriend in downtown Atlanta of all places. She felt comfortable there because Atlanta is a progressive city. It wasn't supposed to be a place where hate crimes happened. As they were walking down the street, a truck slowed down and yelled out, "Eat shit, faggots." As she turned to look at the vehicle, a milkshake hit her in the face. She felt completely humiliated and looked the part as well. "It's not the end of the world, I know that, but I want you to think about it beforehand because there are a lot of hateful people out there."

"You're right, there are hateful people all over the place, but I don't want to let a handful of shitty people stop me from living my life. I want to be who I am, and if anyone has a problem with me liking a black girl, that's their issue, not mine. Wait, is it okay if I call you a black girl?"

"Of course it is. I am a black girl."

"I know, but I don't want to sound racist."

"You don't sound racist. Would I sound racist if I called you a white girl?"

"No."

"Good, then it's settled. I'm a black girl, and you are a white girl, and neither one of us are racist."

"You are smart." Olivia smiled a wide smile that displayed her youth behind her playful lips. Her lips still held the taste of Lindsay's, and she hoped that would never change.

"Oooh, I had an idea. If things ever got too bad," Olivia said, "or if we just wanted a change, we could always move to Austin, Texas or Portland, Oregon. I hear they are super progressive out there."

"Let's not get ahead of ourselves," Lindsay said, "but don't tease me. I absolutely love Portland, Oregon. It's my favorite city in the world. Their motto is 'Keep Portland Weird.' I love that."

"You've been there?" Olivia had traveled quite a bit with her parents, but never to the Pacific Northwest.

"A few times. It's where I was meant to live. I always told myself that I'd end up there one day."

"It's settled then." Olivia hopped back into the car first, and Lindsay joined her after she fixed her sandal. "Portland it is."

CHAPTER 17
'Tis the Season

"THANKS FOR COMING WITH ME. IT means a lot to me. I'm sorry for everything." Carter held Nicole's hand as they walked through his father's new home. "Hey, Dad. We're here."

Isaac leaned around the entryway of the kitchen and spotted his son and Nicole by his side. This was not how he wanted to spend his Christmas Eve. Everything had been headed in the right direction. Now...

"Hey guys, it's great to see you." Isaac greeted his son with a hug and extended an awkward one for Nicole. "Does this mean that you two are back together?"

"It does, Mr. Childs," Nicole answered before Carter could. "Merry Christmas."

Isaac welcomed them in and made his way back toward his Julia in the kitchen.

"I heard you were having twins," Nicole spoke to Julia for what Isaac believed might be the first time. Now that he thought about it, he couldn't remember if they'd ever met.

"Julia, I'd like you to meet Carter's girlfriend. This is Nicole. Nicole, this is my wife, Julia." It was their engagement, after all, that caused her to break up with Carter in the first place. Still, Isaac loved his life and would not let the worst mistake of his life ruin any part of it. He had too much to lose.

"It's lovely to meet you." Julia shook her hand like they were the best of friends and offered her the friendliest smile this world had ever seen. Isaac normally loved how kind and compassionate Julia was, but this time it made him cringe. "You are a beautiful girl."

"Thank you, Julia. You are gorgeous yourself." She reached out and touched Julia's belly. "I hope you don't mind. I'm sorry, I should have asked first. You just look so cute."

"Oh, no, it's fine. Touch away. They've been kicking a lot today, so you might get lucky and feel them."

"I love babies." Nicole made eye contact with Julia as she spoke. "Any time you guys need a babysitter, I will be more than happy to watch them for you."

"That would be wonderful. You are so sweet." Julia walked to the dining room and gathered everyone to eat. "I was ready to eat an hour ago. We can talk more while we enjoy this fantastic meal." She giggled and filled her plate. Isaac tried to recover from the unexpected arrival of Nicole and chose to focus on his delightful family instead.

"Wonderful and fantastic?" Isaac joked. "You sound like our president with all of your adjectives."

"Hey," Julia playfully scoffed, "don't you dare say something like that on Christmas Eve."

"Yeah Dad, didn't you vote for him anyway?" Carter chimed in.

"No politics at the dinner table, not even when it's just us. I'm sorry I said anything. Enjoy your meal."

"Yeah, Carter," Olivia teased, "you wouldn't want to get Dad and Julia fighting on Christmas now, would you?"

"What, are you guys on different sides of the aisle?" Carter asked.

"No, we're not on different sides of the aisle, whatever that means." Isaac wiped his mouth and drank his water. "Your sister is a dork, that's all."

"You know where that word comes from, don't you?" Julia leaned back in her chair as she spoke with her hands resting on her satisfied belly.

"No, but I'm sure you do." Isaac enjoyed her close relationship with the English language. Julia always had a little tidbit or story behind a word or a phrase.

"Well, I'm not going to say, but you should look it up."

"So, you're just going to tease us?" Isaac poked his wife's leg.

"Actually, I'm going to excuse myself for a quick nap. I'm tired. Nicole, it was nice to meet you, and kids, it was lovely to enjoy this dinner with you. I apologize if I'm being rude."

They all assured her that she was fine, and Julia wobbled upstairs to rest. Isaac sat down in the living room and turned on a rerun of *Gold Rush*. Rylee climbed up on the couch, full from everything he'd saved for her at the end of the meal, and she nuzzled her nose into the blanket until she covered herself up. He always thought it would be fun to go to Alaska and mine for gold, except for the freezing temperatures and the fact that he'd never mined before in his life.

Carter and Nicole left so they could spend time together at the house in Woodstock, and Olivia told her father she was going with them. Olivia had waited anxiously all night, wanting nothing more than to finish their dinner so she could go to Lindsay's apartment to spend more time with her. They were not a couple, they made that clear, but they would be. She thoroughly enjoyed these new and exciting feelings. She didn't know how to describe them other than as celestial. That might not technically be the correct word, but she assumed anyone else would use that term if they felt the way she did. It felt somehow correct to her.

"Where are you really going?" Carter asked his little sister after they walked outside. "And why can't you tell Dad? Is it a bad boy?"

"If I tell you, do you promise not to say anything?"

"You know me, now just tell me."

"Fine, but you have to promise not to judge me either. You know I've never really been in a relationship before."

"Liv, just tell me already. I'm not going to judge you. As long as it's not one of your teachers or a forty-year-old man, you're good."

"It's not a man at all. It's a woman. Her name is Lindsay, and she is older. She's twenty-nine." Olivia felt relieved to tell her brother. It seemed like a dry run, like practice for when she would have to eventually break the news to her father.

"Okay... That's not what I was expecting. I didn't know you were, I mean I had no idea... I'm not saying it right. That is great, besides the fact that she's twenty-nine. How long have you two been together?"

"I'm not a lesbian, at least I don't think that I am. I'm bi. I'm still a little confused, but I'm figuring it out. Please don't say anything until I'm ready. After I turn eighteen, I'll tell Daddy, and it won't be so bad then."

"I understand," Carter said. Olivia could tell that he was being truly supportive. "You didn't tell me how long you've been together. When did you two meet?"

"We only met like a month ago, after I was hit by the car. She was my counselor."

"That's kind of odd. Aren't there laws against things like that?" Carter's tone shifted to that of an overprotective brother, though still mainly supportive. Nicole stood by silently, watching them.

"It's not like that. We just started talking, literally yesterday. We talked for hours, and then we met today and talked more and went for a walk. I'm pretty sure the laws are for when the two people are having sex. We're not having sex," she saw Carter wince here, "and we aren't going to be. We are just going to talk until I turn eighteen and then we can date and have a real relationship."

"Just be careful. Relationships can jump to the next level in a hurry. That's what happened with me and Nicole. We were just friends and then all of the sudden," he took her hand in his, "we fell in love."

"I'm happy for you," Nicole finally spoke, "and I can't wait to meet her. Have fun with your friend." She smiled and led Carter to their car so that Olivia could go her own way. They returned to Carter's home in Woodstock, and he poured out all his hard liquor as soon as they walked inside.

"I know it's not perfect, but it's a start." He emptied the fourth and final bottle of liquor down the sink. "Don't move the trash can too much," he said as the bottles clinked together when Nicole pulled it out of the pantry. "It makes me sound like I'm an alcoholic."

"You kind of are." Nicole touched his chest and gave him a soft kiss on the lips. "But you're my alcoholic, and I'm proud of you."

"Yeah? You're proud of me?" He dropped his hands to the small of her back, fixed his eyes on hers.

"Very. I know how hard it is to quit a bad habit. Your drinking is an addiction, and I want you to get better."

"You don't think I'm a failure for keeping the beer?"

"No, I don't think you're a failure. I think you are strong for getting rid of the liquor and deciding that you're going to quit. I believe in you." She kissed him once more and dropped her head onto his shoulder. Carter had developed a small beer belly and a little extra padding, but he still possessed muscular arms and a thick upper body.

"Thank you. I can't do this without you, you know. I drank a lot after we broke up. I know that's not an excuse, it's just how it is, I suppose. I'll be better though; I promise."

They spent the rest of their Christmas Eve night together watching *Elf* and cuddling together on the couch. On the other side of Woodstock, Olivia and Lindsay sat next to each other on Lindsay's couch, watching *A Christmas Story* and enjoying the warmth of her Red Sox blanket.

"How'd you become a Red Sox fan if you're from Alabama?" Olivia held her hand and had already positioned her head on Lindsay's shoulder. It felt wrong to do so, but even more wrong not to.

"I was like sixteen when the Red Sox were down three games to none, and they came back to win it all. It broke their curse of losing for all those years, and something about it spoke to me. I know that sounds strange since it's just a game, and I'm not even a huge baseball fan, but after my parents died when I was twelve, I felt all alone. I remember being out to eat with a few of my friends, and we watched the end of that game on TV. One of the Red Sox players stole second, and it was like watching magic happen right before my eyes. I literally had goosebumps all over my arms and, from then on, I decided to root for the Red Sox."

"Have you ever been there?" Olivia did the math in her head. She would've only been four-years-old when that happened.

"Boston? No, I've never been there. I've never been anywhere in the Northeast, actually. I'd love to go sometime and watch a game at Fenway Park. I think that would be a bucket list type of trip."

"I love traveling." Olivia laid down on the couch and rested her head on Lindsay's lap. She looked up at her as she talked and studied her smile. She noticed how white her teeth were, and the subtle dimple that appeared when she smiled really wide, high on her left cheek.

"Me too. It's probably my favorite thing in the world. If I could, I'd spend an entire year driving to every state and taking a picture in front of the 'Welcome To' signs. I'd love to go for small hikes and eat at local restaurants, and really just see the beauty in all of the states."

"Oh my God." Olivia caressed Lindsay's fingers as they talked. She made up her mind that they would be good, that she would not kiss her again, or anything else, until she turned eighteen. That way, she wouldn't get Lindsay in any trouble, and they wouldn't have to lie about their relationship if it ever came up. "That sounds like the dream year of my life. Seriously, I absolutely love traveling. I want to go to Europe as well and visit Ireland, Scotland, England, and so many other places. I'm about to graduate, you know. We could take off and do a summer trip, just me and you. It could be a celebration for when announce our relationship to the world." Olivia spoke with genuine excitement. She was naive, though she knew that she was. Did that self-awareness count as maturity? Either way, she wanted whatever her heart desired, and she wasn't afraid to simply go for it and make that thing happen.

"I can't just pick up and leave, sweetie." Lindsay grinned down at her young friend, while Olivia melted when she called her names like, 'sweetie' and, 'sweetheart.' Those were words she could easily get used to hearing from Lindsay. "I have a job and a life here, as much as I'd like to just pack up and leave sometimes."

"Well, you never know." Olivia didn't want to tell Lindsay about her family's money so soon. She barely knew her, truth be told. Yes, she overflowed with gushy feelings toward Lindsay, but she remained level-headed enough to understand that it would be best to wait before telling her that her dad had many millions of dollars. She needed to make sure Lindsay truly wanted to be with her before revealing her financial situation. "I like to live spontaneously. I've been thinking about taking a year off after high school and traveling. I've started writing, and I think I'm going to write a novel."

"Look at you." Lindsay beamed as Olivia spoke about her passions. "You said your stepmother is a writer. I actually ordered one of her books after you first told me. I can't wait to read it once it gets here."

"Which one did you get? I've read her first two books now. She is so talented. I'm trying to learn as much as I can from her." Olivia felt a bit guilty for looking up to Julia so much. She wondered what her mother would think if she knew.

"I'm pretty sure it's her first book. *Six Days To Live...* does that sound right?"

"Yep, that's the one. It's so good. You're going to love it if you love creepy, suspense-type novels."

"I do. They scare me a little, but I like it. What type of book do you want to write?"

"I'm not a hundred percent sure yet. I think it will be in that mystery, suspense genre, but I've also been writing some romance and drama-type thoughts as well. I haven't actually started the book yet, but I've written one short story and some ideas for a book. After I write the ideas down, I read them back and see what feels right."

"And?" Lindsay gently ran her hand through Olivia's hair, as if not wanting to disturb her while she dreamed out loud. "What feels right so far?"

"Hmmm, so far I'd have to say it's a blend between the mystery and drama genres. Julia told me not to worry about what genre it is, that it will come once I write. She said to just sit down and write, and then see what comes out. So that's what I've been doing, but just with the ideas for the book so far."

"You are so cute when you talk about your writing."

"Thank you." Olivia blushed. "I think you're cute too."

"And I think you can do it. Write a book, I mean. I'd love to hear some of your ideas if you're comfortable enough sharing them with me."

"I'd love to share them with you." Olivia sat up after she glanced at the clock. "We talked through almost the entire movie. How long has it been over?"

"I don't know." Lindsay said as they both looked at the clock that read midnight. It was now technically Christmas morning. "We've been talking for hours, hun. You better get home before your dad gets worried about you. I don't want you to get into trouble on Christmas. I'm pretty sure that's not how you'd want to spend your Christmas."

"Yeah, you're right. I better get going." Olivia stood from the couch and strapped on her jacket. Lindsay stood as well but remained near the couch. Olivia knew that Lindsay wanted to stay strong and wait until she was of age before kissing her again.

"Goodnight." Olivia turned and waited for Lindsay to walk over and kiss her like the end of the world was just around the corner. She assumed that if they were to kiss outside in that chilly air, she would no longer need her jacket. Their lips pressed together would heat their entire bodies.

"Night." Lindsay raised her hand close to her shoulder and waved awkwardly. As she did, Olivia rushed over and took what belonged to her. She kissed the older woman on the lips and prayed that it would never end. Lindsay embraced Olivia in her arms, squeezing her in as close as she possibly could. Olivia returned her fervor and allowed her body to tingle with anticipation of the unknown and newness.

Just then, Olivia's phone rang. It was Isaac.

"You have to go," Lindsay whispered.

"I know, but I don't want to."

"I don't want you to either, but you have to. Soon, sweetheart, very soon."

Olivia left and skipped to her car, floating in pure raw delight. She drove back to her home in Kennesaw and fell asleep with a permanent grin. She knew she would never need pills again. No, she had a new addiction in her life, and it was one she would not relinquish.

CHAPTER 18
Uber

AGENT FAITH DIALED THE NUMBERS ON her work phone, two days after Christmas. She'd already made two other calls just like this one. Agent Noah had done the same. They'd listened to the heartbreak and the sadness from the parents and husbands of the victims they had to report as partially recovered.

"Hello," Isaac answered as soon as he saw Agent Faith's name pop up on his phone.

"Hello, Isaac." Agent Faith referred to him by his first name. As soon as she did, he realized that this conversation would be different. "Have I caught you at a good time?"

"Yeah, it's fine. What's going on?" Isaac hadn't expected to hear from the FBI again. He had no idea what they could possibly be calling for and immediately felt guilty for not having thought about them in so long. He'd moved on with his life and his past life was slowly fading away.

"We've had a major development in the case. If there's any chance you could meet with us today or tomorrow, we need to update you on our latest discovery."

"Okay, I can be there in thirty minutes."

"Would it be possible to make it for this evening? Say, around 7:00 PM?"

Isaac hung up the phone and decided not to tell Julia or the kids anything until after he met with the agents. His mind raced with possibilities. He wondered if they'd found her body down in Biloxi or possibly somewhere else nearby. Was it feasible that the Butcher was not her killer after all, that they'd just now arrested her true killer? All the *Dateline NBC* episodes and *Criminal Minds* shows began to replay in his mind.

Isaac kissed Julia and went for a walk with Rylee around the neighborhood. She jumped in circles as soon as she heard the word, *walk*. After their stroll around the block, he left to enjoy a coffee, hoping to kill the time before seven PM rolled around. When it finally did, he walked into the station on Lemon Street and prepared for the worst-case scenario. He wasn't quite sure what that would be, but he assumed he would find out shortly.

"Hi, Isaac." Agent Noah greeted him with his partner by his side. "It's nice to see you again. I hope you had a good Christmas."

"We did, thanks for asking." Isaac proceeded to fill them in on his marriage to Julia and the news of the pregnancy. The agents were unaware of all the developments in Isaac's life, but they seemed happy for him.

"That's wonderful to hear." Agent Faith folded her hands as she sat next to her partner, while Isaac watched them from across the desk. They did not take him to an interrogation room for this meeting. The room was cleared of all of the local detectives at 7:00 PM and away from any Marietta police officers who were working at that time. "This isn't going to be an easy conversation," she said as she continued with their news.

"Did you find her body?" Isaac's stomach filled with an uneasy feeling that he did not enjoy. The closest comparison he could think of was the day he pulled into his driveway and saw Nicole's car parked there. Even still, this was more than butterflies or a sick feeling. He couldn't quite describe the sensations. They were entirely new to him.

"Yes and no," Agent Noah politely interrupted. "We discovered something that we've never come across before, Isaac. We searched his properties again after we started the investigation over. All of this came after his suicide note."

"Wait, he left a suicide note?" Isaac had never heard about a suicide note. He only knew the Butcher hanged himself in his cell.

"Yes," Agent Faith answered, "we didn't release that publicly."

"What was in the note?"

"We can't say. I'm sorry, Mr. Childs. I know it must be frustrating for you." He noticed that she referred to him as Mr. Childs again.

"What does it matter now? My wife's dead, and Haney is dead too."

"I understand that it might not make sense, but we need to keep it private in case there are details in the note that may prove useful later." Agent Noah tried to bring their conversation back to the matter at hand. "Isaac, the reason we called you is because we found something after searching his properties again. We did not find anything of significance at his home in Acworth, but we did make a major discovery at his other residence in Cartersville. Hidden on the back of his thirty-acre property was an underground bunker that he camouflaged with grass, leaves, and dirt. Inside of that, we found twenty-five arms belonging to his victims. One of those arms came from Ramie, from your wife, Mr. Childs. We were able to match her fingerprints. I know that I can't relate to how you're feeling, but I am truly sorry for your loss, and for how this must feel coming so long after everything originally happened."

"I don't understand. How did you guys miss this during your original search? I mean, this is what you do for a living, right? How could you have possibly walked past a bunker on his property?"

"You're right," Agent Faith said like an admission. "We should have found it the first time. It's no excuse, but his property was rather large, around thirty acres, as we said, and the bunker was hidden and the door weighted down so that it was invisible to the naked eye. We only found it when I pulled on the rope that was attached to the door, and I felt something slightly move."

"I guess it doesn't make a difference anymore anyway. She was dead before. Does this make her deader?" Isaac realized that he had yet to grieve for the loss of his wife. He did in fact move on too quickly after she passed away by marrying Julia just over a year later. Now, he was about to have twins with his new wife, while they would need to bury Ramie's arm where they placed her empty casket. He didn't know what to do, only that he needed a drink. "Thanks for telling me. I have to go."

"Isaac," Agent Faith called out, as she tried to stop him from hurrying out of the station, "we really are sorry."

"It's fine." Isaac walked out of the station, never once looking back at the agents. He hurried to his truck and simply stared out at the cold, steady rain that had begun falling.

I've been sober for how long now? Isaac thought. *So long that I stopped keeping track of the time. I thought alcoholics never stopped counting. Don't they know how many days it's been since their last drink even like twenty years later? I haven't drunk in over a year, but I can't even quit being a drinker the right way.*

Isaac gripped the steering wheel and thought intently about his next move. He knew what he needed to do. He should drive home and tell his perfect wife about the discovery and allow her to comfort him. Julia always made him feel better when he got down, and the mere sight of her pregnant belly made him smile. Then, after she comforted him, he could tell the kids and be there for them. He didn't want to do any of those things, however. He craved the taste of a bitter beer, the burn only a straight shot of vodka could provide. The rain continued to fall as Isaac pulled out of the parking lot on Lemon Street, and he headed to the closest bar that he remembered from his past.

He drove ten minutes down the road and pulled into the Mazzy's on Roswell Road, the one that still allowed smoking inside. It was one of the few places around that still permitted smoking inside the restaurant. He used to enjoy going to Mazzy's, the one in Kennesaw that didn't allow smoking, because they showed all the sports games and served good burgers. He'd never been a smoker, and he didn't like the smell, but occasionally it made him feel better.

Those were the only times where he enjoyed the smell of smoke and the ability to smell like smoke an hour later, even though he'd never smoked a cigarette before in his life. Isaac sat in his truck for five minutes as he debated what to do next. He ignored the text from Julia and felt like such a baby for wanting to cry yet again.

After clearing Julia's text, he shifted the truck into reverse and began to back up. He tapped his brakes as a car whizzed by and proceeded to roll out of the parking spot. He circled around and parked on the other side of the lot. Isaac turned the truck off and put the keys into the pocket of his Auburn windbreaker. He stroked his clean, freshly shaved face and fixed his eyes upon the rain that seemingly fell in slow motion. The windshield began to fog up after only thirty seconds, and Isaac's stomach repeatedly turned, waiting for him to make a decision.

I'm a thirty-eight-year-old man. I don't need permission to drink. He read these thoughts as they raced across his mind. *I don't deserve to be clean and sober. The Butcher cut Ramie's arm off and buried it, while I managed to fall in love and start a new family. I don't deserve happiness.*

Isaac opened the truck door and jogged into the restaurant with one hand over his head and the other shielding his phone beneath his jacket. The temperature dropped to the mid-thirties as the night progressed. He felt a touch of sleet mix in with the rain, and he welcomed the warm, smoky air that greeted him inside the bar. He found a seat on the far end and sat down away from the six other people scattered around the horseshoe-shaped bar. Isaac wiped his hands on his jeans and understood that this would be the deciding moment in his new life. The bartender greeted him with a smile and handed him a menu.

"What can I get you to drink?" She appeared to be in her early to mid-thirties and was undeniably attractive. Isaac normally didn't like short hair on a woman, but approved of her spiked, pink-streaked black hair. Her revealing tie-dyed tank top stood out as well, though he assumed that she probably wore it so she would receive bigger tips as the alcohol flowed.

"Give me just a minute, please, but I'll take an ice water for now." Isaac hated not ordering a real drink. He always thought that the bartender would think he would turn out to be a bad tipper and not give him good service.

"No problem, hun. Just let me know when you're ready." As she walked to the other side of the bar, Isaac couldn't help but glance in her direction. She looked as good from behind as she did from the front. He began to fear that his weakness might be rising once again. *I'm already having these thoughts, and I haven't even drunk yet.* He thought about his previous transgression and then about his pregnant wife at home whom he loved dearly. He would never cheat on her, and he felt guilty for even looking at another woman. *God, forgive me.*

"Yeah, what's your beer with the highest alcohol content?" Isaac finally spoke after debating with himself for a full minute.

"Do you like IPAs?"

"They're my favorite kind of beer."

"We have a local XPA out of Atlanta. It has a 7.4% alcoholic content. Would you like to sample it first?" She leaned in toward him just a bit. Isaac noticed that she seemed friendly, but that was literally her job, so he wasn't sure if she was actually flirting with him or not.

"That'd be great, thanks." He kept his eyes focused on hers.

"I'm Nikki, by the way." She handed him the quarter-filled pint of the XPA. Isaac thought it more than a coincidence that her name was so close to that of his biggest sin. He quickly looked down at the smooth-looking beer and gave into the craving. He downed the sample of the thick drink and instantly felt his eyes gloss over, even if they did not appear that way just yet.

"I'm Isaac. It's nice to meet you."

"So, did you like it?"

"I did. I'll take a big one of those and some mozzarella sticks as well." He understood fully that he would be buzzed within a half an hour and drunk within two hours. He just hoped that would be the worst thing he did that night.

"Is this your first time here, Isaac?"

"It's been years since I was last here. I actually quit drinking, so I really shouldn't be here." He admitted it out led, yet he continued to drink the beer in front of him.

"I feel bad now." The bartender frowned toward Isaac. "What made you stop in on such a nasty night? Don't you know that it's freezing outside?"

"It's a long story. I don't want to bother you with all of the specifics." He rotated his ring around his finger and looked up at the TV where a random basketball game played in the background.

"I've got time." Nikki looked around the bar to show him there wasn't much else going on. "But you don't have to, if you don't want to."

"I don't know if you remember or not..." Isaac brought up the original disappearance of Ramie, and the story of the Biloxi Butcher. He told her the gist of the story without getting too specific.

"I never heard about that. Oh my God, that is awful. I'm so sorry."

She said the same things that everyone else said. What else could they say, that they weren't sorry? *I'm sorry* was the only appropriate response.

"Thank you, I appreciate that." He ordered his second beer and decided to take a shot as well. "Wanna take a shot with me?" He'd never asked bartenders or women to take shots with him before, especially not pretty women.

"We're not really supposed to, but I desperately need a drink." Nikki smiled and made them both a Fireball shot without even asking what kind of shot he wanted. "Cheers." She tapped her shot glass against Isaac's, and they both downed the spine-shivering liquid together. "So, you look like you're a pretty successful guy. How'd you move on from all of that?"

Isaac told her all about Julia, his two kids, and the twins who were on their way in just a few short months. He assumed that Julia would be disappointed in his drinking, not to mention him getting to know this bartender more than he should. Julia wasn't exactly the jealous type, though he had yet to give her a reason to be jealous. Their relationship was still new, not even a year old, though marriage and twins-on-the-way had a way of accelerating life.

"So, you are married?" She sounded a little disappointed. She could see the ring on his finger, but it didn't seem to deter her. "Please don't take this the wrong way, but how did you find someone else so soon?"

"I didn't mean to. I accidentally met her when I was playing disc golf one day, and we hit it off. She is honestly my soulmate." Isaac finished his second beer and told her all about hitting Julia in the head with his disc. She'd never heard of disc golf, so he explained that to her as well. "Another shot?" He motioned for his third beer as well, not even an hour after his arrival at the bar. Each one of the XPAs equaled two light beers, and his buzz began to grow rather quickly. Nikki made them both another shot of Fireball, and they clinked their shot glasses together once again. "So, I see that you're married, or engaged." He noticed the ring on her finger shortly after the moment he sat down at the bar.

"I am married. We got married four years ago, but it feels like twenty."

"Is that a good thing or a bad thing?"

"Dear God, it's not good." She took a drink of her fountain drink from underneath the bar. Isaac guessed that it might contain a little something extra inside considering her boldness and willingness to take shots with him while she was working. "He's an asshole. If it weren't for the kids, I would have left him years ago."

"Kids? You look too skinny to have kids." He hung his head. "Sorry. How many do you have?"

"Thank you, you're too kind. I have two kids. Joshua is four, and Jaxson is two."

"Wow, you have your hands full then. I'm sorry to hear about your husband. Marriage is tough. Believe me, I know. That didn't sound right. I loved my first wife dearly, and I am very happy now. I love my wife."

Isaac drank more of his beer and found it amusing that one of her kids shared the same name as his brother. He glanced down at his phone and texted Julia back as she'd sent him three texts by this time, wondering where he went and if he was okay. He told her that he was fine, that he just needed to think for a little bit and he'd be home in a little while. Julia responded with only a smiley face, which heightened Isaac's shame.

"You're fine. I understand that marriage is tough, but I've got plans and goals in life. I'm not going to do this forever and live to make him or anyone else happy."

"Good for you, but there's nothing wrong with being a bartender. You get to meet new people, and I heard you guys make pretty good money." Isaac wasn't about to tell her that he made hundreds of thousands of dollars each year in interest alone, much less that he was a millionaire.

"No, you're right." She poured them both another shot after checking with the other patrons at the bar. "I just mean that I want to do something bigger with my life. I want to start my own business and be my own boss. Plus, this job can be fun some nights and depressing at other times. It's sad to see some people drink every single day and leave more miserable than when they came in. I don't like that part of the job."

"I would imagine that'd be tough to watch." He finished his third beer shortly after his third shot of Fireball. He tried to never mix beer and liquor as it gave him horrible headaches and made him feel like death the next day. Tomorrow would surely be miserable since he hadn't drunk is so long, even if he quit drinking now. There was no chance of that happening, however. "What kind of business do you want to start?"

"I always thought it would be fun to be an interior designer. I love decorating, and I don't know, I think I'm pretty good at it." Nikki pulled out her phone and leaned over the bar to show Isaac how she'd decorated her house and a few others homes she'd brought to life as well. She was talented. Her designs held the perfect mixture of modern and vintage with a few bright colors sprinkled among rustic restorations.

"Oh, wow, you do have a knack for this. You know I invest in businesses sometimes, so if you ever get serious about starting your own business, you should let me know."

Except Isaac didn't invest in businesses, and didn't understand now why he said that he did. Probably because she was nice, and attractive, of course.

"Really? What do you do for a living?"

"I buy and sell stocks. I get to work from home, so that's pretty nice, especially with the babies on the way." He hoped that by mentioning the babies again he would keep enough of a buffer there between the two of them.

"I just might take you up on that offer." Nikki wrote her number down on a piece of paper and slid it across the bar. She placed it into Isaac's hand and then poured them both another shot. Isaac felt buzzed two shots ago. Now, he was pretty sure that he was slightly drunk.

"Cool," he said nonchalantly, trying to make Nikki giving him her number not that big of a deal. "I'll call you sometime, and we can talk more about it."

"Definitely. Call me whenever or text me. Whatever is easier for you." She grinned in a way that was devoid of any innocence whatsoever. "Cheers."

"Cheers." Isaac tapped her glass yet again and downed another shot with his new friend. He started to feel sick to his stomach with all the mixing as the mixture of beer and liquor did not belong inside of him. The cheesesticks didn't help any, and he figured he better slow down before the night took even more of a turn for the worse. "Can I get another glass of water?" The only thing saving him were the three glasses of water he'd consumed in between his beers and shots. Nikki refilled his glass with water, and Isaac excused himself to the restroom to regroup and somehow redeem himself.

He stared at the bathroom mirror and locked bloodshot eyes with himself. *What am I doing*? Isaac found some solace in the fact that he held no desire to text Nicole. That was the old Isaac. Now, he was faced with another attractive woman who was unhappy in her marriage. *I love Julia. I can't hurt her. I don't want to hurt her.* He washed his hands, then returned to the bar and opened the door with the paper towels, so he wouldn't bring back any of the germs that disgusting men left on the handle from not washing their hands. He wasn't exactly a germaphobe, but those were germs he did not want to share.

"Can I get you another beer?" Nikki had another shot waiting for him when he sat back down at the bar.

"Yes, please." Perhaps he wasn't a new man after all. Perhaps he would simply make his same old mistake with this new woman. At least it wouldn't bring Nicole back into his life. She and Carter seemed happy together from what he gathered on Christmas Eve. Carter sure acted like his old self again.

"This one's on me." Nikki placed the tall beer in front of Isaac and laid her other hand atop of Isaac's. "What are you doing after you leave here?"

Isaac's nerves began to race even faster. He pulled his hand away, politely, and drank his new beer as quickly as he could. "I have to get home to my wife. She's pregnant, remember? Plus, I've drank way too much tonight."

"You're not driving home, are you?"

"No, of course not. I don't drink and drive. I've got an Uber coming in a little bit." None of that was true. He used to always drink and drive, and he'd never used Uber before.

"Okay, good. I thought maybe you'd had too much to be driving. You don't need an Uber. I get off in an hour. I can give you a ride home."

"No, that's nice of you, but I'll be fine, really. I don't think my wife would like that very much." Isaac tried his best to say the right thing.

He put himself in this situation by stopping at the bar in the first place, and then by talking with the pretty woman too much. He didn't mean for any of this to happen. He simply wanted to drink away his pain and forget about the FBI finding one of Ramie's arms, which he'd have to bury after having the casket exhumed. "I think I'll make this my last beer and check out, if you don't mind."

"Are you sure?" Nikki smiled broadly, her eyes slightly glazed over as well. "I really don't mind. We could hang out for a while too, if you wanted to."

"I appreciate the offer, that's really kind of you." Isaac did not think it was kind. It was mildly tempting, but he did not want to hurt Julia. He finished the last of his beer and left her two one-hundred-dollar bills, more than enough to cover his hundred-dollar tab. "I have to be going. It was nice to meet you, Nikki." He held out his hand and shook hers like a southern gentleman. "I'll be in touch with you about your startup."

"Goodnight, Isaac. Be safe." She watched him walk out of the bar and into the light snow that had begun to fall an hour prior. It wasn't sticking to the roads, but Isaac watched his breath in front of him as he found his way to his truck. A light dusting covered the tips of the grass around the parking lot and an even smaller amount sat atop his truck. He started the truck and rubbed his hands together to try and warm up. The temperature now rested at twenty-nine degrees, and Isaac pulled Nikki's number out of his pocket. He stared at the numbers and the smiley face she drew underneath.

Isaac thought of Ramie, how he'd made the wrong decision with Nicole. He wanted to smash his head into the steering wheel for throwing away more than a year's worth of sobriety. As the truck slowly warmed up, he pictured Julia and the faces of his little girls. He imagined they would be born with a full head of light-colored hair and chubby little cheeks. He looked back down at Nikki's number and made the only decision he could. He pulled out his phone and sealed his fate yet again.

"Hello? Is everything okay?"

"Yeah, everything is fine." Isaac choked up when she answered the phone. *What have I done?* he kept asking himself. "I need you." He finally got the words out.

"What do you mean? Are you hurt?" Julia now spoke in full panic mode. Isaac knew that he didn't sound like his normal self.

"I'm not hurt... I made a big mistake. I'm so sorry." He rolled his window down and threw Nikki's number into the bushes.

"Isaac, what's wrong? What happened? Whatever it is, it's okay."

"I got drunk. I need you to come and pick me up. Be careful though, it started snowing a little bit ago." Isaac felt such relief to admit his mistake to Julia. He never told her that he wouldn't drink, yet it still felt like he'd done something wrong.

Julia made the twenty-minute drive to Mazzy's and embraced Isaac as soon as she pulled into the parking lot. They drove away in her car and left Isaac's truck at the restaurant. Nikki watched them drive away and walked over to his truck. She spotted her number in the bushes and picked it up. She placed it underneath his windshield wiper, so it could be waiting for him when he returned.

CHAPTER 19
Happy Birthday

ISAAC DID NOT KEEP NIKKI'S NUMBER when he returned for his truck the next day. He threw it back into the bushes and tried to pretend that the previous night never happened. Julia reassured him that it was not a big deal. She took the news of the FBI finding one of Ramie's arms the same as Isaac. They were both shocked and saddened. Carter and Olivia said very little. They only hugged each other and agreed not to have another ceremony or anything like that. They did exhume the casket and bury the arm inside, a few weeks later. The only person who attended was Isaac. He said one more final goodbye to his first love and apologized to her. This time he offered more sincerity and spoke to her like it was just the two of them again. After he spent his time alone with the casket, they lowered Ramie into the ground for good.

January wrapped up with a small snowstorm, and February provided the coldest stretch that Georgia had seen in years. The highs rarely reached the thirties, and the lows often dropped to the single digits or the teens. When March arrived, Julia entered her eighth month of pregnancy without any other issues, except for her enormous belly. She carried the babies well, but her stomach swelled to gigantic, though still captivating, dimensions. Meanwhile, Olivia and Lindsay continued their relationship. They texted and talked every day, but they did not date at all. Olivia spent some time at Lindsay's house, yet they both practiced self-control and refrained from anything that might get Lindsay in trouble. As Olivia's birthday finally rolled around, she had a surprise for her father.

"Happy birthday, baby girl." Isaac greeted his daughter in the kitchen with scrambled eggs, thick slices of bacon, soft biscuits, and orange juice, free from any signs of pulp. "I can't believe you're eighteen-years-old already. Time flies."

"Thanks, Daddy. It smells so good in here." Olivia sat down at the table and prepared to eat her first meal as an adult. Julia wobbled in shortly after, smiling her contagious smile.

"I hope you made enough for me and the little ones." Julia poured each of them a glass of orange juice. "Happy birthday, Olivia. Do you have any special plans for your big day? Cigarettes? Lottery tickets?"

"Don't fill her head with ideas like that," Isaac joked, though only half-heartedly. He slipped up and drank one more time after finding out about Ramie's arm, but he did it at the house that time and had been completely sober for the past two months.

"Like she hasn't already thought about it," Julia teased.

"Oh, yes, I am going to be smoking all day and buying as many lottery tickets as I can get my hands on." She took a bite of bacon as her father made her plate first and then Julia's. "There is something that I actually wanted to talk to you about. I told myself that it would be best to break the news to you on my birthday since you couldn't get too angry with me on the day I was born."

"You're not pregnant, are you?" Isaac said, his tone half-serious.

"No, Daddy, you have to have sex to get pregnant. You two should know that better than anyone." Olivia managed to make him feel uncomfortable while Julia worked her way through the delicious meal. Rylee stood over her bowl and guzzled up the bacon fat and bread crust that Isaac left for her.

"That is true," he responded with as few words as possible. He didn't like talking about things like that with her. "What do you need to talk to me about?"

"The truth is that I've met someone."

"Well, look at you. What's his name?"

"Who said it was a he?" Olivia made her best attempt to keep the conversation light and airy.

"Yeah, right. You're not a lesbian. Are you?" Isaac asked. He realized at that moment that she'd never had a boyfriend before, so it was an actual possibility that his daughter liked girls.

"Isaac," Julia said with a look that signaled for him to be supportive.

"I'm sorry, sweetheart. I didn't mean any of that in a bad way. If you are a lesbian, I am fine with that. I also just ruined your coming out conversation, but we'll laugh about it down the road, right?"

"You're a dork, Daddy." Olivia smiled, and he realized that she seemed genuinely happy. All he desired was for his kids to be happy.

"I'm not a lesbian, but I am bi. I honestly don't know what I am exactly, only that I've fallen for a girl; a woman actually."

"Okay, well I have to process all of this. I didn't expect it, that's all." Isaac stumbled with his words. "How old is she? It's not one of your teachers, is it?"

"No, she's not one of my teachers. Her name is Lindsay. She's twenty-nine."

"Okay then." Isaac immediately thought of his transgression with Nicole. His act was worse, but still, twenty-nine? Something about Lindsay being a woman instead of a man made him feel better, but he was unsure why. He understood that made him sound less progressive than he actually was, but it was how he felt. "Tell me more about her. How did you two meet? What does she do for a living? You know, all that good stuff."

"She lives in Woodstock, and we met a few months ago. She's really sweet and kind, and we haven't done anything. We've just talked and gotten to know each other since I was only seventeen. I didn't mean for this to happen, I just kind of fell for her."

"So you really like her then, huh?" Isaac calmed his emotions and determined himself not to get hung up on Lindsay's age. "Wait, wasn't your counselor's name Lindsay? Is this the same Lindsay from after your accident?"

"Yes, but we didn't start talking like that until after I stopped seeing her."

"So, that's why you stopped seeing her so soon. I knew there had to be a reason. You told me how much she was helping you. I guess she'll be a part of your life again." Isaac had learned enough about parenting to know that he shouldn't push her away or condemn her. She was eighteen, and while she still lived in his home, that could all change in just a few short months. He made up his mind that he would support and love his daughter and get to know Lindsay before casting judgment.

"Sort of, honestly. You know me, Daddy. I've never felt like this before. I don't know if it's just young love or what it is, but I love her."

"That's sweet," Julia said as she excused herself from the table and carried the dog upstairs with her.

"I'm happy for you, baby girl. Really, I am. This is a lot to take in, but I'm not mad. I don't like how you met, but I understand that life isn't always clean cut. It's messy sometimes. If you're happy, and if she treats you right, then that's good enough for me."

"I feel so much better now," she said as she walked over and hugged her father. "I've been so nervous about telling you and hiding my relationship with her. I've never looked forward to a birthday so much in my life."

"I'm glad you told me. You can tell me anything. I promise I will do my best not to get mad and to be supportive. As long as it's within reason, I just want you to do what makes you happy."

"There is one more thing." Olivia sat back down on her side of the table and drank the last of her juice. "It's not a big deal, but I don't want you to be surprised when you meet her. Lindsay is black."

"Really? A black lesbian from Woodstock? That's gotta be a rare thing."

"Very funny. She's originally from Mobile. She went to Mercer, and now she lives in Woodstock."

"She sounds nice, and of course I don't care that she's black. The age thing is the only issue I have to work through, but I will."

"Can she come over tonight then?"

"Only because it's your birthday." Isaac teased his daughter and thought to himself that at least she wouldn't be getting pregnant anytime soon. She'd only been seeing a counselor because of the accident, which revealed her pill habit, which traced back to Ramie, which started because of his drinking. This gave him one more reason to never drink again. In the back of his mind, he guessed there would be a day where he messed up again. It's who he was. He seemed to always find a way to slip up, even if it were only one time. He assumed he wasn't the only one who did things like that, but he often felt like it.

Isaac kissed his daughter and headed upstairs to prepare for the day. He walked by the snoring dog and his napping wife. All things considered, his kids were healthy, happy, and the new babies were destined for the same fate. As soon as the water washed over his body in the shower, he craved a beer. No, he craved six or seven beers. *Shit,* Isaac thought as he cleaned his skin and allowed the steam to cover the mirror. *I'm such a failure.* He dried off and put on his favorite pair of jeans and a blue fleece jacket to keep him warm in the March cold. He thought that spring might never push this winter out of the way. As he left the house, he noticed that Olivia had already left, and Julia lay upstairs, sound asleep with the dog. He pulled out of the driveway and prepared to give into his dark desires, on his daughter's birthday.

***

Olivia made it to Lindsay's apartment in the early afternoon, thankful that her birthday landed on a Saturday. She skipped up to the door and let herself in.

"Hey, birthday girl." Lindsay kissed Olivia on the lips and embraced her in a way they'd never embraced before. This time, it felt softer, and it seemed right to Olivia.

"Don't say it like that. You sound like a creeper." Olivia giggled and jumped onto the couch. Lindsay fell down beside her and locked her hand inside of Olivia's.

"Birthday girl," she said again, this time in a deeper, more disturbing voice.

"Stop. You're ruining my birthday."

"Really?"

"No, not really. I told my dad this morning, and he took it pretty well. Well, except for you being black. He had a little problem with that."

"Seriously?"

"No, but that's for using the creeper voice on the day of my birth."

"Oh, you're hilarious." Lindsay squeezed her hand with a playful force and kissed her one more time on the lips. Olivia guessed she would never grow tired of being with this captivating woman. "And he didn't care about how we met?"

"He cared some but not too much. He said that he just wanted me to be happy and that he supported me. He seemed kind of shocked that you were a girl and not a guy. It was sort of funny."

"You don't really know that I'm not a guy, you know." Lindsay laughed as Olivia pictured their future together. She imagined them moving to Portland one day and living downtown in a high-rise apartment overlooking the Columbia River. They would take walks together in the rain and become Trail Blazer fans. They could adopt a child or two and live happily ever after in the Pacific Northwest.

"I guess I don't." Olivia leaned in and nibbled on Lindsay's full lips. The girls moved their hands around and began to explore each others' bodies for the first time. Lindsay beamed with joy, and Olivia overflowed with raw excitement. They fell even more in love as they dreamed together while still being fully awake.

"So, I guess you are my birthday girl," Lindsay said as they lay together on her bed, covered by a sheet and staring into Olivia's eyes.

"I love you," Olivia said those words for the first time in her life that wasn't to a parent or the dog. She loved Lindsay more than she knew was possible for one human being to love another.

"I love you too," Lindsay said, and Olivia knew that she meant it. She wasn't merely repeating the overused phrase to make her happy on her birthday. No, Lindsay truly loved her. In fact, Olivia guessed that she'd never been in love before.

"Hey, there's something I need to tell you." Olivia felt safe now. It was the right time for her to inform Lindsay about her financial situation.

"Sure, sweetheart. You can tell me whatever you like." Lindsay kissed Olivia's cheek and rested her head on her chest.

"Remember how I told you that I really wanted to travel?"

"Of course. I want to travel too."

"Well, here's the thing; I'm kind of rich."

"What do you mean by kind of rich?"

"Like really rich. Like I'd never have to work if I didn't want to, but I do. I'm not like that. I have big dreams. I want to travel, but I also want to be an author and accomplish other goals in my life."

"Why didn't you tell me earlier?" Lindsay asked with a sense of curiosity.

"My dad always taught me to be careful who I tell about our money because money changes people. We hardly ever tell anyone. Only our immediate family knows and a handful of other people, but my dad became a multi-millionaire right after college."

"How? Did he win the lottery or something?"

"That's funny 'cause he jokes sometimes that it felt that way. My mom used to say that as well. He started this internet business and it took off. After a year, he sold it for a ton of money, and we've been rich all my life."

"That must be nice."

"I like it. I mean, money isn't everything, but it does make life easier. So you see, we can travel and do all of the things we talked about."

"I can't travel on your dad's money. I have a job and a life here. I wouldn't feel right about taking his money and going all over the world with it."

"We don't have to go all over the world. We could start with Portland."

"I do love Portland." Lindsay smiled and kissed her skin one more time. Olivia loved the taste it left on her lips and her natural smell that filled the room. She smelled like flowers and some type of berry soap. Both made her incredibly happy and tempted her to want more.

"And I do love you." Olivia slid down and enjoyed the time with her girlfriend. She kept calling her that in her mind, whenever she wasn't referring to her as her love, because it seemed surreal to have an actual girlfriend. "Let's get ready and head back to my house. I'm excited for you to meet my dad and Julia. Julia is enormous by the way. There's no way she's going to last until her due date."

"When is that again?"

"May 1 or May 2, something like that."

Olivia and Lindsay showered together and left Lindsay's apartment hand in hand. They proudly strolled to Olivia's car and made the drive south to Kennesaw. Lindsay commented on the gorgeous home that Olivia still considered as Julia's, though at times, it also felt like her own. As soon as they walked through the front door, Rylee greeted them by jumping in circles and licking Lindsay's leg.

"Rylee, down." Olivia motioned for the excited pug to get down.

"It's fine. She's so cute," Lindsay said as she pressed her fingers into the extra skin on the pug's neck.

"Hey, Julia." Olivia spotted her stepmother in the kitchen and led Lindsay to the welcoming room. "Julia, this is my girlfriend, Lindsay." It felt like heaven to refer to Lindsay as her girlfriend. "Lindsay, this is my stepmom, Julia."

"It's wonderful to meet you." Julia stretched out her hand to greet Lindsay, and Lindsay offered a captivating smile to make a good impression.

"It's great to meet you as well. You have a lovely home, and can I just say that you look amazing? Seriously, you are so pretty."

"Well, aren't you the best?" Julia blushed and rubbed her massive belly. "I can see why Olivia fell for you."

"Where's my dad?" She realized that her father hadn't popped in with a funny or sarcastic comment yet.

"You know what? I'm actually not sure. He left when I was taking a nap, and I haven't heard from him since. I'll call him now." Julia called Isaac, but he did not answer the phone. She tried again but still, no answer. She texted and waited nervously for him to respond. "I'm sure he went to play disc golf or maybe for a run and just left his phone in the car."

"It's kind of cold to play disc golf, no?" Olivia knew that her father hated to play when it was this cold outside. His hands would turn to ice, and he would complain the entire time. He sometimes ran in the cold, but he tried to go in the middle of the day. The sun was about to set, and something did not feel right.

The girls followed Julia to the back porch to enjoy a cup of hot cocoa together. Isaac had two heaters installed so that they could enjoy the screened-in porch all year. The three of them sat together and talked, while Julia waited for Isaac to text or call her back. After another hour passed, they began to genuinely worry that something might be wrong. Just as she was about to call him for the fifth time, they all heard a loud noise from the front of the house.

"What was that?" Olivia jumped up and raced through the house to see what the noise was. Lindsay ran behind her, and Julia walked as quickly as she could. When Olivia opened the front door, she saw her dad's truck smashed into the back of her car. "Daddy, are you okay?"

Isaac stepped out of the truck and surveyed the damage. The front of his truck showed a small dent and a few scratches, but the back end of Olivia's car took the brunt of the collision. Lindsay stayed in the house while Julia walked all the way over to Isaac.

"I tried to call and have been texting you non-stop," Julia said as the smell of alcohol drifted in the air. She lowered her voice. "Honey, you drove like this? What if you got into an accident?"

"I'm fine, honestly. I just didn't expect to see Liv's car in the driveway, that's all." Isaac walked fairly straight toward the front door as he spotted Lindsay standing inside the house. "You must be Lindsay." He leaned in for a hug. Isaac never was an angry drunk. If anything, he became too friendly. "It's great to meet you."

"It's nice to meet you too, Mr. Childs." Lindsay offered a sly smile that embarrassed Olivia. She hoped that Lindsay didn't get the wrong impression about her father, as it was impossible not to know he'd been drinking.

Isaac excused himself and went upstairs to lay down. Seconds after his head hit the pillow, he drifted off to sleep by watching the ceiling spin around. By the time Julia apologized to the girls, especially Lindsay, Isaac was already passed out and their conversation would have to wait. Olivia and Lindsay said goodbye, and they left to eat dinner for Olivia's birthday and escape the awkwardness of her father's drunken arrival.

"I'm so sorry about my dad. He's not usually like that." She told her all about her dad's struggle with drinking, the parts she knew anyway.

"You don't have to apologize. Trust me, we all have family problems."

"No, but you don't understand. My dad is the greatest guy there is. He literally never does this. The only other time I've seen him come home like this was like a year and a half ago, after my mom died. Please come back tomorrow and meet him again when he's his normal self. I hope this didn't scare you off."

"Sweetheart," Lindsay said as she squeezed her hand, "I'm not going anywhere. You can't scare me off. I get it, trust me. In fact, there's something about me that you need to know. I was going to wait to tell you, but I feel like you need to know this."

"You're not really a lesbian, are you?" Olivia tried her best to deflect and lighten the mood.

"I think you know that I am. No, I have to tell you something about my past, something huge. I just need to know that you won't ever say anything to anyone."

"Of course, I promise." Olivia sensed that this would be a life-changing revelation. Whatever it was, she believed that it would be fine.

"I've never told anyone what I'm about to tell you. This is beyond big," Lindsay said, visibly nervous.

"Okay, okay, just tell me. You can trust me. I'm not going to tell anyone. I love you."

Lindsay waited for Olivia to put the car in park after they pulled into the parking lot for Olivia's birthday dinner. Olivia gazed into the eyes of her love, waiting for the news that might test that love.

CHAPTER 20
Old Search Engines

"I FOUND SOMETHING." AGENT NOAH LEANED against his partner's desk and grinned with anticipation. "I think this is what we've been looking for."

Agent Faith scanned through the papers that Agent Noah set down in front of her. As she did, one name kept popping up: John Smith.

"What is this?" Agent Faith asked, beyond curious at this point.

"You said yourself that Haney must have had another place where he dismembered the women. We still haven't found that place. I got to digging online, and I just kept searching Charles Haney on all these different search engines. Nothing new. Nothing until I stumbled upon something on this search engine that looked like it came from the nineties." Agent Noah slowly built to his climactic discovery. "I found a site that lists all of the names ever used at an address for mail delivery. Guess what I uncovered at his place up in Cartersville?"

"John Smith?" Agent Faith suddenly felt shame for not thinking of searching his mail records earlier.

"Exactly. John Smith. I kept searching, and it didn't stop there. He's been getting mail in his name and in John Smith's name for the past twenty years."

"Do you think he has a partner?" They'd worked this angle early on, but never found any evidence that pointed toward a partner.

"I don't think so, but I'm not completely sure yet. I think he used an alias."

"John Fucking Smith." Agent Faith rarely cursed, but her frustration shone through at this point in the conversation. "He picked the most common name in the United States so that it would take an eternity to find his other identity."

"That's what I'm thinking. It's not too difficult to create a second identity with a social security number and to get it complete with a fake background if you've got a little money and you know the right people. He had some money, so I'd bet that's what he did."

"Let's track down some of the most recent mail he received and see if he paid any bills in that name. Maybe he had another residence in his alias' name. There has to be."

"And I bet you there are bodies there," Agent Noah said what she was thinking. "At the very least, I'd guess he had another home or deserted property where he cut the women up."

"I'll work the mail angle and you start searching for homes under the name of John Smith," Agent Faith spoke with excitement. She understood that this was the break they'd been searching for. "Start with Cartersville, Acworth, Woodstock, Marietta, and Kennesaw. Then spread out to Roswell, Calhoun, Rome, and Canton."

They began their search through the hundreds of John Smiths' who resided in Georgia. Agent Faith spoke with the local postal inspector who confirmed that John Smith and Charles Haney both received mail at the trailer in Cartersville. That mail obviously hadn't been delivered in approximately a year and a half since Haney was arrested. Agent Faith received little else from the postal inspector and decided to check Haney's tax returns. She went through them all for his past twenty years but nothing stood out. She put in a call to the IRS to see if there might have been another tax return filed for one of Haney's addresses or possibly even with his social security number. While she waited to hear back, she and Agent Noah called everyone with the name of John Smith, one by one. Each John Smith they spoke with narrowed their search for the John Smith they believed to be Charles Haney.

CHAPTER 21
I Was Twelve

"TELL ME, JUST REMEMBER THAT IT is my birthday," Olivia nervously joked. She believed that whatever it was that Lindsay needed to tell her, it couldn't be worse than what she'd gone through with her mother and her pill habit.

"I told you that my parents died in a fire when I was twelve. That's true; they did. What I didn't tell you was how the fire got started." Lindsay appeared shaken and panicked. Olivia could see the fear of Lindsay unburdening herself. She felt special to be the one that she chose to share it with, even if it was an unpleasant part of her past.

"You know who did it?" Olivia asked. She sensed that she did, but she needed to hear her say it.

"It was me. I started the fire." Lindsay waited a moment before Olivia finally responded.

"On purpose? Why would you do that?"

"Because my father had been abusing me since I turned ten. I developed early, and he drank heavily. He always hit me and my mother, but I thought that was normal. I figured that every father hit their kids when they got angry or if they deserved it. I didn't know that it wasn't normal. But once he started touching me and doing other things to me, I died on the inside. I hated myself, and I hated my mom. She knew exactly what he was doing because I watched her walk by my room a dozen times over those last two years, yet she did nothing."

"Oh, sweetie, I'm so sorry." Olivia placed her hand on Lindsay's leg and listened to her pour out her heart and spill her pain all over the inside of that car.

"I know she was scared of him, but I was scared of him too. She could have called the police or moved us away, but she just let him beat me and keep touching me. So, shortly after I turned twelve, he got me pregnant. When he found out, he beat me so badly that he broke my arm, and I had to go to the hospital. They told the doctor that I fell off the monkey bars at the park down the road, and no one suspected anything. My mom is the one who figured out I was pregnant. I got my first period when I was eleven, so after two months of not having one when I was twelve, I told my mom that something wasn't right."

Lindsay rested her hands on Olivia's and continued to tell her long-buried past.

"My dad said that my mom would take me to get an abortion and that I was a slut for getting pregnant. He pretended like he wasn't the one who got me pregnant. He acted like my mom didn't know because she was too terrified to ever say anything to him. The night he told me that he was going to make me have an abortion, I decided that I would kill them both. I got a can of gas from the garage and poured it all over the downstairs of the house, up the stairs, and down the hall to their bedroom door. I used a lighter to start the fire, and I ran out of the house around three in the morning and watched it burn from my front yard. A little while later, when the house filled with smoke and flames, I ran to the neighbor's house and told them to call 911. By the time they arrived, it was too late. My parents were both dead."

Olivia didn't know quite what to say. She listened, silently, before she finally spoke again. "They didn't suspect you? I mean, they didn't wonder how you got out of the house?"

"They questioned me, but there was no evidence tying me to the fire. I was pretty smart for a twelve-year-old. I put the gas can back in the garage, washed my hands thoroughly, and then rubbed them in laundry detergent before washing them again. There was no trace of gas on me and no proof that I did anything wrong. I told them that I woke up to a sound in the living room. See, I slept downstairs while my parents stayed upstairs. When I walked out into the living room, I told them I saw a masked man running out of the house and the house was already on fire. My dad had a lot of enemies, so they thought it might have been one of the people he screwed over from his past. He used to be a drug dealer, for like ten years actually, so it wasn't that hard for them to believe. I said that I called for my parents but that the stairs were on fire so there was nothing I could do. No one could believe that a twelve-year-old girl would commit such a crime."

"That is such a horrible story." Olivia leaned over and kissed Lindsay tenderly on the lips. She wanted her to know that she wasn't going anywhere. "You did what you thought was right, and you were just a kid. It's not like you're a murderer or anything. I mean, you grew up and went to college, and you're a counselor now. You help people. You did something with your life and overcame your past."

"I try. You know I still have nightmares sometimes? There are nights where I wake up in a sweat or jump straight up in bed because I've just dreamed about my father for the millionth time."

"I can't imagine. I don't know what I would have done since I've never been in a situation like that. I'm so sorry you had to grow up with that."

"It's fine; it's not your fault. Like I said, I've never told anyone that before in my life. I'm trusting you, you know."

"I know." Olivia felt grown up before, but now she sensed that there was no turning back in their relationship. This propelled them to a new level of love and trust that she took immense delight in.

"I feel so free to have that off my chest. You don't understand what it's like to have a secret that big and not be able to share it with anyone for all of these years."

"You're right. I don't know what that feels like, but can I ask you something?"

"Of course." Lindsay stared eagerly at her love.

"What happened to the baby?"

"Well, I went to foster care because we had no other family. I was only two months pregnant, and nobody knew when I first arrived. I obviously wasn't showing, so my foster parents thought I got pregnant there. They gave me back, and I bounced around foster homes for the rest of my junior high and high school years. Long story short is that I ended up having the baby and giving him up for adoption. I didn't even name him or anything."

"Wow... So you have a son out there somewhere?"

"Yeah, he'd be sixteen now."

"Do you ever think about trying to contact him?"

"I've thought about it many times, but I don't think it's a good idea. I don't want anything to do with that part of my life, and if he looks like my dad did, I wouldn't be able to handle that. Some things are better left in the past, and I feel like that is one of them."

The girls finished their conversation and ate the birthday dinner together with as much normalcy as possible. Olivia pictured herself as such an adult now. She had a real-life girlfriend, and they shared a secret together that was bigger than any she'd ever known. After they finished their evening out, she dropped Lindsay off at her apartment and went back home to find her father still asleep. Olivia gathered Rylee up and went to her room for the night. She fell asleep to the image of Lindsay and her together, holding hands and talking about anything but the fire.

***

In the morning, Isaac woke with a pounding headache.

"Good morning." Julia turned toward him in the bed. "How are you feeling?"

"Terrible. Was it bad?" Isaac vaguely remembered his entrance the previous night and his first impression with Lindsay.

"Isaac, you can't do this anymore. I don't like you drinking, but I'm not going to tell you that you can't drink. However, I *am* going to tell you that you can't drink and drive. What would I do without you? How would I raise the girls by myself? I don't want to have to go through life alone because you couldn't stop yourself from getting drunk and driving."

"I know. I'm a horrible person. I'm so sorry. I'll start going to meetings. Maybe that will help. I just hate myself sometimes. I mean, I go for such a long time without drinking, and then out of nowhere, I start again. And it's not like I just drink a few and have a good time. I drink until I'm drunk, and I do something as stupid as driving."

"I love you, and that's why I'm talking to you. When I picked you up from the restaurant, I didn't care. I was happy that you called me. When you drank at the house after that, I was fine with that too. But this is not something that I'm okay with. You could have hurt yourself or someone else. You could be dead or in jail right now, having ruined someone's family. I know it's not easy, but I need you to look at me and tell me you're not going to drink and drive again. If you slip up and drink again, we can deal with that, but not the driving part."

"I promise. I won't drink and drive again. I want to promise that I won't drink again, but I just don't know if I can do that. I want to, but I know myself. I'm weak."

"You're not weak. You have a problem. We all have our problems."

"Except for you." Isaac loved Julia dearly, but he sometimes found himself jealous of her. She did in fact seem perfect. He'd yet to find a real flaw with her as being too nice was not an actual flaw.

"I have my flaws too. My ex-husband tried to kill me, remember?" They both grinned though it didn't make Isaac feel any better. It only reminded him that it was her ex-husband's drinking that led to him shooting Julia, and now he was bringing that aspect of her past back into her life. He believed that his drinking led to the problems for everyone he loved.

"At least I'm a happy drunk."

"And a tired drunk." She poked his side. "You passed out right when you hit the bed last night. That's another reason I don't want you driving. You could have fallen asleep at the wheel and left me and the girls all alone."

Isaac apologized again before he showered and asked God for help with quitting. He'd been addicted for nearly twenty years at this point, and he thought he beat it last year, but here it was again, back in full force. It not only lurked within, it also watched him and enjoyed its ability to control his life at a whim.

This was day one of his sobriety. He looked online and found the number for a local A.A. meeting. He hated talking about his problems with other people, but his family deserved better. He needed to do something different in order to actually be different.

CHAPTER 22
Say Their Names

"PUSH. COME ON, YOU CAN DO it." The doctor encouraged Julia during her third hour of giving birth. "We're almost there. I can see the head."

April Fools' Day would never be the same again for Isaac and Julia. When she told him that her water broke, Isaac laughed. As soon as he saw the floor, he knew that the babies would be born a month early. It didn't surprise him all that much given how big her belly had grown, but he also figured that was largely due to her carrying twins. Olivia and Lindsay sat in the waiting room, and Carter arrived after making the drive in from Auburn. Nicole walked in with him as they had news of their own, though now they would wait to share it since this day belonged to the babies.

"You're doing great, sweetie." Isaac held her hand and allowed her to squeeze it as tightly as she needed to. He thought back to being in a similar looking room with Ramie, all those years ago. When Carter was finally born, he'd nearly passed out as he hadn't eaten all day, and he felt sick to his stomach by the sight of the umbilical cord. He'd done much better with Olivia, since Ramie had to have a C-section. He wasn't inside for that birth, though he waited just outside the room with Carter's little hand inside of his. "The first one is out. She's so gross," he joked. "But she's unbelievably pretty, just like her mother."

"Let me see her." Julia smiled at her baby girl as she prepared to bring the next one into the world.

"We're almost done." The doctor handed the baby off to one of the nurses and encouraged Julia to stay focused for a little while longer. "Just a few more pushes, and it will all be over."

Julia continued to push, and no more than ten minutes later, the second girl was born. She had a little more hair than the first baby, both darker than Isaac imagined, but she was a bit smaller.

"They're beautiful." Julia couldn't stop herself from crying. She'd waited all her life to have children, and now at age forty-five, she was the beaming mother of two little girls.

"They're perfect," Isaac said. He kissed each baby on the cheek as the nurse carefully placed them into Julia's arms. "So, what names did we decide on?" They'd discussed so many that Isaac couldn't remember which names they finally landed on.

"We never did agree on names," Julia said. "How about I pick this one, and you choose the other girl?" It felt funny to Isaac referring to them as anything other than by their names, yet there was nothing else they could call them yet, aside from perfect.

"Of course. That would be the only fair solution," Isaac teased. "We could also draw names out of a hat. Or, I could ask the nurses what their names are, and we could name them that."

"Very funny," Julia said as they considered their long list of names. Isaac assumed this would be the easy part, but they both found it difficult to actually pick the name that their daughters would live with for the rest of their lives. Finally, after thirty seconds of deliberation, Julia chose the one name that rang true to Isaac's ears. "Bailey Madison," she said those words like they were meant to exist, and Isaac believed it was the only name that truly fit.

"I love it." He kissed Bailey on the cheek and tried to remember which baby was his. They appeared nearly identical. "Okay, my turn." He thought about his list of names and quickly landed on the one that reminded him the most of England. He wasn't sure why that made it more appealing to him, but for some reason it did. "Victoria Grace." The name fell from his lips with such grace that the name could not be anything else.

"That's so pretty." Julia smelled their little heads and kissed both of her girls. Isaac delivered the news to his kids in the waiting room. He'd gotten to know Lindsay better since his last drunken mishap. He felt embarrassed by the incident, but he was now three weeks sober and still counting the days.

It was still a daily struggle for him not to drink, though he hoped the new babies would be another reason for him not to give in again. As more time went by, it became less awkward to see Nicole. At times, he almost forgot that he'd slept with her, something he never would have thought possible this time a year ago. She and Carter didn't just seem happy together, they were happy according to Carter. She made the move to Auburn with him, and they'd gotten an apartment together a little over a month ago. It appeared that she might not be going away anytime soon. He thanked God that she never revealed their secret, though he assumed that she would be as ashamed as he would be for anyone to find out.

Once they moved Julia into her own room, Isaac led the kids inside to see their little sisters. Lindsay and Nicole joined them as they quickly became fixtures at all family functions or discussions. Carter held Victoria first while Olivia carefully carried the smaller Bailey. Both girls slept peacefully, and everyone fell in love with them at the same moment. They switched babies, delicately, and breathed in their new baby smell.

"They really do smell so good," Olivia said as she kissed Victoria on the forehead.

"Just don't get any ideas," Isaac teased his daughter.

"I'm not the one you should be telling that to." Olivia glanced at her brother and then over toward Nicole. "These two are irresponsible, you know. Plus, it would be pretty hard for me to get pregnant, don't you think?"

Isaac laughed, yet he didn't find it all that funny. Talking about sex or anything related to sex with his kids always made him uncomfortable. It didn't matter to him that they were both adults now, eighteen and twenty-years-old, it still seemed weird to him. Carter and Olivia seemed to find it amusing, especially Olivia. Julia appeared to enjoy seeing him squirm as well.

"Okay," Isaac joked, "you're all are ruining baby day. When they get older, I'm going to tell them that you tried to take the spotlight from them on their day." Isaac took Victoria and Bailey in his arms and snuggled them into his chest. He wondered what Rylee would think about the new babies. She'd never seen a baby before, so it would all be new to her.

Julia and the babies went home three days later as they both arrived into the world healthy. They breathed pure relief that there were no problems. Isaac and Julia had read all the articles online about women over forty having complications in their pregnancies. She thanked her daily walks and writing for keeping her sane and healthy. Now that they were home, there was nothing to do except live. This was the first day of the rest of their lives.

CHAPTER 23
Dirt Road

AGENT FAITH AND AGENT NOAH CONTINUED their search for the real John Smith. They made more phone calls looking for Charles Haney's alias than they had in their entire careers, or it seemed that way at least. They visited the homes of ten John Smiths' that fit their profile, but each one turned out to be a living, breathing John Smith. On May 1, one month after Isaac and Julia welcomed their twins into the world, the agents pulled up on a vacant property tucked into the woods of Calhoun. Calhoun sat about thirty minutes north of Cartersville and a good hour north of Woodstock.

"Where the hell is the house?" Agent Noah looked into the thick line of trees in front of him. They parked along the road where a mailbox sat alone, at the end of a gravel road they guessed was just short of a mile in length. Once the gravel ran out, slightly in front of their SUV, a dirt path led into the woods. There were no other homes nearby, and both the agents prepared themselves for the unknown.

"I don't know," Agent Faith said, keeping her hand near her gun. She'd learned to trust her intuition over the years, though she often wondered whether it was her woman's or agent's intuition that took over. "Something's not right about this place."

"Should we call for backup?" Agent Noah asked as they ventured into the woods about twenty yards. The dirt path narrowed as they stepped further into the woods, but it didn't appear that anything resided within.

"There's nothing to backup yet," she responded. "We haven't found anything."

They continued to walk into the wooded property as the road seemed to lead nowhere. They walked for at least two hundred yards before they both spotted a small home in the distance. It looked run down and abandoned with no cars parked on the property or plants growing around the outside. There was no grass or toys or anything that signaled that people lived there. They made it to the front door where Agent Faith knocked loudly. Agent Noah peered through a small window to the left of the tiny front porch. The house had a window on both sides of the porch. Each one looked like it belonged in a bathroom rather than on the front of a home. The structure couldn't have held more than two bedrooms inside. After twenty seconds of silence, Agent Faith knocked again while Agent Noah looked through the other window, though he could not see through due to the blankets hung on the inside.

"Should we go in?" Agent Noah asked as he began to walk around the side of the house.

"We'd better try to get a warrant first, and I'm not sure that we'd be able to. We don't have much to go on besides our gut feelings. But I'll tell you this much..." Agent Faith failed to complete her thought. As soon as that last word left her mouth, the front door flew open and knocked her down the three steps and onto the ground. A woman rushed from the house wielding a medium-sized knife.

"Put the knife down!" Agent Noah yelled with his gun drawn toward the unkempt woman. Agent Faith reached for her gun, but the woman lunged on top of her and dropped the knife into her chest with one swift motion. Agent Faith gasped and wondered where the adrenaline was that should take over in a situation like this. Before the woman had a chance to pull the knife out, Agent Noah fired one shot. The bullet went into the side of the woman's head, and she fell over next to Agent Faith, the lower half of her body still strung across the agent's.

"Shit, shit, shit." Agent Noah ran over to his partner and felt for a pulse on the woman. The bullet killed her, but they didn't know who or what else might lay inside. The knife stood straight out of Agent Faith's chest, and there was no way he could remove it without any means to stop the bleeding or ability to treat the wound. The woman had stabbed her on the right side of her chest, so it didn't pierce the heart. Still, she lay in shock and struggled to speak more than a few words.

"Clear the house," she whispered as she managed to get the words out. She stared up at the blue sky, most of which hid behind the lofty trees. Agent Noah stood to his feet and walked up the steps with his gun pointed in front of him.

"This is the FBI! If there's anyone else in the house, identify yourself now!" he shouted the commands. They hadn't expected to see anyone, much less a crazed woman with a knife. He walked over to the bedroom on the right and took notice of how little there was in the home. It sat almost completely empty without any electricity, from what he could gather, and no furniture. There wasn't even a fridge in the kitchen. He shouted out the command again and opened the door. He entered the room and aimed the gun toward an empty mattress and a few scattered shirts and other clothes. The smell nearly overwhelmed him. It smelled like body odor and metal, mixed with the stench of decaying flesh and possibly stale urine.

He left the room and walked to the other side of the house. "If there's anyone in there, say something, or you will be shot!" He counted to three and turned the knob. The door opened, and Agent Noah shrieked from the sight in front of him. He assessed the situation and made his best effort to process what he saw inside that room. He ran out of the house and gasped for air.

"I'll be right back," he said to his partner. "I don't have any cell service. I'm going to call for help." Agent Noah sprinted down the dirt driveway until his phone registered one bar. He called for assistance and rushed back to be with his partner.

"It's going to be okay. You're going to be fine. An ambulance will be here in just a little bit. Stay strong. You're going to make it." Agent Noah went back inside the house and looked inside the second bedroom again. He thought he'd seen everything in his twenty years of service, but this was unlike anything he'd ever seen or heard of. He knelt and tried his best to offer some sort of comfort until the ambulance arrived.

CHAPTER 24
Family Meeting

"WHO'S A BIG GIRL," ISAAC SAID in a high-pitched voice and held Victoria's tiny fingers. "Is it you? Are you my big girl? And how about you?" He looked over at Bailey and kissed her cheek. Both girls opened their mouths wide and kicked their legs. He could tell them apart easily now as Bailey displayed a noticeable freckle on the left side of her head. They stretched out on his bed while Julia wrote in the other room. Isaac picked them up and took them to see their mommy.

"Look who's here." He held the girls like a football and proudly displayed them to Julia. He felt that he was just now ready to be a father. All the times he became easily frustrated with Carter and Nicole when they were younger, he wished he could go back in time and be more patient. He didn't regret much in his life. He tried to learn from his mistakes and grow from them, rather than look at them as failures. He was able to do that with most things, save his mistake with Nicole and how impatient he'd been as a young father. He knew that fatherhood was something where you learned as you went, but still, he let too much get to him, and it took him many years to let things go and allow his kids to be kids.

"Say hi to Mommy."

"Hey girls." Julia smiled and leaned in toward her beautiful twins. "They are one month old today. It's crazy how fast the time goes by. People say that all the time, I say it all the time, but it really is true."

"You don't have to tell me." Isaac kissed both the girls on top of their heads and delivered one to Julia as well. "I've got a twenty-year-old, an eighteen-year-old, and now two little babies. See, I told you I loved babies," he said the last part in his high-pitched voice that he enjoyed using with his newborn girls.

"Yes, you did. You are a great father. We are lucky to have you." Julia reached for Bailey and breathed in her smell of baby powder and milk. Both of those smells inundated them with joy.

"Are you kidding me?" Isaac kissed Victoria's cheek repeatedly until the baby turned and tried her best to eat his face. "I'm the lucky one. You've been so patient with me and understanding. Less than two years ago I thought my life was over. Now, I honestly couldn't be happier."

"I'm glad we make each other happy then. And you've done so good going to your meetings and not drinking since your last little slip up." Julia traded Bailey for Victoria and showered her with the same kisses. "What time are we meeting with the kids tonight?"

"Around seven, I think. I'll text Carter and ask him."

"They still haven't told you what it's about?"

"No, I think they take joy in making me wonder. Actually, I know they do."

"And where on earth could they get that from?" Julia teased. "You do that to us whenever you get the chance. This is what you get for being so sarcastic all the time."

"Yeah, yeah." He stole Bailey from his wife and tucked her back in between his arm and his chest. The girls loved to look out at the world around them and play with their hands as they did. Rylee sat perfectly still next to Julia, waiting for someone to pet her. Julia obliged the quiet pug and squeezed the fat around her neck that had begun to roll over her harness. "As long as Nicole's not pregnant, I'll be good with whatever it is."

"And how about Olivia and Lindsay? What is it that they can't tell you in order for you to remain okay?"

"That they're getting married, I suppose. Liv is too young. Anything else, and I'm good."

"I doubt it's that, but didn't you get married at eighteen?" Julia reminded Isaac in case that is what Olivia and Lindsay wanted to talk to them about.

"Yeah but that's different."

"How so?"

"I don't know, but it is. I'm taking the girls for a walk." Rylee perked up when she heard Isaac say that magical word. "Do you need anything?"

"No, you guys have fun. I'll be writing for a while, and then I think I'll take a nap before the big meeting tonight."

"Stop it. It's not that big of a deal."

"How often do they call meetings like this?"

"Well, never, but still, just stop it." He kissed Julia and carried the girls downstairs to get them ready for a walk around the neighborhood. He let Rylee join them as he felt bad watching her one eye bulge from excitement. Isaac buckled the girls into the double stroller and tucked them in with a blanket, even though it was fairly pleasant outside. Both the girls enjoyed being wrapped up tightly with nothing but their heads free to look around. When they wanted their arms out, they would wiggle them out, even at a month old. Isaac took joy in this simple act and cherished every moment with the twins. He spent time with Carter and Olivia, but he made up his mind that he would be the best possible father to Bailey and Victoria. He would not only be patient and kind, but he would also simply be there for them and place a high value on the little aspects of life.

The day sped by, surprisingly, and when seven PM rolled around the kids arrived at nearly the same time. Carter and Nicole pulled in first, followed moments later by Olivia and Lindsay. Olivia was graduating in a few weeks, so Isaac guessed that their news might have something to do with her college plans. It was late to be deciding on where to attend, but he hoped she would go to Auburn like the rest of the family. He told himself that he would support her no matter where she chose to go. His best guess for Carter's news was that they were pregnant. He would pretend to be happy, but that would not be good news for him. Something on the inside told him to ready himself for disturbing news from his son.

"They are so freaking cute," Olivia said as she held Victoria and made silly faces to the adorable baby. "I can't wait to be a mom one day."

"One day," Isaac quickly responded.

"Leave her alone." Julia handed Victoria's binky to Olivia and tickled Isaac without him being able to stop her. He hated being tickled, and she loved sneaking up on him from behind and squeezing his sides with a gentle pressing. He enjoyed it too, though he would never admit it.

"Seriously," Nicole chimed in as she held Bailey, "you guys made the perfect babies. They never cry, and they are beyond gorgeous. They look like little model babies."

"Thank you." Julia received her compliment as humbly as she could. "They are more than I could have ever hoped for."

"All right, all right," Isaac interrupted the love fest all around for his beloved twins. "That's enough with trying to butter me up. Why did you guys call the meeting?"

"Butter you up?" Carter laughed. "Who the hell is trying to butter you up? Isn't that a Mike Myers SNL line or something like that?"

"You're hilarious, son. What's the news? What's going on?"

"Fine, I guess we'll go first," Carter said as he looked at his sister and slyly smiled.

"So, Olivia knows what you have to say?" Isaac asked the question, yet he assumed she already knew. Olivia nodded her head and grinned with contained anticipation for what she and her brother were about to say.

"Okay, here it is. I asked Nicole to marry me, and she said yes. We're getting married, but we're going to wait until I graduate."

"Congratulations," Julia spoke first and hugged Nicole and then Carter.

"That's great news, son. I'm happy for you. I'm happy for the both of you." He looked at Nicole and gave her the most natural hug of his life. This hug seemed genuine to him, and while it must have been awkward on some level, it somehow felt right. "That's not that bad," Isaac continued, "I thought you were going to tell me that you guys were pregnant."

"First off, I can't get pregnant," Carter teased his father. "Secondly, that wouldn't be horrible news, would it? I mean, you and Julia got pregnant out of wedlock and you have like the perfect babies. I swear, this lack of crying makes me think the whole parenting thing is easier than everyone says. I think maybe we will have some kids of our own really soon."

"Easy, parenting is the most difficult thing you'll ever do," Isaac reminded his son.

"Thanks, Dad. Love you too." Olivia frowned sarcastically toward her father.

"You know what I mean. It's hard to raise kids. The twins seem easy now, but they do cry, and they are a lot of work. You are seeing them after they've been fed and loved on non-stop. Leave them alone for a while and you'll see how difficult they can be. Plus, do you know how many diapers I've changed this past month?"

"He's changed more than me," Julia giggled. Isaac smirked every time she did. It brought him a sense of pure happiness to see her smile.

"I'm just kidding, Dad." Carter took Bailey from Nicole and rubbed his cheek against her chubby cheek. It seemed to be the most normal thing for all of them to do when they picked up either of the twins. "We aren't having kids anytime soon, and we won't actually be getting married for two more years. We figured that will give us enough time to plan a wedding and decide where we want to live and all that good stuff."

"Where you want to live?" Isaac asked. "You aren't moving back here?"

"I don't know yet. It depends on if I go for my master's or what my job opportunities are after graduation. It's too early to say, that's all."

"I support you no matter what, but just know that I truly want you close by. We are lucky to have money where we don't have to worry about finances too much. If there's one thing I've learned in life it's that there is nothing more important than family. Julia and I were just talking this morning about how fast time flies. It really does, and I want to spend as much time with all of you as possible."

"Don't get all mushy on me," Carter joked, yet he seemed to receive the heartfelt sentiments from his father.

"Well, this is going to make my news a bit more awkward." Olivia jumped in to share her news.

"You're not getting married, are you?" Isaac asked, unable to hide his fear for what she was about to say.

"No, we're not getting married. Not yet at least. We've decided that we're moving to Portland after I graduate."

Isaac wasn't sure how to respond. His baby girl was going to move across the country, as far away as she possibly could? Yes, he had two more baby girls now, but still, he didn't want any of his kids to be so far away from him.

"I don't understand. Where did this come from? Why Portland? Which Portland?"

"Portland, Oregon. We've talked about it for the last few months and decided to just do it."

"What about college?" Isaac looked directly at Olivia, ignoring everyone else in the room.

"I'm still going to go to college. I'm just going to take one year off to experience life and write. I know it's not what you wanted for me, Daddy, but please, I need you to trust me. And this wasn't Lindsay's idea." Lindsay stood silently behind Olivia as Liv tried her best to convince her father that this was a good plan. "I had to convince her to come with me. She didn't want to leave her job or her life here, but this is something I feel like I need to do."

"What about work for Lindsay? What are you going to do?"

"I have a job lined up with the city of Happy Valley," Lindsay spoke for the first time. "It's just outside of Portland. I'm really sorry, Mr. Childs. I can't say that I know how you feel, because I don't, but I do love your daughter, and this is what we want to do."

"And it's just for a year, Daddy. If we don't like it, we'll move right back."

"And if you do like it?" Isaac began to cry thick tears. He wiped at his cheeks and apologized to everyone. "I don't know why I'm crying. I'm sorry; I just didn't expect this. I'm such a girl."

"You know," Olivia tried to lighten the mood, "you cry more than I do. I don't think it's fair for you to say that you're such a girl when we don't cry nearly as much as you do." Everyone laughed, and Carter and Olivia closed in for a hug with their father. Isaac let the tears flow as he squeezed his kids tightly and held their heads.

"I just love you guys so much, and I'm sorry for not being a good dad." Isaac didn't know where any of this was coming from, but since he was already crying, he decided to go with it.

"You're a great dad," Carter reassured him.

"You're the best dad in the world," Olivia agreed with her brother.

"So, Portland, Oregon?" Isaac wiped the last tears from his face and composed himself. "I do love the Northwest. I guess I'll be flying a lot over the next year. You girls don't mind if I come visit once a month or so, do you? I'll stay in a hotel so I won't impose. I just want to see you, that's all."

"Of course, Daddy. You can come as often as you want. I didn't think you would care this much now that the twins are here."

"You are all my children. I can't just replace you with new babies, despite the fact that they are the cutest babies in the world."

Isaac realized that his life would never be the same. Carter already lived two hours away, but after he and Nicole got married, who knew where they would end up. Once Olivia and Lindsay made it to Oregon, he feared they would never return. He'd visited that part of the country several times and absolutely loved it. At least this would give him an excuse to travel out there again, but still, he felt like he just lost both of his kids. The only saving grace was Julia and the twins. It's like life was telling him, *Out with the old and in with the new.* That sounded incredibly callous, even in his mind, but it appeared to be the reality.

"So, you might be a Duck or a Beaver if you go to school out there?" Isaac remembered how much he enjoyed walking around the campus of Oregon State University during one of his visits, many years ago. He spent an afternoon on the University of Oregon campus as well, but it didn't have the same feel to him.

"Let's not get ahead of ourselves, Daddy. With mascots like those, I think I'm better off moving back to Auburn after a year and becoming a Tiger."

They finished the night together with pizza and stories. Carter and Olivia talked about funny moments from their childhood, including that one time their father broke the garage door window with a basketball after passing it to no one. They laughed and realized that they were a family. They sat there, flawed and imperfect, but they sat there together. They looked at the babies and understood that they would make a better life for the twins, a life that would not include addictions, or cheating, or death in their futures. They would shower them with love and help them learn from their past mistakes.

CHAPTER 25
A Dog

ISAAC WOKE THE FOLLOWING MORNING TO the gentle cries of his girls. He lifted them from their cribs and quickly transferred them to their changing tables. Each girl had to lay on her own changing table, otherwise one would swat at the other.

"No wonder you were crying." He grinned down toward Victoria while plugging the binky into Bailey's mouth. After changing Victoria, he did the same for Bailey and carried them downstairs to make them a bottle. Isaac liked to let Julia sleep in and take care of the girls in the morning so she could get her rest. When they cried in the middle of the night, it was usually Julia who tended to them. Isaac figured it was a fair trade. He had the routine down fairly well at this point, able to hold both girls at the same time and keep the bottles in their mouths. He often stared at them as they ate and wondered how he'd lucked out with the twins. He couldn't have imagined caring for kids like Carter and Olivia, yet Victoria and Bailey swooped in and stole his heart.

"Look who it is, girls. It's your mommy."

Julia came down the stairs in her vintage *Simpsons* t-shirt, the same one she wore when they met on the disc golf course. She'd lost nearly all the baby weight, and her old clothes were starting to fit her again. She liked to sleep in that shirt as it reminded them both of how they met.

"Hey, girls." She bent over and kissed the twins on their foreheads as they stared, wide-eyed, yet they continued to drink from their bottles. She kissed Isaac on the cheek, and he lifted the back of her shirt to see if she was wearing her matching *Simpsons* boxer shorts. She was. "Easy there," she teased. "We already have two babies. I don't think we can handle anymore."

"I like the babies." Isaac said in his baby voice and handed Victoria to Julia, while he began to pat Bailey's back to get her to burp. "Are you saying that you don't like babies?"

"Quiet you," she said in her best Dwight Schrute imitation. "What are your plans for the day?"

"I'm going to talk to Liv and Lindsay about the money thing, and then I'm going to surprise Carter with the truck."

"Remind me again why you're doing this," Julia teased. Any chance she received to give him a hard time about money, she did.

"I know it's a lot, but I just want them both to know that I support them and that I love them. I don't want Liv to have to stress about money for the next year. Portland is way more expensive than here, and I'm not sure they realize how tough it will be for them to live on Lindsay's income if Olivia doesn't work as well. I want her to really live this year. If she's going to put off college and try something this big and new, I want her to do it right."

"And you don't think that a hundred thousand dollars is a bit much?" Julia needled him and smirked at her best friend.

"Yeah, it's probably too much, but it means they can have some fun and not have to worry about anything. You know we are good when it comes to money. I showed you the bank statement, right?" Isaac smiled.

"Yes, you did. Thank you so much, sir. I appreciate you letting me see how much money you have."

"God, you really are hilarious, aren't you?" Isaac set Bailey in the bouncer and then Victoria in the one next to her. He grabbed Julia, and playfully tossed her onto the couch and tickled her. "Do you still think you're funny now?" Isaac tickled her and squeezed the areas he enjoyed so much underneath her *Simpsons* clothing.

"Not in front of the babies," she protested, though not with a wholehearted rejection.

"They're one-month-old; they don't know anything." Victoria kicked her little legs and put the bouncer to work while Bailey gave her a run for her money.

"They know enough," Julia said as she kissed him deeply and then pushed him off. "Later, when they are napping."

"They nap all the time." Isaac stood up and helped Julia to her feet as well. He gave her a playful smack and stretched his arms. "We're not that young anymore, you know."

"I'm the one who's hilarious?" Julia laughed. "How much is the truck you are buying for Carter again? Eighty thousand dollars?"

"No, it's not eighty thousand dollars." Isaac headed toward the stairs to get ready for the busy day of buying his kid's love. "It's only fifty thousand."

"You're right, that's much better," Julia joked. He knew that she didn't care about the money or the gifts.

Isaac showered and put on his favorite pair of athletic shorts that displayed a strange collection of top hats and bow ties. He received a handful of bewildered looks when he wore them, which was about once a week, but it just made him like the shorts even more. There was also something about paying fifty thousand dollars in cash for Carter's truck, dressed the way he dressed, that made him feel good about himself. He met Carter at the car lot in Kennesaw and surprised him there, before he headed back to Auburn the next day.

"I don't understand," Carter said as he took in the greatness of his new truck. The red paint showed his reflection and the four doors gave him the same room that his Lexus currently offered. He'd driven the Lexus since he turned sixteen and never even thought about getting a new car, though he had mentioned getting a truck one day. "What did I do to deserve this?"

"You didn't do anything. You're just you, and I love you. This is to show you how proud I am of you, and it should take care of you and Nicole for quite some time."

"Thank you. I really appreciate it." Carter hugged his father and looked through the truck. It appeared to be equipped with everything he could possibly imagine. The back of the headrests had TVs built into them, and the truck came with Wi-Fi. The seats were genuine black leather with a red pinstripe trim that really popped. The amenities appeared to overwhelm Carter, and he left there with the biggest smile of his life. Isaac watched him drive off after they cleaned out Carter's car. Isaac traded it in as part of the deal, as they had no need for the car after the shiny new truck came into the picture.

He started his drive back home to deliver the good news to Olivia. She'd still been asleep when he left, so this would be a great way for her to wake up.

"Hello," Isaac answered the phone even though he did not recognize the number.

"Hello, Isaac? This is Agent Noah. Isaac, I need to speak with you. It's important." Lucas Noah had made dozens of calls to families over his career but never one like this.

"Okay, what's going on?" Isaac felt his stomach turn. He hated conversations like this, and each time the FBI had called him before, it never turned out to be good news.

"I need you to come up to Gordon Hospital in Calhoun. Something has happened, Isaac, and I need to speak with you in person. Please come right away."

Isaac called Julia and informed her of the phone call from Agent Noah. "I'll call you as soon as I know something," he said as he turned around and jumped on 75 North toward Calhoun. The drive would take him close to an hour from where he was in Kennesaw, and it offered him ample time to worry about what they could have discovered. He wasn't sure how he would respond if they found the rest of Ramie's remains. He would have to exhume the casket for a second time and say goodbye all over again. He pulled into the parking lot of the hospital and spotted Agent Noah in front of the main entrance, waiting for him with the most somber look he'd ever seen in his life. As he parked his truck, Agent Noah walked over and met him there.

"Isaac," Agent Noah spoke first and stretched his hand out to greet him, "it's good to see you."

"You too," Isaac responded, though it was not good to see the agent. He guessed that Agent Noah felt the same way about seeing him. It was simply something that people say to calm their nerves.

"Follow me over here." The agent motioned toward a bench that sat on the edge of the property, away from anyone else. The sun shined brightly yet there was enough of a breeze to still be pleasant. They sat down on the bench, and Agent Noah turned toward Isaac. "There's no easy way to say this, Isaac, so I'm just going to say it the best that I can."

"What is it? Did you find Ramie's body?"

"We found a third property that belonged to Charles Haney. It was under an alias he created with a fake social security number and a life that never existed, under the name of John Smith. We've been searching for quite some time now for this John Smith, and after more dead ends than we could count, we finally located his third property here in Calhoun. When we walked up to the house yesterday, a woman rushed through the front door and stabbed Agent Faith in the chest. Thankfully, she's going to be just fine. She's actually recovering in the hospital right now."

"Who was this woman?" Isaac asked, shocked by the latest development.

"We believe she was a woman he abducted more than twenty years ago, likely his first victim or close to it."

"What do you mean? Have you spoken to the woman? Does she know what happened to Ramie?"

"The woman is dead. I was forced to shoot her before she stabbed Agent Faith again. There's more to the story, Isaac. After I searched the house, I found two women inside of the home... still alive. One of them was your wife. Ramie is alive."

"That can't be. She's dead. You guys found her arm. You said the prints matched," Isaac spoke frantically. He couldn't accept what Agent Noah was telling him.

"I'm sure this must be overwhelming, Isaac, but let me explain. It is Ramie, and while she's gone through a literal hell, she is alive. She's missing her left arm, but the rest of her is still there. Now, I should warn you that she looks very different. She's lost a lot of weight, she's barely been outside for close to two years, and she's experienced an immense amount of trauma."

"I don't understand. Is she in the hospital? Can I see her? Wait, Haney has been dead for a while now. Why weren't they able to escape? Was that woman working with him?"

"I know you must have a million questions, and I'll do my best to answer all of them that I can. Ramie is inside, and I will take you to see her in just a moment. She and the other victim who survived both had their arms cut off by Haney. He had some medical training, so he was able to sew their wounds up and treat them with basic care. The woman who attacked my partner was apparently brainwashed after all those years, and they all lived in fear of Haney. Ramie and the other surviving victim informed us that the woman who stabbed my partner seemed to love Haney in a twisted sort of way. It wasn't uncommon for him to leave for long periods of time. This is all secondhand information as we can't speak with her, but we believe that she feared for her life, and that's why she attacked Agent Faith. They were unable to leave the property because all three of the women were fitted with high voltage shock collars around their necks and ankles. If they made an attempt to leave the property, they would have been shocked with such a high voltage that they could have been killed. Actually..."

"How did they live?" Isaac interrupted Agent Noah. "How did they have food if Haney was dead and they couldn't leave? Did he have a partner, or was the woman who stabbed Agent Faith able to leave?"

"He didn't have a partner. What he did have was a massive storm shelter that was stocked with two years' worth of food and water. It was like a prepper's storm shelter who believed the world was going to end. The house didn't have electricity or running water, but the women were able to go to the underground shelter for food and bottled water. Apparently, there was one other woman left there by Haney. The women told us that she tried to escape shortly after Haney left one night. We found her remains along the shock line. It appears that she tried to escape, but the voltage took her life."

Isaac couldn't get the mental picture out of his head. Ramie had been kept like a dog for nearly two years while he remarried and raised a new family. How was he supposed to explain this to her? Did this mean that he had two wives now? Isaac's stomach raced with worry, and he wasn't sure how to proceed.

"Does Ramie know that I've got a wife and two new babies?"

"We haven't told her anything. We thought that would be best coming from you." Agent Noah stood and led Isaac toward the hospital. They walked in and waited for the elevator to open. Isaac felt a panic attack coming over him, and he thought of Julia and the twins for the first time. He knew that this was not fair for anyone. No matter what he chose, he was going to hurt someone he loved. They stepped out of the elevator on the fifth floor, and Agent Noah showed him to Ramie's room. Isaac knocked lightly on the door and peeked inside.

"Ramie?" he whispered, not wanting to wake her if she were sleeping. He imagined that she must be exhausted. He swallowed hard and forced himself not to cry. This was not about him. This was about Ramie. She was back from the dead. Carter and Olivia would be overcome with joy to learn that their mother was alive, and while she was going to need months, and probably even years of healing, she was still here.

"Isaac," she spoke softly through squinted eyes. "Isaac," she said his name again and began to sob uncontrollably. He walked to her right side and gently placed his hand on top of hers. She looked weak and frail, weighing no more than eighty-five pounds. She was pale, but not completely pale as she had been outside some each day. He could see her veins on top of her arms, and her hand felt bony, not like his Ramie.

"Ramie, I'm so sorry." He gave in and cried anyway. There was nothing he could do once he saw her tears flow. He cried because he'd forsaken his wife. He moved on too soon, and if he had just waited like a normal person, he wouldn't be faced with this impossible decision. He leaned in, delicately embraced her face, and followed with a kiss on top of her head. He struggled for anything to say, anything at all that would make any kind of sense to her. The only thing he knew at that moment was that he needed a drink.

CHAPTER 26
Life

"DOES IT HURT?" ISAAC ASKED, THOUGH he knew that it must. He tried his best to look into her eyes and not over toward where her missing arm should be. He held her hand as they spoke and debated over how much he should tell her, not wanting to cause her anymore pain so soon.

"I don't know," she still spoke softly. Her voice sounded different, like it had been chronically weakened over the course of her abduction. "They've got me on a lot of medicine. The doctor said they will be able to put a prosthetic arm on, so that's good news. My stomach hurts. I haven't eaten real food since all of this happened. They said it was two Septembers ago that he took me? I can't believe it's been that long."

"Yeah, I can't imagine what you've gone through. I'm so sorry. Was it difficult to keep track of the time?"

"Not at first, but then after he took my arm off, I lost track of everything. I don't even remember when that was, just that he was there in the beginning, and then he suddenly disappeared. There was another woman, but she died trying to escape. I don't know if they told you."

"Yeah, the agent told me a little bit ago. I don't know what to say." Isaac shifted in his chair. "I can't believe you're actually alive. We buried your arm."

"The kids must be heartbroken. How are they? When are they going to come see me?"

"They actually don't know yet. I just found out, right before I walked in. I can go call them now if you want me to."

"Yes, please. I need to see my kids."

"Let me step outside of the room and call them. I'll be right back." Isaac stood to call Carter and Olivia, but Ramie squeezed his hand to stop him from leaving.

"No, please don't leave me. Please, call them here. I don't want to be alone."

"Okay, I'm sorry. I'll call them here."

"You know how he got me?" Ramie stared off toward the door as Isaac held his phone in his hand. "He hit me with his car while I was running. I fell into a ditch like two streets from our house, over toward the lake, and I thought he was getting out of the car to help me. Instead, he hit me in the head with a shovel, and the next thing I remember was being in that house with a shock collar around my neck and ankles. It was hell, Isaac. I never thought I'd see you guys again. I thought he was going to kill me for sure. I watched him kill one other woman. It was awful."

"I can't imagine. I really can't. Some things have changed, Ramie. I feel like I should update you some before I call the kids."

"Like what? Is everyone okay?" She sounded worried, like her motherly instinct had not been used properly for nearly two years.

"The kids are fine. Carter is finishing his second year at Auburn, and do you remember Nicole?"

"Emerson?"

"Yeah, that Nicole. They've been together for a while now, and they literally told us about their engagement yesterday. Now, they're not getting married until he graduates, but she's already moved down there with him, and they have their own place now. He started out in the dorms, but they couldn't live there together, so he moved out."

"And what about Liv? How is she? She must be getting ready to graduate this month. I can't believe it, Isaac. I missed so much." Ramie's tears streamed down once again.

"Liv is great. She took it pretty hard after you went missing, and well, I guess it's not your death anymore. We've been saying that for so long now. The guy confessed to killing you. It's still surreal to be here with you right now."

"They said that he hung himself in prison?"

"Yeah, that's how they found you. He left a suicide note and apparently they started their search over again because of it, though they wouldn't tell me what it said."

"I don't want to talk about him. Tell me about Liv. She's good?"

"She's great. She battled through a pill habit, but she made it through it. A car actually hit her in the fall, during cross country practice, and that's how we found out about it."

"A car hit her too? Was she hurt badly? A pill habit?" When Ramie said those words, it brought up the dark memories of their past, prior to her abduction. That life seemed like one that existed in a book somewhere, not a life that truly belonged to Isaac. Nothing seemed real anymore. He couldn't even imagine what it felt like to her.

"She had a broken pelvis but nothing major. She has been clean since then, but the biggest thing about Olivia is that she finally met someone."

"That's wonderful. Who is he? Do I know him?"

"It's a girl, a woman actually."

"She's a lesbian? What do you mean by a woman?"

"She said she's bi. What she said specifically was that she wasn't sure what she was, but she fell for an older woman. She told us on her eighteenth birthday. Her name is Lindsay, she's twenty-nine, and she is really nice."

"I guess that makes sense. The girl part, not the older woman part. She never did have a boyfriend. I just never thought about either of our kids being gay. Did you take it okay?"

"No, I kicked her out of the house and told her to repent before she ever came back."

"Very funny," Ramie spoke that phrase as they often had in their past. As soon as she did, Isaac thought about he and Julia using those two words so often as well. They were the best words in the world besides I love you.

"No, I took it fine, but it did surprise me as well. She just told us yesterday that they were moving to Portland, Oregon after she graduates, but that might change now that you're here. You are here. I am still shocked, obviously."

"What about you? What's changed with you? You look different. You look better."

"Thanks," he said sarcastically.

"I meant that you've lost some weight. You look thinner."

"I quit drinking for the most part. I've only had a few mishaps since you went missing. I've recently started going to A.A. meetings to help me beat it for good, and I think it's working."

"Did you meet anyone else while I was gone?" The way she asked told Isaac that she already knew. He could feel a shift in the air, as if she could read his mind and see his beautiful babies.

"I did. I'm sorry, Ramie. It's not fair to you, but I thought you were dead. We had a memorial service for you, and then we had to exhume your casket to bury your arm."

"It hasn't even been two years. How did you meet someone else already? I thought we were soulmates?" She stopped crying by this point, but he could almost literally see the pain growing inside her chest. He thought that she might actually have a broken heart, and that it could explode at any moment.

"We can talk about this later." Isaac tried to hold her hand, but she pulled away. "We don't have to do this right now."

"Do what? Do you love her?"

"Ramie, please."

"No, I want to hear you say it. Do you love her?"

"Ramie."

"Just answer me. What's her name? When did you meet her?"

"Her name is Julia. I met her a while ago while playing disc golf."

"What's a while ago?"

"This isn't going to help you. Let's talk about this later, after you've seen the kids and had more time to rest."

"You don't care about me," she began to cry softly. "You only care about yourself. You moved on with your life just fine. I see how important I really was to you."

"Ramie, it's not like that." He tried to apologize. He longed for the right words to say, yet he understood those words did not exist.

"Get out," she spoke more loudly now, though still much softer than how her old voice would have sounded.

"Ramie, please."

"Just leave."

Isaac left the room and glared down the empty hallway. He didn't see any other patients or hospital workers nearby. It's as if he were alone.

I stole her life from her, he thought.

He called Carter first and then Olivia. He told them where to meet him but did not explain why over the phone. He then called Julia from outside the hospital and explained what was going on. He didn't have time to make the hour drive and tell her in person, not with needing to wait for his kids to arrive. He broke the news to his wife that Ramie was in fact alive.

"Isaac," Julia teared up on the other end, "I'm so terribly sorry. How are Carter and Olivia?"

"They are on their way here, but they don't know yet. I didn't want to tell them over the phone."

"How are you handling it?"

"Not well. I thought she was dead, Julia. What am I supposed to do now? She kicked me out of the room when she found out that I'd met someone else. I haven't even told her that we're married or have twins yet. How am I supposed to feel? I'm literally the worst person in the world."

"Don't say that, sweetie. I know this must be tough, but we'll get through it. She will too; it's just going to take time."

"I don't know how we'll get through it. I mean, are Carter and Olivia still going to want to have a relationship with me when they find out their mother is alive?"

"I'm sure they will. They love you, Isaac. I love you."

"I love you too. That's what makes this even worse. If I didn't love you, I could just go back to my old wife and try to make that life work again, but I love you more than anything. You and the girls are my life."

"We love you too." Julia spoke like the other woman in a love triangle. He knew that she didn't want to hurt Ramie either, yet he also understood that neither one of them were willing to give the other up. Before him, he guessed that she loved only her writing and her mugs. Now, she had him and the girls, and they were a complete family with the brightest future imaginable. He didn't know what the future would look like anymore.

Isaac spotted Carter's new truck as it pulled into the parking lot, and he walked over to meet his son. Until Olivia arrived, he would have to stall.

"What's going on?" Carter asked as soon as he stepped out of the truck. "Are you okay? You look fine."

"I'm fine, son. Let's wait until your sister gets here, and then I'll explain everything."

Isaac waited with Carter for ten minutes, the longest ten minutes of his life. Once Olivia pulled in, he walked them over to the same bench where Agent Noah broke the news to him.

"There's no right way to say this, so I'll just say it. Your mother is alive."

Silence. Carter and Olivia looked at each other and then directed their bewilderment toward their father.

"Is this some kind of a joke? If so, it's not funny, Daddy." Olivia said what her brother must have been thinking.

"I'm not joking." Isaac proceeded to fill his kids in on everything he knew. He braced them for their mother's appearance, her state of mind, and the fact that she was not happy with him.

"How is she supposed to feel?" Olivia said angrily. "You're her husband, and you left her. She's been held in some shit hole for two years while you married a new woman and had two new babies."

"Please don't mention that I'm married or that we have twins. Your mother asked me to leave before I had a chance to tell her everything. She only knows that I met someone."

"This is just perfect," Olivia continued, "just when everything is going great. And not just for me, but for you and for Carter too. Everyone is happy, and now Mom is back, but we can't be happy? Life is so messed up. Why did it have to happen like this? Why?" Olivia hugged her father and began to cry while Carter stood quietly to the side.

"You guys can be mad at me; I deserve it. But please be kind to your mother. She's gone through more than any of us know. I can't even imagine how she's feeling."

"What are you going to do?" Carter spoke, for the first time.

"What do you mean?"

"Well, you're still technically married to Mom, aren't you? Is your marriage to Julia even legal now that Mom is alive?"

"I don't know about that; I hadn't thought of it that way. I love your mother, I really do, but I love Julia too. We have the babies now. I can't leave them. No matter what I choose, I'm going to hurt someone."

"Well, you do have to choose," Olivia said.

"Who do you love more?" Carter asked. "I mean, you were married to mom for nearly twenty years. You've only known Julia for a year and a half."

"I'm sorry." Isaac didn't think that any good could come from rating his love for the two women and sharing it with his kids. The truth is that he was madly in love with Julia. His love for Ramie was a familiar love, but one that he had let go. He didn't think it was an option anymore, so it was difficult for him to picture himself with her again. "I can't leave Julia. I can't leave the girls. I don't know how to handle any of this, but please know that I love you both."

"Take us to see Mom," Olivia said as soon as her father finished speaking.

"Of course."

Isaac led his kids into the hospital and back to the fifth floor where Ramie lay in her bed. He stood outside the door and listened to their joyous reunion. He stepped into the doorway and waved to Ramie. He didn't want to just walk away, but he also couldn't bear her asking him to leave again.

"Wait," Ramie softly called out. Isaac took a step into the room and made a face toward his kids that begged for forgiveness. "Do the kids know?"

"Yes," Isaac admitted, "the kids know."

"Is it serious?"

"Can we talk about this alone?"

"We're a family," Ramie said, "and they're adults now. We can talk about this together." Carter and Olivia stepped back silently, and Isaac inched closer to the bed.

"Ramie," Isaac said, suddenly lightheaded, "I married her. We just had twin girls who were born a month ago."

"So, you really didn't waste any time, did you? It's nice to know that while I was held in captivity by a monster, by a monster who cut off my arm, that you all just moved on with your lives like nothing ever happened."

"Mom," Carter spoke from behind his sister, "it's not like that."

"Did you and your sister approve of this Julia woman?"

"I mean, we did, but it's only because we thought you were dead."

"I wish he'd killed me." Ramie's tears flowed and ran down her neck.

"Don't say that, Mom." Olivia grabbed her hand and sat down next to her. "We love you. You have to understand that we believed you were dead. The guy confessed, and the FBI told us you were dead. They found your arm, Mom. What else were we supposed to think? But you're back now. We can make this work. We are still a family."

"Your father has a new family, Liv. I have nothing."

"Mom." Carter tried to show his mother that they were happy to see her, that they were elated to have her back.

"Just leave, all of you. I want to be alone."

"Mommy." Olivia fought back the tears that flowed freely when she first walked into the room.

"Go," Ramie whimpered and turned away from her kids. Isaac knew that all of this was unfair. There was no way she could have expected any of this. Of course she knew that things would have changed. She knew Carter would be in college and that possibly he and Olivia might have met someone, but he understood that what he'd done was unforgivable.

"I love you," Olivia said as they walked out of the room.

"Love you, Mom," Carter added after his sister.

Isaac did not say anything. He looked at Ramie, though she would not look directly at him. He waved and followed his kids out of the room. Ramie closed her eyes and wished dearly that she would never open them again. Isaac walked with his kids to the elevator and nobody said a word until they stepped outside of the hospital.

"Guys," Isaac spoke through the tears, struggling to maintain his composure. "Please forgive me." He stretched out his arms and pulled them in close. They'd been through hell over the past two years, and he wasn't about to let Ramie's homecoming divide them. He didn't know how he would do it, but he was determined to keep his family together and not allow something that should be good news to destroy them. "This isn't your mother's fault. Be mad at me. Be angry with me. I'm the one to blame." Carter and Olivia sobbed on their father's shoulder and felt the afternoon sun shine down on their necks. The warmth made them feel at peace and offered them hope for some sort of reconciliation. They wrapped their arms around each other and believed that they were a family.

ABOUT THE AUTHOR

Jackson Baer is a professional thrifter who is happily married, the father of four children, and an avid runner. He was born and raised in Georgia, and spent time in Oklahoma, California, Connecticut, and then Oregon, as an adult. He's a graduate of Oregon State University and now resides in North Georgia, raising his family, near family.

He's a bit of a free spirit who enjoys working from home, traveling around, looking for treasures to share, and creating worlds that otherwise would not exist. Thrifting and writing are his two passions, and he's fortunate to be able to do both.

For more, please visit Jackson Baer online at:
Website: www.JacksonBaer.com
Goodreads: JacksonPaulBaer
Twitter: @JacksonPaulBaer
Facebook: JacksonPaulBaer
Instagram: JacksonPaulBaer
Pinterest: JacksonPaulBaer

WHAT'S NEXT?

Watch for the second book in this "An American Family" series, *Life after Death*, to release in November 2018.

Then, watch for his novel *Clouds Fall Like Fire* to release shortly thereafter.

To keep up with all of Jackson Baer's books from Evolved Publishing, please stay tuned to our website page linked below.

www.EvolvedPub.com/JBaer

MORE FROM
EVOLVED PUBLISHING

We offer great books across multiple genres, featuring hiqh-quality editing (which we believe is second-to-none) and fantastic covers.

As a hybrid small press, your support as loyal readers is so important to us, and we have strived, with tireless dedication and sheer determination, to deliver on the promise of our motto:
QUALITY IS PRIORITY #1!

Please check out all of our great books,
which you can find at this link:
www.EvolvedPub.com/Catalog/

Thank you!